The Royle D
A Colonel Tom Royle Adventure

Gerry Sammon

© Gerry Sammon 2017

Gerry Sammon has asserted his rights under the Copyright, Design and Patents Act, 1988, to be identified as the author of this work.

First published by Endeavour Press Ltd in 2017.

*This book is dedicated to my loving wife Diane,
and my two wonderful daughters, Rachel and Jessica,
who have encouraged, supported and cajoled me into
finally finishing this novel.*

The Royle Deception is a work of fiction, based on many factual events – "secret" histories. Some names have been changed in the process of writing this novel, a political thriller taking us from wartime South East Asia, Britain's involvement in South Vietnam immediately after the Second World War, The Malay Emergency that followed, and Britain's role in sending unofficial advisors into Vietnam when the Americans came on the scene.

It is true that British and Commonwealth soldiers and airmen fought the then Viet Minh in Vietnam in late 1945, after the Second World War had ended, and before the French returned to rule their former colony – using defeated Japanese soldiers to keep law and order.

In writing this story I acknowledge the brave dedication of all the journalists who risked their lives in what we call the Vietnam War, and what the Vietnamese refer to as the American War. Some of these journalists – both western and Vietnamese, north and south, died to get their stories out. Their sacrifice is commemorated in Ho Chi Minh City, formerly Saigon.

*Gerry Sammon
Bolton, Lancashire, UK
December 2016*

Table of Contents

THE SKIES OVER MONGOLIA, SEPTEMBER 13, 1971	7
COCHIN CHINA, OCTOBER 1945	8
OCTOBER 1974	33
YUNNAN – INDOCHINA BORDER, EARLY NOVEMBER 1944	44
HULL, OCTOBER 1974	52
YENAN, CHINA, OCTOBER 1944	54
HULL, ENGLAND 1974	61
MALAYA, NOVEMBER 1951	74
LONDON, OCTOBER 1974	85
MALAYA, JULY 1957	86
SAIGON, DECEMBER 1974	96
CHONGQING, EARLY NOVEMBER 1944	100
SAIGON, DECEMBER 1974	106
QUY NHON, SOUTH VIETNAM, SEPTEMBER 1965	115
DECEMBER 21 1974, HULL, ENGLAND	135
MONDAY 23 DECEMBER 1974, DON LUAN, SOUTH VIETNAM	140
TUESDAY 24 DECEMBER 1974, BANGKOK, THAILAND	145

TUESDAY DECEMBER 24 1974, SAIGON	146
CHRISTMAS MORNING 1974, CAMP FRIENDSHIP, THAILAND	152
HONG KONG, DECEMBER 1974	161
LATE DECEMBER 1974, HULL, ENGLAND	178
CENTURY HOUSE, LONDON, 30th JANUARY 1975	220
FEBRUARY 1975	224

THE SKIES OVER MONGOLIA, SEPTEMBER 13, 1971

The First-ranked Vice Premier of the People's Republic of China, Vice-Chairman of the Chinese Communist Party, and Minister for National Defence held back a scream of terror as his aircraft plummeted to the ground in a trail of flame and fire. He was the third most important person in the People's Republic of China, holding that nation's most important positions. How had it come to this?

Bin Lao had seen his wife and children die in the attack on his private plane as a mystery fighter aircraft shot white hot cannon shells into the passenger jet. The jet fighter had no markings. Bin Lao asked himself, *how could my secret have been revealed?*

Escape was now impossible. The pilots were dead and only he remained alive as smoke filled the luxurious passenger cabin of his private plane and he watched the steppes of Mongolia rushing towards him.

COCHIN CHINA, OCTOBER 1945

The blast sent soil and tree branches flying into Tom's face, stinging and lacerating his skin.

Lieutenant Tom Royle's Japanese sergeant was already on his feet and racing towards the sound inside the dark jungle thicket. The screams stopped.

Captain Pascal Thierry, a Free French officer, lay flat on the leaf-covered jungle floor to Tom's right. It was steamy and humid in the half-light of the rainforest. The Frenchman raised his head, his face covered in moss and grime, and barked a short, sharp laugh.

'It is good to send the Japs on ahead, no? They make excellent mine hunters,' said Thierry. Tom looked at the French officer and shook his head in an expression of dismay. Royle had embarked in-country two months earlier ahead of the official British mission to Saigon. Thierry was attached to the Free French 5th RIC – the Regiment d'Infanterie Coloniale. The French regiment had arrived only recently, some time after the famed British 20th Indian Division, which had already won two Victoria Crosses – Britain's highest award for military gallantry - during the Burma Campaign to drive back the fierce Japanese forces. The RIC's mission, so far, was simply to observe.

The British officer's face caught the dim light filtering through the tree line and his care-worn features immediately returned to a state of alert as he waited. He removed his cap and wiped his sweating face with the same hand, sweeping the peaked hat back on to his brown-haired head. A whistle, the sound of an English cuckoo, sounded from the trees. His Japanese sergeant's signal. Waiting time was over.

Royle waved the two Gurkhas and the Japanese soldiers to their feet and shouted 'Advance!' Royle knew that by now Sergeant Kanaka would have taken cover.

The group ran into the tangle of trees, firing as they went. Royle signalled for the firing to stop, and Thierry strolled up to join them. The charge and shoot tactic had been developed by Royle during his years of jungle warfare to ensure no enemy soldiers lay in wait.

There was certainly no love for the Japanese in this Frenchman's heart... nor in his. And Royle had more reason to hate them than this French observer. But Royle now had to work with them, and use his new found diplomatic skills as well as the fighting skills he had honed as the Second World War raged. Almost four years ago the Japanese had stormed Tom's home in Singapore with irresistible strength. The deaths of his parents – occurring separately and horribly – flashed back to him as he remembered how his training with the Manchester Regiment stepped up to a higher gear when the news reached him, and he vowed to avenge them.

Tom's mother Emily had been evacuated with hundreds of other women and children from Singapore on a civilian passenger vessel that never reached the safety of Sumatra. He heard later how it had been dive-bombed crossing the Straits of Malacca by Japanese aircraft and sunk. Survivors had been strafed in the water. Later still Tom had heard that the Japanese had known the ship had been carrying civilian refugees fleeing their onslaught.

His father Harry, a veteran first of the Boer War in South Africa as a young man and later the First World War, both with the Manchester Regiment, owned a small family-run rubber plantation on the island and had remained in Singapore to help defend the colony, knowing the situation was lost. Although he was too old to join the regular army he helped – and towards the end fought – with the 6th Territorial Battalion of the Manchesters as the Japanese poured out of Indochina, through Siam, and down into Malaya, finally reaching and occupying Singapore in February 1942. He was captured alive and incarcerated in Changi Prison. He had lasted a nightmarish two years before beri-beri, forced labour, and the jail's infamous cruelty killed him. Tom's Uncle Jim had owned a small rubber plantation at Baling in Kedah on the Malay Peninsula, just south of the Siamese border. He was bayoneted to death as the Japanese swept through the unprepared British colony. Aunt Helen was shot, but not before being gang raped in their own home – a popular punishment distributed by some of the more ruthless soldiers of the Imperial Japanese Army. The two children, Veronica and Charlie, were taken to a prison camp. He still hadn't heard about them, but the war had only just ended and there seemed to be more missing people in the world now than ever. Thankfully, he knew his sister Amelia was safe in Britain.

She had been sent to the "old country" before the European war had started to be with relatives in Manchester. Safe now, but she had endured the daily danger of Hitler's aerial attacks by Goering's bombers. He had never been told why Mel had been sent to live with their aunt and uncle in England. Tom had heard rumours of some sort of scandal, but no more.

How ironic, thought Tom. Here he was, in the jungle 35 kilometres north of Saigon. The very place where the Japanese launched their South East Asia offensive against his Malay home in December 1941. Yet now, in October 1945, he was leading a scouting party with two Gurkha troopers, a dozen defeated Japanese soldiers under orders to work for the new British Control Commission in Saigon, and this sneering Frenchman as an observer.

Only he and Thierry among them knew that the French would eventually be handed back control of Indochina.

It was the Nazi-collaborating Vichy authorities who had delivered the country over to the invading Japanese, after the capitulation of Indochina's French rulers to Germany in 1940. In August Royle had been told in confidence it would become French Indochina again in person by the Supreme Allied Commander in South East Asia, Lord Louis Mountbatten, just prior to flying out of Ceylon to Tan Son Nhut airport in Saigon for his mission in-country. The rest of the world thought Indochina would be given a form of independence. At one stage Britain had even dallied over the idea of Indochina becoming a part of the British Empire, but this would have upset the Americans who currently held a great big pay-cheque to dig Britain out of crippling wartime debt. Instead the deal was done for Indochina's French masters to return, and the country would again become French Indochina. US President Roosevelt, British Prime Minister Churchill, and Soviet dictator Stalin had decided that stability was the answer in South East Asia during their wartime conferences, where the world would be carved up between the victors. A return to the pre-war status quo would bring that stability, they had agreed. Nothing could now stop that happening; Tom had had the plan confirmed by his divisional commanding officer, General Douglas Gracey, immediately before setting out up country three gruelling days ago. His orders: lead a squad made up from two men of the 100th Indian Infantry Brigade's 1/1 Gurkha Rifles – incomparably brave and loyal soldiers; a dozen Japanese infantrymen now taking British orders; and a French observer from the RIC.

Gracey's British Military Control Commission had been initially welcomed by the Viet Minh, the most powerful political faction in Saigon at the time, mainly but not exclusively communist, when the British arrived soon after the Japanese surrender. Good will soon ebbed away into suspicion and violence, and now the small British force found itself embroiled in a guerrilla war it did not want and had not been prepared for. By October the fighting had intensified, and the British brigades all began taking losses. For this reason disarmed Japanese troops were reactivated as front-line forces, shielding the British and Indian forces to some extent, but taking terrible losses themselves.

October saw the cities pacified and under military control. The British then began to change their tactics, taking the guerrilla war into the countryside. The British had cut their jungle teeth in the brutal Burma battles, and now they adjusted again, this time to fight alongside their erstwhile Japanese foes.

Viet Minh guerrillas had moved back into the jungle, concentrating their forces into a large strategic triangle formed between the cities of Thu Duc, Bien Hoa and Thu Dau Mot, which is where Royle and his squad now found themselves.

'Thierry, kindly keep your prejudices to yourself at the moment, would you?' said Royle.

'*Captain* Thierry to you, *Lieutenant*,' announced the Frenchman, haughtily.

'Of course, sir. But your rank has no authority here. You are an observer and nothing more. Like my men, including these Japanese troops seconded to me, I give the orders, and you are obliged to obey them,' spat Royle, now heartily sick of the French officer's attitude and false bravado.

'Tell me, Captain Thierry, how much jungle fighting have you done, sir?'

Thierry looked blankly at Royle, knowing he had overstepped the mark with this veteran bushman.

'Sir, I have lived and fought in the jungles of Malaya, Indochina and Burma, pretty much throughout this war with the Japanese. I have lost most of my family over here, while I am certain you have spent the whole time in England until only recently this year, with General de Gaulle and his government in exile. Your mission is to observe, mine is to keep you safe, and among those keeping you safe, sir, are these Japanese soldiers who have been ordered by their commander in chief to obey our commands. And while we are in this God-forsaken place, those commands are my commands. Understood, sir?'

'Perfectly, Lieutenant. I apologise,' Thierry nodded in acknowledgement of the younger man's position and experience, then wiped the perspiration from his brow.

*

Late in 1941 Tom Royle had enlisted in the 6th Territorials and was sent with all the new recruits wishing to fight Hitler to England. He had taken a steamer from Singapore to Southampton and travelled north by train to the home of the Manchester Regiment at Ladysmith Barracks in Ashton-under-Lyne. It was his family's regiment. Tom's father Harry had been a lieutenant then later a major in the Manchesters 26 years earlier during the Great War. He had seen horrors never to be spoken off during those four years of war on the muddy battlefields of Europe. Now it was Tom's turn.

He had wanted to fight the Nazis in Europe. Dressed in his 6th Territorials uniform, Tom waved an eager goodbye to his parents on the dockside, alongside his Uncle Jim, Aunt Helen, and his younger cousins Charlie and Veronica, in the heat of a Singapore morning as his ship sailed away, destination Southampton. On disembarkation he had caught a train to the capital and had seen and been shocked by the effects of the aerial blitz on London. And on arrival in Manchester, traditionally his family home, he had been stunned by the devastation of the Christmas blitz in the city.

After a brief but joyous reunion with his 15-year-old sister, Amelia, at the age of 19 Tom Royle embarked on six weeks of army training and soon got himself recognised as a crack shot – the legacy of a boyhood shooting snakes and rats in the jungle outside his Malay home. He missed his family in Malaya on the long sea crossing, and meeting his sister again was a wonderful boost to his personal morale. She had been sent to Manchester for safety, Royle reflected, and instead had been close to death a number of times as Goering's bombers flattened much of the city. *Such a cruel irony*, thought Tom.

Tom's younger sister Amelia, or Mel as Tom called her, had created her own life while a schoolgirl in the city. The 15-year-old had always been a free spirit, with strongly held, if controversial, views. Despite the war Tom learned she had made many friends and had settled in to her new life, which she knew would end either with victory over Hitler, or defeat at the hands of the Nazis. Mel was sure it would be the former, and after that she would be able to return to her parents' estate in Singapore when life returned to normal.

Amelia had been unable to keep still with excitement when she received a telegram from Tom to say he was on his way to Manchester and wanted to meet up. She didn't wait for arrangement to be made, but instead caught a bus to Tom's barracks, and ran directly to the guardhouse where she asked to see her brother. At first the soldiers on guard duty refused her request, but Amelia told them the story of how the siblings had been separated and how much she needed to see her brother. Amelia could be very persuasive.

Twenty minutes later she saw Tom walking quickly towards the guardhouse, waving to her. Amelia ducked under the barrier and ran towards her brother, squealing with excitement. She jumped into his arms and he swung her round, kissing her on the cheeks and her hair, both laughing and crying in equal measure.

'Tommy, oh Tommy. You're here. I was so excited when I heard. Let's go somewhere? When can we have a talk? How's mum and dad? Why don't you ...'

'Mel,' Tom laughed, 'Give me a chance to breathe will you.' Tom hugged his sister tightly then let her go. 'They say absence makes the heart grow fonder, Mel.'

This time Amelia laughed. 'I know. We used to fight like cat and dog, remember?'

'That I do, and I have missed you terribly,' said Tom as he led his sister back towards the guardhouse. The two soldiers on guard duty at the main entrance looked on with amusement.

'Look Mel,' said Royle. 'I've just arrived and I have some introductory training and basic familiarisation to undergo, so I'm afraid you can't stay.' Amelia looked disappointed. 'The sergeant-major will have my guts for garters if I don't do that.

'But I have a weekend pass before the real training starts, so I will come over to see you then. Deal?'

'Deal,' smiled Amelia. 'I will show you the sights, and we can have long talks about old times.'

Tom waved goodbye to his sister, then walked back across the parade ground.

Tom felt proud at the way his sister was coping with the rigours of war on the home front. He discovered every Tuesday night Amelia would brave the blackout to travel into the city centre by bus – a truly perilous journey in the pitch black. She told her brother she was attending meetings to prepare her for volunteering as a Red Cross worker to help people in need who had been affected by the war. Tom Royle had too much on his mind to consider that she could be lying to him.

Tom had been a serious jungle walker with his father as a boy and he wanted to return to the tropical forest as soon as Hitler had been dealt with. In 1941 Royle believed, as did the wartime British government, a Japanese threat to Malaya was inconceivable. The months that followed soon changed that view.

Leadership qualities brought him to the attention of his Regimental Sergeant-Major, Ernest Muthers, a small, wiry man carrying battle honours from pre-war tours of duty with the 1st Battalion in Palestine and Egypt in 1938, Burma in 1929 with the 2nd Battalion, and the more recent evacuation of the British Expeditionary Force from Dunkirk, again with the 2nd Battalion, fighting a fierce rear-guard action to allow the huge British force to retreat from overwhelming odds. Muthers won the Military Cross for valour then, after being wounded by shrapnel in the stomach. He was evacuated home on one of the legendary small ships, the volunteer civilian boats that crossed the English Channel to help the Royal Navy rescue the British force, allowing them to fight another day.

Royle was soon wearing a platoon leader's flash on his shoulder. On passing out into the regiment Tom had the lowly rank of private soldier, but was immediately diverted into a sharp-shooter detail. Tom Royle was to become a sniper.

Tom Royle was having the time of his life as he drilled, trained, drilled and trained, all the while with thoughts of glory and honour at the forefront of his mind. Hope rose when he heard that a brigade from his regiment had been stationed in Singapore. Royle had requested a transfer so he could be near home. As he waited a response to his transfer request leave was spent in neighbouring Oldham, the Prime Ministerial constituency of Winston Churchill, and the excitement of Manchester's city centre, a short bus or train ride away. Local pubs were the ideal release, as were the local girls, and there were frequent visits to see his sister whenever possible. Whenever he could, Tom spent his time reading the newspapers, visiting News Theatres in the hope of hearing about how the war was faring elsewhere in Europe, and listening to the BBC on the wireless. He spent as much time as possible with his sister, who was living with their uncle Sidney and aunt Florence, both childless, to the north of the city centre in leafy Cheetham Hill, at that time a prosperous district of the city. From there she witnessed the nightly bombing raids, while inexplicably all around the citizens of Manchester were carrying on with a steely determination to enjoy the Christmas festivities, come what may.

But the bombing raids eventually stopped. There had been setbacks – the retreat at Dunkirk – they called it a tactical withdrawal – the German blitzes on major cities. Britain stood back and licked its wounds, then pooled its remaining resources to get tough.

All seemed to be going well again, then came the shock news of the fall of Singapore in February 1942. News of his mother's death took a long time to reach him. His father's fate was even more uncertain. His world came crashing down and Tom's war suddenly became real. Now he wanted to fight the Japanese and help win back his home in Singapore and Malaya. Thoughts of honour and glory vanished like wisps of smoke, to be replaced by an urgent demand for cold, hard, personal vengeance.

Royle trained longer and harder. When he wasn't taking part in training with his platoon and the rest of the battalion, Royle would train on his own during any free time and during leave periods. Again Royle came to the attention of Sergeant-Major Muthers.

Muthers watched through slitted eyes in the early morning sunlight as Royle began what was becoming a daily ritual on the assault course. Royle had no weapon. They were locked away and in the safe keeping of the quartermaster, only to be released when they were officially required. Instead, Royle used a straight tree branch, which he slung over his shoulder when not in use with a length of string tied at either end, like a crude rifle strap.

'Royle,' bellowed Muthers. Royle stopped his bayonet practice and looked around. Muthers simply pointed to the ground in front of him and Royle loped slowly towards him. 'On the double, lad!' shouted Muthers. Royle picked up the pace and halted at attention in front of the sergeant-major.

'At ease, then stand easy Royle,' said Muthers. The sergeant-major looked Royle in the eye and noticed his face was streaked with tears.

'At this rate you are not going to be fit to use a pea-shooter, let alone a sniper's rifle. You're doing twice the training anyone else in your platoon is doing. I would wager you're doing twice as much as anyone in the regiment. What do you say?'

'Sorry sarn't- major,' said Royle.

Muthers sighed loudly and led Royle away from the assault course and across the parade ground. 'Is it on account of your mum, lad?' Royle remained silent. Muthers glared at him until he spoke.

'I suppose so, sarn't-major,' said Royle, who then went silent again.

'Well?' said Muthers, demanding more information.

'Sarn't-major I just feel so angry. If I didn't do all this extra training I feel I would burst,' said Royle eventually. 'She was trying to get to safety, Mr Muthers. They murdered her. She was a civilian, trying to swim ashore after the Japs sank the refugee ship she was on. They machine-gunned her and the other survivors before she could reach land. It was pure bloody murder.' Muthers nodded in sympathy.

'It's no good bottling it up, lad. And all this extra training will make you fit for nothing when the time comes. And the time is coming, very soon indeed. I understand what you're going through, but you need to take a step back,' cautioned Muthers.

'I want to get them. Get back at them for what they've done,' said Royle through gritted teeth. 'I don't know what's happened to my dad now the Japs have got Singapore. Impregnable my arse,' Royle looked abashed at Muthers, who was well known for disliking any vocal use of any expletive. 'I don't have a large family. My aunt and uncle and two cousins are in Malaya, on the mainland, but it's not looking good for them either. I just want to get back at them. They need to pay for what they've done. And I want to make them pay.'

'I know, lad. And you will, you can take my word for that,'

It was an ill wind that blew a degree of strategic good. In the same series of raids that struck Malaya and Singapore, the Japanese also attacked the United States' naval base at Pearl Harbor in Hawaii, and American interests in the Philippines. That was enough to bring the United States into the war and provide Britain with a powerful ally.

Soon after his pep-talk from Sergeant-Major Muthers there came a visit by a man from Whitehall. The man, bowler hatted, wearing an immaculate pin-striped suit, winged collar and tie, approached him, with the permission of his commanding officer, and took him to afternoon tea at the still luxurious Midland Hotel in Manchester, driving him there in a government issued Packard 6, the type he later learned were in use at the ultra-secret decoding station at Bletchley Park in Buckinghamshire. The man was from the Ministry of Economic Warfare, the government department then in charge of the Special Operations Executive. He had heard of Tom's jungle experience, his fine shooting skills, and his fluency in Malay and Cantonese. He also knew of Royle's recent bereavement in the colony and his recent transfer request.

'So Royle, my condolences. The loss of your mother in such tragic circumstances must be hard to come to terms with. After all, it isn't that long ago since you last saw her,' the smartly dressed man said.

Royle gritted his teeth at the mention of his mother. 'Thank you, sir.' Royle looked around at the opulence inside the Midland. The expensive wallpaper, the brass trimmings, the ornate windows, now covered in tape to prevent glass injuries in case of air raids. Heavy blackout curtains stood waiting to be closed at a moment's notice.

The man in the suit picked up a large teapot and poured the amber liquid into Royle's dainty china cup, then offered him a sandwich off a decorative plate. Royle took one as the man poured a splash of milk in Royle's tea cup.

'You have a chance to avenge her, young man,' said the man, picking his own cup up and taking a sip.

Royle said nothing, but watched the man as he picked up a tiny sandwich, containing thinly sliced cucumber with the bread crusts removed and cut into neat triangles, and popped it into his mouth. The man smiled as he chewed.

'Your request for a transfer has come to our notice, as have your special skills,' said the man. 'We want to offer you a job.'

'Thank you, sir. I already have a job,' said Royle.

The man smiled again. 'Yes, and I have had a full report on your progress. The job I am offering is like no other. And it is right up your street. Stay with the Manchesters and you will be sent to fight in either Europe or North Africa. Come with me, and you will fight on your home turf.'

SOE had established a special clandestine fighting force called Force 136 based at Singapore, but it had not been given time to become effective before the Japanese overran the island. Tom was told he would be on the next troop ship to New Delhi, where the surviving members of Force 136 had been relocated, and from here he would be sent for guerrilla training with the elevated rank of sergeant. The man told him his experience in bushcraft and his being a more than adequate rifle shot would then combine his guerrilla warfare training with that of instructor, with its enhanced pay, before being fast-track trained as an officer at the military school in Quetta. He would then be let loose against the Japanese, as a member of the newly formed and toughened Special Operations Executive Force 136, following special forces training near Poona. His military path had been laid out before him.

'Royle,' said the man, dabbing his lips with a linen napkin, 'Your job will be to become a piece of grit within the Japanese haemorrhoid cream over on the Malay mainland. You will harrie them, sabotage their supply lines, then melt back into the jungle.'

For the first time during his meeting with this mystery man, Royle smiled. 'I can be more than that, sir. I think I can be the unhealed scab that they won't be able to resist to keep picking at.'

It was only after the man had given Tom his orders and left, after paying the bill, that Tom realised his host had not introduced himself by name. All Royle retained as a reminder of his chat – he corrected himself, it was a recruitment interview – was a travel warrant for an SOE assessment centre in the south of England.

Royle looked again at his orders. He would leave in two days, after putting his affairs with the Manchesters in order. He would go for initial assessment to what had been the exclusive private school for girls at Roedean, now closed and commandeered for wartime service.

On arrival, Royle found that he would be sharing a dormitory with five other men who had been signed up to train for undercover work in various theatres of war, mostly France and Norway. It seemed he was the only one destined for Asia. The six men introduced themselves as they made themselves at home in the former girls' dormitory. The room was a high ceilinged affair with three dim light bulbs dangling from the ceiling to offer less than adequate light. A wash stand and basin stood at one end of the room and each man had a towel hung over their metal-framed bedstead which surrounded a very hard mattress covered in rough army bedding.

On the opposite side to the light switch on the right of the door was a small white button attached to a bell somewhere else in the grand, rambling building. Above the button was a notice printed in black on white card. The notice read: "Ring if you require a mistress". It was the cause of great hilarity for the six men billeted there on their first night before initial training began in earnest. Indeed, one of the trainees, a French-speaking lieutenant in the Tank Regiment who would be trained as an SOE operator in France, never to be seen again, even tried ringing the bell for a joke. Unsurprisingly, no mistress arrived in the room. Just as well, because they had been warned to keep away from the local girls during their secret training.

Roedean was an unlikely training base for the fighters and linguists destined to become a silent force of saboteurs and intelligence gatherers in what everyone now realised would be a long, drawn out battle for survival. And thus the school was the ideal cover. Its ample grounds – 118 acres on a cliff-top overlooking the English Channel on the rolling Sussex Downs outside the seaside town of Brighton - served well as a base for secret military exercises in espionage and basic training; in outbuildings the young recruits learned about wireless telegraphy and bomb making.

The exclusive school for girls had been established in 1885 to provide a female route into the university colleges at Cambridge, among others. Instilled in all the servicemen sent there for training, however was the school's inspirational motto, Honneur aulx digny – Honour the Worthy.

For a week the trainees were packed off to the Government Code and Cipher School in London and separated into groups for their designated theatre of operations.

Royle went to the GC & CS Far East section, where he was given a brief introduction to code breaking and how to create ciphered messages from remote locations. He learned Morse code over the following weeks until he was literally thinking in dots and dashes. Then Royle was given details of the GC & CS outpost in South East Asia, the Far East Combined Bureau, or FECB, at first based in Hong Kong, then moved to Singapore ahead of the Japanese invasions in both colonies. The FECB eventually settled in Ceylon, the base for Lord Louis Mountbatten's South East Asia Command. What the men were unaware of was that Japanese messages were being intercepted by FECB and GC & CS, then sent to Japanese language cryptographers at the ultra-top secret Bletchley Park for decoding.

*

And now at the tender age of 24, a junior British officer, late 1945, the big war over, in the jungle again, and fighting an invisible enemy – this time the zealous rebels who called themselves Vietnamese nationalists – the Viet Minh - who threatened to knock askew Britain's - and France's - imperial interests in the region.

Sergeant Tenga, one of Royle's Gurkhas, crawled up to Tom's left, his rifle slung across his back and his curve-bladed kukri drawn.

'I will see what has happened, sir,' Tenga said. Royle nodded, the noise of the explosion still ringing in his ears.

Tenga crawled low along the jungle floor towards the trees from where the acrid blue-black smoke of the blast was filtering. Out of the smoke walked Sgt Kanaka, formerly of the fearsome Japanese Southern Expeditionary Army Group, clutching his colleague's blood-stained khaki cap and a wallet containing identification and mementos of a soldier who would not return.

Royle and Tenga stood simultaneously and walked towards the stone-faced Japanese sergeant.

'Who was it, Kanaka?' asked Royle.

Kanaka saluted smartly. 'My apologies for this breach in security. Corporal Ishito was careless and trod on a booby-trap mine. He is dead. The enemy is long gone.'

Kanaka bowed and stuffed Ishito's wallet and cap into his tunic. They would be sent to his family in Osaka along with a letter of condolence from Sgt Kanaka. Even now Ishito had only been 21 years old and had been fighting with the Japanese Imperial Army for six years. First in China, then across South East Asia during the Japanese springboard of occupation, Operation Ichigo, and finally here in Indochina.

Royle had to admire the discipline of the Japanese soldiers, despite their ruthless wartime reputation when it came to dealing with prisoners and civilians. Royle had never rated the Japanese for their bushcraft in jungle fighting. He had found he could out-manoeuvre all but the most skilled Japanese jungle fighters, and had done so on numerous occasions during this long war. All thanks to his father and uncle.

*

Tom Royle was just 12 years old when his father, Harry, and uncle Jim took him hunting in the jungles of Kedah, close to Jim Royle's rubber plantation at Baling. Jim's eight-year-old son Charlie, Tom's cousin, accompanied them, to Harry's annoyance, but Charlie had gone into a tantrum at the prospect of being left behind. He was given the safe and undemanding task of carrying the empty sacks the hunting party hoped to place their prey in to take home.

Harry had already taken Tom on forays around his own Singapore estate, where Tom would display his skill with a rifle, stalking and hunting small animals and snakes.

But here, in Kedah, Tom was being taken on, and taking part in, a real hunting trip, away from the relative safety of the family plantation, and in the thick of the real Malay jungle.

Today they were hunting gaur, a powerful bovine beast with spear-sharp horns. It was also known as seladang. Along the way they hoped to also get a crack at three possible types of deer - sambar deer, mouse deer or barking deer – and some wild boar. The hunting party would be camping under the trees in Kedah for a week, and a half dozen ethnic Chinese porters carried their tents, cooking equipment and rifles on three ponies as they snaked their way around winding jungle trails.

Uncle Jim was leading the way, slashing through vines and branches with a sharp machete. Tom and his father were close behind, with young Charlie proudly carrying the sacks at the rear, all followed by the porters and their ponies.

Harry laughed as Jim slashed his way through the undergrowth, 'Carry on doing that, Jim, and we won't see anything with four legs at all.'

Jim shook his head and continued hacking his way through the green tangle.

They continued for another twenty minutes, then Jim stopped and called for a rest break. He sat, sweating and breathing hard, where he had stood. He took a long drink from his water bottle, then looked at his brother. 'All right, Harry. See if you can do any better. We are about six miles from a clearing where we can make camp.'

'We will, come on Tom.' Harry and Tom stood and made their way to the front. Tom picked up a machete from a sheath tied to one of the ponies. Harry stood there, his hands free.

'And what do you intend cutting through with?' said Jim. 'Or will you make young Tom do all the work?'

'I can cut through with my machete, Uncle Jim,' said Tom, raising the sharp weapon in his hand and moving to the very front of the line.

'Not so fast you two,' said Harry. 'With all the racket we're making we won't see another animal until we're greeted by Amelia's dog, Baldwin back home. Anything we want to hunt will run a mile. Here's a trick I learned from the Boers.' Harry Royle reached in to his knapsack and brought out a pair of heavy duty, stainless steel hand secateurs. He flourished them at his brother, then handed a pair to Tom and proceeded to silently cut through the undergrowth.

'Lesson One,' said Harry Royle, laughing. 'When stalking, don't let them hear you coming.'

That night they made camp and enjoyed a meal provided by their Chinese cook. Early the next morning they set off with three of their six porters.

Harry and Tom again began to silently, but painstakingly, snip their way through the branches and vines that impeded their progress, while Jim carried the loaded rifle to protect the party from marauding tigers or leopards. Every few minutes they stopped to listen, then continued, all the time ensuring the thin breeze blowing within the rainforest was in their faces.

Harry stopped suddenly and raised his hand to indicate a general halt. Everyone stopped and Harry, a renowned and expert tracker, sniffed the air. He indicated Tom should do the same. Beyond the undergrowth, in a small clearing, they heard rustling and animal noises. And then Tom detected the faint musky odour of an animal. Tom's father put his finger to his lips to indicate silence, then beckoned his brother over with the rifle. Harry took the weapon and handed it to Tom. Tom had never fired a Lee Enfield .303 rifle before. It felt much heavier than the weapon he was used to back home.

Harry Royle quietly parted the greenery before them, and there stood a mouse deer. The smallest deer in the world, it was an adult male and was feeding on plant matter on the floor of the clearing. Tom silently knelt and aimed the heavy rifle, moving the bolt as quietly as possible to feed a round into the breech.

'Take a deep breath and hold it, then aim and fire,' whispered Tom's dad.

Tom did as he was told. He had shot small wildlife before, but with his own smaller calibre .22 rifle. And while the mouse deer was the smallest of the deer species, it was the largest animal he had ever had in his gun sights.

The red-brown animal with white neck stripes continued to feed from the canopy floor. The deer was in Tom's sights. He squeezed the trigger and fired.

Recoil from the rifle, the standard British army rifle since 1895, knocked Tom on to his back and almost dislocated Tom's right shoulder. Tom's ears rang with the crack of the discharged shot. He managed to raise his head in time to see the mouse deer leap away into the treeline.

Harry hoisted Tom back on his feet and Tom rubbed his sore, bruised, right shoulder. Uncle Jim laughed lightly while cousin Charlie looked at Tom wide-eyed.

'Lesson Number Two, Tom,' said Tom's father. 'This is the weapon we will be hunting with. It has an effective firing range of about 550 yards and maximum range of 3,000 yards or one and three-quarter miles. It can fire up to 30 aimed shots per minute and has a ten-round magazine. And, you will already have noticed, it delivers a hell of a kick. Shoulder all right?'

Tom nodded as he continued to rub his bruised shoulder.

'Good,' said his father. 'The lesson is, learn all you can about the type of weapon you are using. They are all different and knowledge can save your life in an emergency. But there is nothing quite like experience when it comes to using a weapon.'

Tom nodded, and walked to his knapsack to sulkily take a sip of water.

Two hours later they encountered a wild boar snuffling for food in the undergrowth. This time Tom did not miss.

*

Tom Royle's path as a covert operator with Force 136 had sent him behind enemy lines for much of his war, and his early training in bushcraft and hunting had made him the ideal individual to ghost in and out of enemy territory. He knew he would be tortured and killed if discovered, and he knew the experience would neither be quick nor pleasant. Royle had returned to Malaya under Japanese occupation, as well as Burma and northern Indochina, carrying out sabotage missions and causing as much mayhem as possible, occasionally linking up with fellow Force 136 officers and members of the American equivalent, the OSS. He had forged links with anti-Japanese nationalist groups and trained them to fight guerrilla-style. Many were already efficient in bushcraft, which made his job all the easier. He had particularly good fortune with the Malayan Communist guerrillas who had quickly organised themselves into an effective fighting force in the jungles of Malaya. Royle was able to group them into fierce fighting units who lived in the bush for years, fought with the invaders as often as possible, disrupted supply lines, and then melted back into the relative safety of the canopy.

It was December 1943 and Royle was back in the jungle in Malaya, in Kedah, where he had been taken by his father and uncle on his first hunting trip. It was on this trip to the mainland on another mission to sabotage Japanese supply lines and cause general havoc that one of his Communist guerrilla contacts had told him about his father. News had just filtered through about Harry Royle's death in Changi Jail. His death had happened quite recently, but there were no details about how he had died. Royle took the news silently, gritting his teeth so his jaw muscles throbbed beneath his skin. So, now he was without a mother and a father. Thank God his sister remained in England. Relatively safe at least. Royle and his company of guerrillas took a short break beneath the rainforest, even though they did not feel fatigued. It was more so Royle could compose himself. They were still in enemy territory and any loss of concentration could mean discovery and death. Royle wandered away from his men and into the darkness provided by a clump of trees, where he silently wept for a few moments, then took a deep breath, wiped the tears from his face, and returned to his guerrilla soldiers.

Speaking in Malay, Royle gathered his men around him. 'Time to carry on, lads. Our next rest break will be at nightfall, and we have a lot of ground to cover until then. Onward!' The group set off, stealthily cutting through the undergrowth with steel secateurs.

Royle had become used to the sight of murdered civilians and burnt-out villages. Hardened as he had become to the horrors of war, and with a visceral fury after learning of the nightmarish deaths of family members in Malaya and Singapore, it was a terrifying and nightmarish incident during this period of his life that would remain with him for the rest of his life. During his jungle forays and sabotage missions in the jungles of Malaya, Royle soon learned that an atrocity could be detected by smell up to a mile away, with the stench of rotting or burned corpses, and the organic smoke stink of smouldering village buildings.

No civilian deaths had been as horrific as those on this particular day, the day he had learned of the death of his father, when Royle had been leading a small group of communist guerrillas to a village just within the canopy. Before they even reached the village they knew it had been made an example of by the local Japanese force. Usually the head man would be executed and the buildings put to the torch for some, often minor, rebellion or misdemeanour.

As they walked into this particular village – no-one knew its name – they knew immediately that this was no ordinary punishment. They were led to the killing ground by smell. The buildings were burned, many to the ground, as they had expected. But every man, woman and child had been murdered, either by bayonet, to save on ammunition, or by being barricaded into buildings and then burned alive. Royle walked around the site of the atrocity until he came to the village chicken pen. All the chickens had been taken away, no doubt for the Japanese garrison to enjoy a feast with. Lying by the broken, bamboo fence that had been used to corral the birds lay a teenage boy, barely alive, but still breathing. He must have lain there for days. Royle assumed he too had been bayoneted and left to die. But Royle was unable to ascertain any bayonet wound for the pack of starving hounds that were savaging the boy. Four of them were tearing his stomach open and eating his flesh. The boy was so near death he did not move and no sound came from his mouth. But his agony could be told with a look into his horror-stricken eyes. The youth's intestines had been pulled from the gaping hole that was his stomach and the starving dogs were feasting on him. Royle had kicked at the animals, who had in turn snarled and bit him too. A blind fury then took hold of Royle. This, on the day he discovered his father had died, sent Royle into a fugue state of temporary insanity. In a frenzy of violence, Royle took out his pistol and shot all four dogs dead. He emptied his pistol on them until they lay quiet and bloody in the dust. The noise of the gunfire echoed through the trees. Royle's guerrilla comrades dashed to the scene then stared at their usually stoic Force 136 leader as he stood staring at the dead animals white-faced with anger, his revolver still smoking from the discharged rounds.

Then, with tears now unashamedly running down his sweat-grimed face, Royle walked over to the boy, caressed his hair gently, spoke softly reassuring words in Malay while refilling his revolver, then fired a bullet into the boy's brain to deliver him from his agony. And for the first, and last time in that war, Thomas Royle vomited against a tree, in an outflowing of all that he had seen to date, brought to a head by this single senseless horror, and after the all-consuming grief he felt after hearing of his father's death.

It was an incident that would endure and shackle Royle with a phobia of dogs for the rest of his life.

*

'It wasn't a good death, Lieutenant,' said the sergeant, a survivor from what was left of the 6th Territorials Battalion of the Manchester Regiment. 'He bore it well, sir.'

Sergeant Alfred McKinney sat across the bare table from Tom Royle, in the grounds of what had been the Saigon Tennis Club. It was late August 1945, the war had just ended and the British had arrived with the intention of bringing order out of chaos. The two men sat under the shade of the derelict pavilion terrace, where French colons would once have sipped their liqueurs and wines as tennis matches were played. No tennis had been played here since the Japanese takeover. McKinney was impossibly thin and dressed in what could only be described as rags, although closer inspection revealed they were what was left of his army uniform. Replacement clothing had not yet arrived for McKinney, or for the hundreds of Allied ex-prisoners of war now liberated from the Japanese.

'May I get you anything, sergeant? A drink, water perhaps? Something to eat? Before we start,' said Royle, concerned by the greyness in the man's freshly shaven face. McKinney was deeply tanned by years in forced labour under the brutal tropical sun, first in Singapore, where he had been taken prisoner with Royle's father, Harry. But his unhealthy pallor could still be detected. Later McKinney would be transported by Malaya's new Japanese overlords to work on railway bridges across rivers in Siam, which would be used to carry troops and supplies from the Japanese stronghold in Indochina into Malaya and other parts of South East Asia.

McKinney shook his head sadly. 'Just water, thank you, sir. Doctors have given me a strict diet to observe.' McKinney laughed bitterly. 'Look at me, as if I need to be on a diet. But too much food and drink could kill me, they say. Especially after being deprived of it for so long.'

'I'm sorry,' said Royle, reaching for his army-issue water bottle and handing it to McKinney. 'What can you tell me about my father?'

'Harry Royle was a true gent, sir. I was with him at the end. We had been together in work parties repairing damage to the docks at Singapore. The Japanese had caused a pretty awful mess when they assaulted the island, and the docks and harbour were a primary target. The oil storage tanks burned for months, all the derricks and hoists were damaged beyond repair, and the structural damage was extremely severe. The place still stank of burning oil, petrol and spent munitions for many months, sir.

'Harry and I were taken prisoner together when the governor-general ordered our surrender. We were ready to fight on, although by that time it was pretty clear that we couldn't win.

'But we followed our orders and laid down our weapons. The first thing the Japanese did was to execute some of our senior officers. Then we were carted off in a long line, bound and tied by the neck to Changi. That place was never good, even when we ran it. With the Japanese in charge Changi became a whole new level of hell. There was a serious lack of food and water. Sanitation was non-existent, and we were held ten to a tiny cell, with only a small window slit giving natural light. It was grim and damp, and it stank like you have never encountered, sir.

There was just one fetid bucket in a corner for all of us to piss and shit in, sir. We had to take it in turns to empty it every other day, by which time it had got pretty full, attracting clouds of flies.'

'Yes, I've read the report on Changi Jail. How did you end up here in Saigon?' asked Royle.

McKinney's hands shook as he took a cigarette out of his top pocket and placed it between his dry, cracked lips. Royle lit the cigarette for him.

'Like I said, sir. Your dad and I were put to work repairing the docks. We had to work eighteen-hour days. Hard labour it was, sir. Then we would be taken back to our cell at night. Then early next morning, same again. It was a relief to be taken out of the cell, but the work outside was very difficult. Very hard. We did that for getting on for two years, sir.

'When I injured my arm with a pickaxe, Harry told me to pretend to work, while he did his work and mine as well. He did that for four days, until I was able to work again. But your dad knew, sir, that if the Japanese had found out I was injured, I would have been killed there and then. He saved my life by covering for me, sir.

'Some time later, I can't be too exact, sir. We lost all sense of time. But some time later, your dad became ill.

'He began to hallucinate. He had great pain in his limbs and was eventually unable to walk. The illness caused his limbs and body to swell, and I'm sorry to say, he was in excruciating pain.

'Harry started to be ill in our cell and the army doctor, himself a prisoner, demanded he be taken to the prison hospital. The Japanese commander agreed and your father was taken to the hospital, but there was nothing there to treat him with. No medicines were available for prisoners, and the same terrible food continued, even for the sick. I'll never eat a bowl of rice again, sir, and that's the truth.'

McKinney took a long drag of his cigarette, then looked Royle in the eye. 'The doctor came to me a few days after he had been taken to the hospital and told me Harry had died of heart failure brought on by the illness. He said it was beri-beri. I would see many more die from that horrible disease while I was a PoW.

'By this time the work on the docks was virtually complete. Next thing I knew I was being force marched with a group of other prisoners north through Malaya and into Siam. We built bridges across wide rivers so that Japanese trains could transport supplies and troops to wherever they were needed. Very often the bridges were bombed by the Allies, so we were then forced to rebuild them.

'Around May or June of this year we were put on a train travelling north into Indochina and we ended up here in Saigon. Things were starting to look serious as the Japs started losing ground and I thought that could be very bad news for us. Our guards became even more brutal and sadistic. Some prisoners were killed out of hand, sometimes just for being cheeky or talking back to them, like any good Tommy would do. Killed them, I tell you.

'We were put to work in the freight yards on the Saigon River, working as stevedores at the docks unloading ships and then loading the freight on to trains, which would then go across the bridges we had built earlier.

'Then the surrender came, and we were given some freedom. Members of the Viet Minh looked after us. They treated our injuries and illnesses, fed us, clothed us, and we waited. In the meantime the French, who had worked alongside the Japanese all these years, were rounded up and put into the prison camps.

'Then the British arrived, sir. You were a welcome sight, I can tell you, sir.'

'Thank you, sergeant. Thank you very much,' said Royle. He could feel his lips and chin start to tremble and tears began to well up in his eyes. 'You will be repatriated as soon as you are well enough, sergeant. The same goes for the rest of the British prisoners. I appreciate your kind remarks about my father,' said Royle.

'He saved my life sir. Harry Royle was a true hero.'

*

Despite the excesses of some, Royle recognised that the Japanese Army was fierce. Its soldiers had proven themselves to be determined and unremitting fighters and had used every fighting skill known to them, including that of the ambush. Many of his Chindit colleagues, especially officers of the old school, had condemned this tactic as being either cowardly or lauded it as being superior bushcraft. The latter view would linger on through apocryphal history as being the main reason for Japan's success in South East Asia. But Royle recognised it for what it was, simply a good jungle tactic, which the Chindits began to take note of and copy to great effect.

Tenga moved forward into the darkness of the trees, followed by Royle. They would need to find any tracks left by the nationalists in order to continue their pursuit – a tall order. The booby trap had been small but effective. It had killed one of his squad and had obliterated traces within a three-foot diameter crater.

Royle turned back before entering the bush. 'Captain Thierry, please remain where you are until we return. The trail has gone cold and we need to establish a trace again.'

Thierry gave a disdainful half-salute and rolled on his back, his hands behind his head and a blade of grass in his mouth, feigning relaxation. In fact Captain Pascal Thierry was afraid, not of the nationalists whom he had orders to hunt down and track to their hidden hideouts – the order had come from de Gaulle himself – but he was quite wary of the wildlife. The mighty water buffalo, never averse to a sudden stampede; the sharp pointed horns of the wild black seladang, magnificent and deadly if one came across an angry bull; the slithering snakes; but most of all the insects. Royle had seen the poorly disguised horror in Thierry's craggy yet handsome face as soon as they entered the tree line, and the bugs seemed to know too. Royle had seen it before, among the raw recruits who made up the early Chindit force into Burma. Royle had grown used to them during his jungle forays at home in Malaya. The raw recruits soon got used to it, and Royle expected the same of the Frenchman. But for now, Captain Thierry hated this jungle.

Tom turned back towards the dark depths of the jungle perimeter and entered the gloom. He crouched low and allowed his eyes to become accustomed to the half-light before scanning the area for Sgt Tenga. Tenga was crouched beside a tree scanning 180 degrees ahead of him. He turned as Royle slowly approached him with a stealth that had become second nature. He walked with the precise, uneven, crouched and silent steps of a highly trained scout. Tom took a position at the other side of Tenga's tree, watched and listened.

The only sounds they could hear came from squawking birds and squabbling monkeys. The enemy must have simply vanished into the bush. Tom stepped forward, carefully tracking for more booby-traps. There were none. It seemed the rebels had only a limited supply of explosive. Tom's force must have been close to catching them, he realised. The trap had been hastily contrived to give the rebels the chance to escape quickly, while Tom's group reeled in the confusion of the trap. Well, they hadn't been so confused, but a man had died and the delay that caused was all the rebel soldiers needed.

Tom and Tenga looked carefully for signs of the rebel group. Royle had to admit, these Viet Minh guerrillas were expert in the ancient art of deception and concealment. Then, there it was. The one trace they needed to pick up the trail again. A cartridge from a captured Japanese rifle, a Type 44 carbine, half hidden in the undergrowth. One of the rebels must have fired a shot too, Royle thought. But no-one heard it because of the blast. Tenga pointed to a tree near the site of the explosion. The remains of Cpl Ishito smouldered in three pieces to the tree's left. Tenga loped over to touch part of the tree where the wood showed through red, the bark torn away by the bullet. It was a tree known locally as a Dragon's Blood Tree, where red wood showed when the bark was stripped away. The shot had detonated the booby-trap which killed Ishito. A rebel had stayed behind to set the trap while the main group had escaped.

Royle beckoned Kanaka to the spot and pointed to the site. 'Ishito wasn't careless. He didn't step on a mine or a trip wire. The booby-trap was exploded by a single bullet. The mark can be seen in this tree after it had exploded the detonator.'

Kanaka bowed low and said, 'I thank you for your kind words, Lt Royle. I will tell Ishito's family that he died a warrior's death, still in the service of the Emperor.'

At that moment a hail of rifle fire blazed out of thick bushes just over 100 metres away. Three more Japanese soldiers were killed as Royle's patrol leapt to the ground for cover. Tenga crawled left, his fellow Gurkha went right in an effort to outflank the Viet Minh, while Royle waved the Japanese troops to crawl forward, firing as they went. The Frenchman Thierry bravely crawled towards them and pulled his pistol from his holster, gripping it tightly as he searched for a target.

A whistle from the left and then from the right – again the imitation of an English cuckoo, a bird not found in the jungles of South East Asia – told Royle his Gurkhas were in position. It was a signal devised by Royle.

'Rapid fire into that area now!' ordered Royle. Jungle sounds were drowned out as British, Japanese rifles and a lone French revolver, poured leaden death into the target bushes. The leaves and branches were obliterated under the onslaught, then came the screams of the guerrilla fighters caught in what had become a semi-circle of death.

'Cease firing!' shouted Royle.

Silence ensued, and the sharp stench of cordite hung over the patrol for some minutes before drifting off in a haze of blue-grey smoke on the light breeze.

Royle stood, followed by the Gurkhas, Thierry and the surviving Japanese soldiers. Royle waved Tenga's men to investigate the killing ground.

Five dead Vietnamese guerrillas lay there, shot to death.

Tenga returned to the booby-trapped tree, placed his finger in the bullet hole, twisted it and turned his body perpendicular to the point of entry.

'The shot was fired from that direction, Lieutenant.' Tenga pointed to a position 50 yards to Royle's left. 'I would guess they escaped that way too.'

'All right, sergeant. One last survey for booby-traps, then we'll pick up the pursuit.'

OCTOBER 1974

The door seemed to crash open in the silent examination room.

Dr Tom Royle was shaken from his daydream of past adventures by the University of Hull's History Department admin secretary tip-toeing into the room towards the desk where he sat, invigilating a start of term mathematics exam. The academic was no expert in mathematics. Royle's expertise was South East Asian history and culture. But supervising first-year faculty examinations under strict test conditions required no knowledge of the subject these poor students were required to have learned.

Slim, attractive, smartly dressed and hair dyed blonde, Alison Naylor, the department's administrative wizard, drew closer to whisper in his ear. Momentarily Royle was distracted by the fragrance of the scent she was wearing. He'd had little interest in any woman since Meg, his wife, had died twelve years earlier. Besides, at 53, Royle was old enough to be her father. Even so, Dr Thomas Royle was still fit, well built and healthy. His dark brown hair had lightened a little over the years, but there was still no grey in sight. And his broad, craggy face could always light up a room with a ready, broad smile. Women saw him as athletic for his age, slightly dishevelled, a little bit distant and eccentric, but a thorough gentleman with a ready wit and an old school colonial charm many were unable to place.

'Excuse me, Dr Royle, but there are two policemen outside to see you. They said it was urgent.'

Royle nodded curtly and stepped away from the invigilation desk as Alison remained on guard, and he walked quietly out of the hall. Students watched the mini-drama surreptitiously as they feigned disinterest. Alison had said the police officers were waiting for him in his room in the History Department. As Royle walked, absent-mindedly wondering what the police could want with him, he deftly side-stepped his colleague, Dr Adrian Schulman, who was rushing through the hall's revolving doors to take Royle's place of invigilation. The examination still had over an hour to run. Royle nodded a quick acknowledgement to the younger man, but did not slow his pace towards the revolving doors and the university campus. Royle smiled to himself as he realised his jungle sixth sense had not deserted him, even in such halls of academe. The events of the wars he had fought in were still clear in his mind all these years later, and so was the training.

Tom Royle made his way out of the university sports hall, where a number of examinations were taking place that day, down the concrete path between a tower block of student halls, past the multi-storey university student union building and the ornate rococo-style administration building on the right, towards the newly built arts and humanities building, where his cramped rooms were located. As he walked through the heavy double-glazed doors and turned right into the History Department, the smell of polish and clean new wood filled his senses. Dr Tom Royle walked into his room, fourth door on the left down the corridor, for the last time.

The room was covered wall to floor with books, some authored by him, standing on wooden shelves fixed to three of the four walls. Had a large window and radiator not dominated the fourth wall, that too would have been filled with knowledge had it been possible.

Royle's desk was positioned so that he could look through the window on his left at the gardens outside. His work station was littered with student essays, published documents from the State Department of the United States relating to a final-year student dissertation, a telephone and an unwashed coffee mug. Plugged in on a filing cabinet by the window was an electric coffee percolator. Perpendicular to Royle's desk were two other desks, creating the effect of a long conference table, surrounded by eight chairs. This was where he presided over his student tutorials. At two of these chairs the officers sat. Both were smartly dressed in civilian clothes. CID, he thought. Members of the Humberside Constabulary's Criminal Investigation Department.

The two men stood. The first, who seemed to be in his late thirties, spoke: 'Dr Thomas Royle?' Royle nodded, hearing the familiar policeman's tone often heard on TV when a person was about to be placed under arrest.

'I am Detective Sergeant Sweeney, this is Detective Constable Redpath.'

'Please sit down. How can I help you? Coffee?'

'No thank you, sir.' Royle noticed the two men each had a cup of what looked like tea before them. Alison was a gem, but even she was unable to delay the detectives for long. Royle inspected his unwashed mug, shrugged slightly, then poured himself a black coffee and sat at his desk.

'Dr Royle, we have just returned from your house. There appears to have been a burglary and a fire, and we would like to ask you a few questions about some of the items in your house.'

Royle looked at the two men in shock. 'A fire? Burglary? My sister, she lives with me. Is she all right?'

DC Redpath smiled and said: 'That would be Mrs Amelia Harper, sir?' Royle nodded. 'She is unhurt and helping with our enquiries also, sir.'

A sixth sense put Thomas Royle on alert. *Helping with our inquiries also*, he thought. Royle nodded and waved his coffee cup at the detectives in a signal for them to continue.

'Dr Royle, we found weapons and explosives in your house after the fire brigade had made the area safe. The bomb squad are on their way there now to deal with the explosives. Can you explain this please?' DS Sweeney looked into Royle's eyes. His politeness belied an underlying menace.

Royle smiled. 'Why of course. I have a number of hand guns, decommissioned hand grenades and some plastique – minus fuses of course. All kept safely in my safe. Souvenirs of the war. I have the appropriate licences.'

'Well, Dr Royle. Your safe is open and the weapons and explosives are littered around the house and your front garden. We have seen no evidence of any licences or permits,' said Sweeney. 'Please come with us to your house to identify these items. We may have to charge you with possession of explosives, which is a very serious offence. If you need to follow in your car DC Redpath will accompany you.'

Surely they don't think I'm Provisional IRA, thought Royle. Still, there were heightened tensions since the Provos had started their mainland bombing campaign. Royle smiled a reassuring smile.

'That's quite all right, officer. I travel to work on my bicycle. I can come with you in your car,' said Royle, wondering what the devil was going on.

They drove out of the visitors' car park at the front of the university in an unmarked police Ford Granada, turned right on to Cottingham Road for the short journey to Tom Royle's home in the village of Cottingham, a small conurbation outside Hull's urban centre. The car had to stop at a level crossing as the train from Hull's Paragon Station drew slowly towards the platform, destined for Beverley and the seaside resort of Scarborough. Music blared from the car behind – a Mini Cooper - *Killer Queen*, by Queen, playing on the car's tape cassette player until the warning bells from the level crossing alerted motorists and pedestrians that the barriers were about to rise and allow traffic to cross the tracks.

Inside the car, impeccably clean and tidy, Royle detected the smell of newly applied polish to the dashboard and steering wheel, and probably the leather seats too. But even that failed to smother the faint background fragrance of old greasy chip paper.

All the while Royle was wondering what had happened at his house. If his permits had gone missing he could be suspected as an IRA terrorist.

The car drew up to Royle's house and the damage was immediately apparent. The small, yet smart, two-bedroomed detached bungalow in a quiet cul-de-sac of the village had suddenly become the blight of the street. On the front lawn partially destroyed furniture lay scattered, dumped by the firefighters as they tackled the blaze. The windows and curtains of the house were smoke blackened, but still intact. The door had been smashed open, presumably by the firemen as they entered the house. Otherwise the building seemed structurally sound. All three men stepped out of the car. A neighbour's dog ran up to Royle yapping in a friendly fashion. Royle was startled and kicked out at the animal, sending it yelping away. Royle broke into a cold sweat as the memory of those man-eating dogs in that Malay village forced its way up from his subconscious memory. He hated dogs.

'Are you all right, sir?' asked Sweeney, looking at the suddenly disturbed academic.

Royle quickly wiped the beads of sweat from his brow. 'Yes, thank you. Just a slight aberration.'

Sweeney looked at him more closely, a puzzled expression forming on his face.

'Wartime memories, sergeant,' said Royle, forcing a smile. Sweeney nodded and indicated for Royle to head into the smouldering mess that was his house. A uniformed police constable stood guard over the weapons and explosives – from a distance. Sweeney and Redpath led Royle towards the cache.

'Are these yours, sir?' asked Sweeney. Royle inspected his wartime souvenirs for a minute or two.

'They do appear to be, yes. Let me explain …,'

'No need to, sir. Can you come inside now, please?' Sweeney lightly gripped Royle's arm and gingerly led him through the battered doorway – part of the door was still attached to the hinges, but most of the wood had been smashed into large splinters. They entered the lounge. The smoke was still choking, but other than that there was little fire damage. The fire had been started by burning a pile of papers on the bed. This was the seat of the fire, said the white-helmeted fire chief in charge of the firefighters on the scene. Royle's bedroom was a total shambles and was badly damaged. In the corner of the room the safe hung open and empty. Royle looked at the pile of ashes on the bed and despair hit him. The house could be repaired, but almost a year of hard work on his latest academic publication lay destroyed. He had almost completed the work and Royle had intended making it the subject of a new course on the Malayan Emergency next year. He had included some new and exciting facts after some extensive – and personally experienced - research. Royle found himself sitting on a step to his front gate, breathing in the fresh air and slowly recovering from his shock. He had been led outside by the two detectives.

'Sir, I'd like to ask you about the contents of your safe,' Redpath spoke quietly into Royle's ear.

'You mean my weapons? As I said I have a licence to keep guns and the explosives are decommissioned. I have permits for those also, although the documents may lie in that pile of ashes in my bedroom.'

'No, Dr Royle. I mean the papers you kept in your safe.'

Strange, thought Royle. *Why are they no longer interested in my ordnance. Surely that was why they brought me here in the first place.*

'I see,' said Royle. 'They were academic papers; the work of the best part of a year. My latest book on Li Pengfei and the Malay Emergency. I must inform my publisher, we were to launch it in six weeks.'

'Why would someone destroy your work, Dr Royle?' asked Sweeney. 'Professional rivalry, vandalism?'

Angry now, Royle looked at the men. 'I have no idea. Isn't that your job to find out?'

'And the passports, sir?'

Royle gave the detective a quizzical look, then walked to his bedside table and opened a drawer, pulling out his passport.

'Is this what you mean?' he asked Sweeney, now visibly annoyed, as he showed the navy blue document with its gold-embossed crown of the United Kingdom to the detective.

'No sir, I mean these,' Sweeney reached into a pocket of his coat and pulled out a plastic evidence bag containing what appeared to be coloured paper and cardboard, and a large amount of ash. 'We recovered these from your safe, sir. They appear to be passports for different nationalities.'

Royle gaped at the policeman. In the past he had used false passports to get in and out of places while working in his intelligence capacity. But since his retirement he had retained only one – his own British passport.

'I have no idea what those are,' Royle finally said, and went back outside to sit on the front step. He sat there for a while wondering just what the hell was going on, watched all the time by the two police officers.

Royle got back to his feet. 'Now, I would like to see my sister.'

'She's down at the station, sir. We can go now.'

A light drizzle began to fall as the police Granada drove away from the scene.

Cottingham police station was an austere, stone late Victorian building with a small complement of uniformed police officers, headed by a police inspector, and a custody suite in the charge of a custody sergeant. Amelia was waiting in one of the station's bleak interview rooms, seated on a wood and tubular steel stacking chair. She was chain-smoking, resting her elbows on a stained, scratched and scarred table which was in urgent need of a coat of varnish.

Royle walked into the room, followed by the detectives, kissed his sister on the cheek – she returned a wink – then whirled round to face the detectives. 'All right, this isn't going anything like the book. Are we under arrest for something or not?' Sweeney turned to the uniformed female officer guarding the interview room door and with a quick flick of the head indicated for her to leave the room. This was going to be no ordinary interview. Sweeney smiled at Royle and his sister.

'No sir, you are not under arrest.'

Royle decided to push his luck. 'What about my little stash of seemingly unlicensed firearms? I don't want to tempt fate, but I would have thought you have grounds to prosecute me for this at least, considering my permits have disappeared.'

'No sir, that's not our intention. The truth is, we had been on our way to see you an hour and a half prior to arriving at your rooms. We were diverted by the report of your burglary and house fire. We know you are licensed to keep those weapons. We know you had kept them locked up safely, until someone expertly opened your safe.

Amelia pulled a paper tissue from her sleeve, blew her nose and whispered 'Not again, Tommy.' A tear glistened down her cheek. She was four years younger than Tom. A widow, she still carried herself with a trim figure and a handsome face. She wore an orange and black woollen suit and appeared slightly ruffled after her rush into the burning house, her quick departure to call the fire service, and her confusing trip to the police station.

Royle looked at his sister. The detectives ignored her cryptic remark. 'There's someone here to see you,' said Sweeney. 'We thought it best that you come down to the station to speak to him. I can take you to him now, if you like.'

'And who is this mysterious person I've been dragged all the way from my place of employment to meet?' said Royle. Training began to kick in. He began to say things to put his opponent off guard, to measure the distance to the unlocked door of the interview room, his trajectory as he forced his way past the two policemen, through the public waiting area and out of the front door. Then what? No, best to meet the mystery man someone had gone to an immense amount of trouble to bring about.

'Lead on,' said Royle. 'But first, I want my sister properly looked after. She certainly can't go home, and it would be unsafe for her to do so.' Royle looked at his sister and she returned a knowing shake of the head as her eyes turned skyward. 'I want her booked into a hotel and I want my house repaired. And I want you to organise that right now, before I see anyone.'

Redpath let out a laugh. 'We're police, not nurse-maids. We've got better things to do than …,'

Sweeney cut him short. 'We'll do all you ask Dr Royle. DC Redpath will personally take Mrs Harper to a city centre hotel and I will arrange for all the necessary repairs to your house. You have my word.'

'Sarge?' Redpath looked puzzled.

'Do it, Redpath.'

'Yes, Sgt Sweeney.' Redpath turned to Amelia. 'This way please.' The detective constable stomped out with Amelia. He was certainly going to report this one to his Police Federation rep when he got the chance.

Royle gave his sister a reassuring wave as she left the room. Things were starting to fall into place. Redpath was obviously a Humberside detective constable, as he claimed. Sweeney, however, was undoubtedly SB. What would Special Branch want with him after all these years?

'All right Sgt Sweeney. I assume you're Special Branch. What's this all about? I expect you have been briefed about my background?'

'To some extent, sir.'

'Look, I've been retired for the last 14 years. What's going on?'

'Could you come with me now, sir? Everything will be explained in full, I'm sure.'

Sweeney led Royle out of the interview room and up a flight of clean stone steps to the first floor. They walked along a corridor, the linoleum tiled floor shone as if newly polished. Both travelled past a variety of wooden doors, some open. Most were empty of people. Then through double doors and into the canteen. Only a few tables were occupied. Through another set of double doors and they were back on the corridor. A few doors further down they stopped. It was the office of the inspector in charge. Sweeney knocked once and walked in, followed by Royle. A dapper, balding man stood as they entered. Sweeney nodded to him and left the room, closing the door behind him.

'Bill?' Royle asked, unsure, yet at the same time certain that this was the Special Branch officer who had planned Royle's secret operations during the Malayan Emergency twenty years ago.

'Good to see you, Tommy.' Bill Ferney strode around the tidy desk, his arm and hand outstretched. Tom Royle took it. He enjoyed reunions, but this certainly wasn't one of those.

'Bill,' said Royle. 'You're not still in this game are you?'

'No,' laughed Ferney. 'At least not until a week ago. I've been recalled, and now so have you.'

Royle sat in a chair opposite the desk and shook his head. 'Not a chance, Bill. I gave all that up a long time ago. I've got a quiet, respectable life and I've got a hundred or so students who have just started my course. I've got commitments. I've got a life. And most important of all, I've got security and peace of mind.'

'It all sounds a bit boring to me. Not the Tommy Royle I know,' said the older man. Ferney sat down at the desk and opened a red box file. He started to read the contents aloud: 'Thomas Reginald Royle, born 5th December 1920 ... Singapore, blah, blah. Don't need to go into the early years, do we?

'Left the island in November 1940 to fight for the old country,' Ferney paraphrased, 'Against Hitler – admirable if I may say so, blah, blah. From the Manchester Regiment it was a transfer to Quetta after most of your family died, thanks to the Japanese. Ah, yes, then it was the start of your cloak and dagger days. You were recruited to the Special Operations Executive Force 136 because of your jungle and language skills. Your job was to infiltrate enemy lines, cause sabotage, and basically be a complete pain in the arse to the Japanese, slowing their advance as much as possible. Trained at the India Mission's Eastern Warfare School at Western Ghats near Poona, and later at the Advanced Training School at Arugam Bay in Ceylon, or Sri Lanka as we call it these days. Correct?'

'If that's what it says, then it must be,' said Royle. 'But you know all this anyway, why bring it all up now?' Royle was not relishing the reintroduction of his past in such a cavalier manner. During his years under cover he had seen plenty of death. He had killed a lot of people in the course of his duty, and he had seen a lot of people killed, some because of him. Some of the horrors he had been through should not be spoken of so lightly, and certainly not in polite conversation. But he knew this conversation was anything but polite. And it was slowly leading somewhere.

Ferney went on: 'You excelled in Burma. In Malaya you were even more successful, recruiting ethnic Chinese to fight the enemy – both communist and Kuomintang nationalists - and recruiting members of the indigenous Orang Asli jungle dwellers in your subversive activities. You know, Tommy, I remember the Orang Asli well. They were excellent during the Emergency, as I recall.'

'They were pretty good during the war too,' said Royle. 'Ruthless killers and expert trackers. Their bushcraft was the best I had ever seen. Amazingly loyal too. I was in Malaya to prepare for the British invasion at the end of the war, but the Japanese surrendered first.'

'Prior to the surrender, Tommy, you were spirited away via submarine to French Indochina, it says here.'

'Though it wasn't French Indochina by then,' Royle smiled grimly. 'It was part of the Japanese Greater East Asia Co-Prosperity Sphere. I could give you a lecture on the history of it if you like, but I would really like to speed things up and get to the bottom of what the devil you want with me.'

'Won't be much longer,' smiled Ferney, fixing Royle with a steely glare. 'The notes in your file are a little sketchy. Did you recruit members of the Free French in Indochina?'

'I think you know I didn't. Don't tell me this is all about making my file more comprehensive.' Ferney shook his head, still smiling. Royle would have described the smile as being inscrutable, if that didn't produce a frankly hilarious stereotype. 'My speciality was the indigenous population. I went in from the Chinese border to the north, with the help of our American cousins, and a couple of Free French agents seconded to SOE. The Viet Minh were on our side during the war and took me south to the capital, Saigon. We harried the Japanese a little, and the Vichy French, their collaborators. Then the Japanese interned their erstwhile French allies when they realised how badly things were going in Europe for their Axis friends. I returned back north and over the border again.'

'Had a little trouble with the Chinese government, didn't you?'

'I did. Chiang Kai-Shek's nationalist government had me arrested at the border. Said they thought I was a Vichy spy.'

'But you were released shortly afterwards?'

'Correct, after a week in jail and assurances from South East Asia Command.'

'Next you were attached to the 20th Indian Division for the British occupation of southern Indochina, south of the 17th Parallel, mainly concentrating on Saigon. There your mission was … what?'

'The war was over and I joined up with Free French officers as part of my continuing Force 136 operations. Our mission was to prevent the Vietnamese communists from taking control of Saigon, as they had done in Hanoi. Our mission was to clear the path for the return of a French administration, the status quo before the war.'

YUNNAN – INDOCHINA BORDER, EARLY NOVEMBER 1944

Back in his uniform as a lieutenant with the Manchester Regiment, but with a sewn-in SEAC flash on his shoulders, Royle managed to hitch a lift on a US Army truck.

It was a long, dusty and bumpy 800 miles from Chongqing, across the Szechuan border and into Yunnan. The truck was only going as far as Kunming, current headquarters of Chennault's 14th Air Force group – the Flying Tigers. It meant a hastily arranged stay in a US Army bunkhouse, sharing with half a dozen GIs, then an early start to find transport to take him to the border.

His SEAC orders secured him a jeep and driver to take him a further 200 miles to a secret Indochina border crossing near Lao Cai along the Red River.

There the jeep turned back and left Royle to figure out how to cross the wide and quickly flowing river.

A pre-war bridge across the Red River had been destroyed long ago in an air strike by Chennault's Flying Tigers. The river was far too wide and fast flowing to attempt to swim across. Royle dropped his heavy pack and crouched on the river bank wondering how to get across the muddy, silted divide into Japanese occupied Indochina. It was late afternoon and the sun was still hot through the clouds, when Royle heard a sound behind him. It was a young boy, no more than 12 years of age, staring at him intently.

Royle stood and turned to face the boy, who he noticed was dressed in black peasant's clothing and wearing a pair of too-large boots.

'Ni-hao,' Royle said in a general Mandarin greeting, nodding to the boy in a friendly way.

'Ni jiao shenme mingzi?' said Royle in a calm voice, what's your name?

The boy continued to stare at the man in the British army uniform.

The boy spoke. 'Ni zai gamma? Shangnar qu?' What are you doing? Where are you going? The boy pointed across the water and said simply, 'Huai ...' Bad.

'Shi,' said Royle. Yes. Royle's Mandarin was rusty, but he managed to add, 'Wo yao qu Tonkin.' I am going to Tonkin. Tonkin was the French colonial name for that part of Indochina.

The boy turned on his heel and ran off. Royle sighed, then sat back on the river bank and continued to consider a way across.

A half hour later Royle had begun to sweat through his shirt in the afternoon sun when he heard a man's shout.

'Hey there!' The shout was in English. American English. Royle stood to see a man built like a rugby player – or an American quarter-back, he decided – striding down the grassy river bank toward him, his arm extended and his hand stretched out in greeting.

'Howdy, you must be Royle?' Tom shook hands with the burly American and smiled.

'Yes, I'm Royle. I was just wondering the best way to get across the river without getting my feet too wet.'

'Well, Royle, you just leave that to me and my young compadre.' He swung his thumb in the direction of the young boy, now standing behind him. 'Name's Kravitz, Charlie Kravitz. You can call me Chuck. Been in this God-forsaken neck of the woods about a year, so a friendly white face is something of a novelty. C'mon Royle, we need to get started and across before nightfall. I've had my young watcher on the look-out for you.'

Royle retrieved his pack and the three of them trudged away from the river and over a hillock, where a small hamlet stood.

Kravitz entered one of the houses, said something indistinguishable to the unseen occupant, then emerged with his own pack, which he hefted on to his back.

The two of them walked about a mile downriver until they came to an almost invisible zip wire attached to trees on either side.

Kravitz swiped Royle on his pack and laughed. 'My big mistake was directing the Tigers into an air attack on the bridge where you were stood just upriver. Now I've had to rig up this gizmo to get us across. Less obtrusive and a whole lotta fun.' Kravitz laughed again, then told Royle to hold on tight to the rollers that would zip down the taught wire to the other side. One end of the wire was higher than the other so gravity could work its magic. Further down the river there was another zipwire to cross the opposite way. A tether was attached to the roller device allowing it to be pulled back for re-use.

'It's a little difficult getting supplies across, but we've got an attachment so we can pull a boat across when needed. You ready?'

'As I'll ever be,' said Royle through gritted teeth, sure he would end up in the river to be swept miles downstream.

Kravitz gave Royle a push and the Force 136 man literally zipped across the expanse of the river to reach the other side in less than 30 seconds. Royle took a deep breath, planted his feet firmly on the river bank now in Indochina, and gave Kravitz the thumbs-up sign.

Kravitz returned the gesture, then began pulling the roller device back towards him. Five minutes later both men were trekking through the jungle of northern Tonkin.

They were soon completely under the cover of the forest canopy. And it was dark. Added to the deepening gloom of the natural darkness as the sun began to set, the going became tough and a little bit treacherous.

'Mind how you go, Royle. We ain't in Knightsbridge now.'

'Never been there, *Charles*, I grew up in Malaya.' Royle deliberately used Kravitz's forename in full in a half-hearted effort to slightly annoy the blustering OSS officer. Kravitz just snorted a laugh.

'Jungle bum eh? Well you should feel right at home here, *Thomas*.' Royle laughed out loud. He was starting to like this American troubleshooter.

'Another hour or so and we should be at base,' said Kravitz, adjusting his pack and taking a sip from his water bottle.

'Many there?' asked Royle.

'Only a small army wanting to fight on our side to get rid of the Japs. And they're pretty good in a fight. Tough, determined, courageous, and inventive. I'd have these little guys on my side any day of the week.'

'Good to know, Charles,' this time Royle used not a hint of sarcasm in Kravitz's name. It just seemed to feel right using his full forename.

Soon they began to hear the crackle of a fire ahead of them and the faint woodland trail they had been following became more prominent.

A bird screeched in the trees, or was it a forward look out?

Kravitz waved in the direction of the sound, and another different bird-sound emerged from the same tree. It was definitely a lookout.

'Xin chao!' Hello, shouted Kravitz in a loud voice for all to hear. He turned to Royle and said, 'Don't worry, Tommy boy. There aren't any Japs or Frenchies anywhere near here. Our Viet Minh friends here control this whole area.'

It was the first time Tom Royle had heard the name Viet Minh. It wouldn't be the last.

Both special forces officers emerged from the trees into a clearing, where a large bonfire was burning, despite the warmth of the evening. There a small contingent of men waved. All of them wore the black pyjama-style clothing of a peasant.

The group waved the two men over to a cluster of tents, all internally lit. One lifted a tent flap. Both men dropped their packs and crouched to enter.

Inside a small, stocky man was writing at a desk. He looked up and waved the Briton and American to two of half a dozen chairs around the sides of the tent. The man continued to write for a few more seconds then put down his pen, blotted the paper, moved it to one side, then sat with his hands clasped in front of him.

'Lau qua khong gap,' said Kravitz, smiling. Long time, no see.

The man, who Royle now saw wore the khaki uniform and pips of a military officer, stood, and shook Kravitz's hand. Then beaming at Royle, shook his hand too.

'So, Chuck. You met your man,' then turning to Royle said, 'I am so very pleased to meet you Lieutenant Royle.' The Viet Minh officer's English was unexpectedly excellent, and spoken with a slight French accent..

'Tom, I'd like you to meet Colonel Chang Anh. He pretty much runs things around here.'

'Colonel, the pleasure is mine,' said Royle.

'Come, let us eat first, then we can talk. There is much to discuss.'

They ate pho - a nutritious, if bland, meal of fish, vegetables and rice, mixed in with a little broth, then retired to sit by the fire at the centre of the Viet Minh camp.

Anh looked directly into the eyes of the newcomer, the British officer Tom Royle. 'You do not have the look of a jungle "virgin", lieutenant.'

'I grew up in Malaya, colonel. I spent my childhood and most of the rest of my life padding around the forests and jungles at home.'

'He knows his way around a jungle, colonel,' said Kravitz. 'I can vouch for that.'

Anh gave a slight nod of the head, then continued his piercing gaze into Royle's eyes.

'Lieutenant Royle, do you know who we are? What we are about?'

'Sir, I know that you are the sworn enemies of the Japanese invaders and that you have harassed them constantly with sabotage and disobedience.'

'That is true, lieutenant. Unlike our American friend here,' Anh gave a sideways nod to Kravitz, 'you are British, and from what you tell me you also have an imperialist agenda in the country you call home, that of Malaya. We are not only fighting the Japanese, but we are also totally opposed to the French, who have ruined our country for many years while we have lived under their yoke.'

'Yes sir, I understand. The Vichy French are also our enemies and …' Anh interrupted.

'Not just the Vichy French, lieutenant. The French! When we win this war in our country, our intention is to evict the Japanese and the French and run our own affairs. We are called the Viet Minh. We are the Viet Nam Doc Lap Dong Minh Hoi – it means League for the Independence of Vietnam, which is the name of our country. Not Tonkin, Annam and Cochin China, the names the French gave when they split our country into three administrative areas. We want to unite our land, without the French. Do you have a problem with that lieutenant? Are you worried that we intend to cast out your French imperialist brothers at the end of this war?'

'No sir,' said Royle. 'One thing I have learned these past five years is that countries should not be ruled by other countries. Our American allies constantly remind us of this, and it is a poorly kept secret that after this war, if we are victorious, Britain will start to relinquish its colonies. For one thing, I doubt we will be able to afford them.' Royle smiled, knowing the last remark was probably true.

'And your French allies?' continued Anh.

'Well, sir, the way I see it, the French are partly responsible for what's happened here. In Europe, when the Germans invaded France, Britain attempted to stop them at Dunkirk. That failed. Many French senior officials fled back across the English Channel with us to lick their wounds. The French capitulation in Europe has had far reaching consequences, as you have witnessed to your cost here. As the Vichy regime began to collaborate with the Nazis, Germany's ally, Japan, was given free rein to march into your country back in 1941. From here they launched attacks on Malaya, the Dutch East Indies, the Philippines and Pearl Harbor in Hawaii. If we could have stopped the Germans in Europe, this would never have happened.'

Royle looked directly at Anh. 'So yes, colonel. Britain is committed to getting rid of Japan from these shores, and from the shores of their other conquests in the so-called Greater East Asian Co-Prosperity Sphere, and if that means giving nations their own future, then so be it.'

The Viet Minh colonel seemed to relax, then rose and bade the two foreigners a good night. Both turned in to sleep an exhausted, dreamless sleep.

Early the next morning a party of what seemed to be hunters arrived at the camp. They carried the bodies of two deer and packs of rice together with tinned goods.

The noise from their arrival awoke Royle and Kravitz, who got out of their camping cots, splashed water on their faces, then emerged into the dappled sunlight of a forest morning.

The food supplies were being unloaded by teams of men, all dressed in what now seemed to be traditional black baggy trousers and tunic. All wore reed sandals, and most wore what Royle termed a coolie hat, either on their heads or dangling on the backs with a piece of twine.

Those men disappeared into the trees once they had discarded their supplies. The food supplies were then taken up by men from the camp, who Royle noted were now dressed in khaki uniforms. In place of the coolie hats were what appeared to be green camouflaged pith helmets.

Laughter could be heard from Anh's tent, followed by muffled conversation.

Kravitz nudged Royle in the ribs and smiled. 'You're in for a real treat now, kid.'

Emerging from the tent, first came Anh, followed by a slight, ascetic looking man, also wearing khaki. The man had dark hair turning slightly grey and a wispy dark beard. The man looked up at the sky, set a pile of papers down on a bamboo-topped desk outside the tent, then strode over to Royle and Kravitz, his arm outstretched.

Smiling, he gripped Kravitz's hand and gave it a vigorous shake.

'Lieutenant Royle,' said Kravitz. 'Let me introduce you to the leader of the Viet Minh, Mr Nguyen Ai Quoc.'

'It's an honour, sir,' said Royle, shaking his hand.

'You are welcome here, lieutenant,' said Nguyen Ai Quoc. 'Anh here has been telling me all about you and your wish to defeat the Japanese. We are all of the same mind here. We have been helped by the Americans and the Republic of China, and now to have the help of the British is a great coup.' He laughed.

'Sir, I am here to gain intelligence that will help us – the British and America – prepare for an invasion of all the occupied territories. We will want to know the Japanese strengths and their capability of counter-attacking such an invasion force.'

Nguyen Ai Quoc nodded approval, and again interrogated the eyes of the British officer with his own. 'I will leave these talks of military strategy with Anh here, and with my commander-in-chief Vo Nguyen Giap, who is in radio contact. Now I have reams of work to do. Gentlemen ...' With that Nguyen Ai Quoc walked over to his bamboo writing desk, sat in a wooden chair and began working.

The man would become known the world over as Ho Chi Minh.

Giap organised their transport down river. It was 500 miles to the coast and Haiphong, which they would be avoiding. A major port, there was far too much enemy activity. Royle and Kravitz saw a fraction of the strength of the Japanese invasion force in Indochina as they drifted down the Red River and they were worried. The occupying power had settled in to a full neo-colonial force that treated the natives with contempt and cruelty, and their French collaborators with the barely concealed disdain of unequal partners, Japan holding the lion's share of ownership.

Troop numbers were high, supplies were adequate thanks to good links with their occupied territories in mainland China, and it looked like the Japanese could hold on to Indo-China for a long time to come.

But the Viet Minh leader and his generals would be able to support an invasion by land and sea with their own unique local knowledge and their fighting force, which Kravitz assured Royle was fierce, but with its full extent so far unknown.

They spent six weeks in Tonkin, missing Christmas completely, as they drew up their plans. Royle told Kravitz of the communist resistance in Malaya; Kravitz told Royle of the growing anti-Japanese resistance in the Philippines. Things were going the right way, but slowly, much too slowly.

On the Gulf of Tonkin coast, Royle waved goodbye to Kravitz on this, his first foray into Indochina with Force 136 and the OSS. It was the new year and he knew he would rendezvous with Kravitz again in this small but strategic country. A rubber inflatable appeared in the darkness as the surf crashed over the beach north of Do Son, to the south of Haiphong. A sailor silently paddled the boat to the near-invisible Royal Navy submarine, where he was welcomed aboard with a strong cup of tea. The sub slid silently beneath the waves en route to Ceylon, where Royle would report his findings to Mountbatten's staff at SEAC.

HULL, OCTOBER 1974

'And then?' Ferney turned a page in the file.

'And then, when the status quo was established, we left French Indochina. I was demobbed in 1950 after a few stints elsewhere in the world, mostly India and Palestine, and returned home to Singapore. My home was gone, of course. I discovered I was beneficiary of my uncle's rubber plantation in Malaya, along with my sister Amelia. Our cousins, their children, had also not survived the war.'

'Then came the Emergency,' added Ferney.

'Which we both remember well, Bill.'

'Indulge me,' smiled the Special Branch officer.

'The communists began to cause mayhem in 1948. They had a lot of popular backing and things were looking bleak for the British. I was never properly in the rubber business. I was persuaded that I would be of more use in the Malayan Civil Service. I joined and I was brought in to the security operation against the communists because of my SOE background, and I went in-jungle again to see what was happening on the ground. Matters began to turn in our favour around 1951 and for the next nine years or so we had the communists on the run, until they finally collapsed in 1960. And that's when I hung up my cloak and dagger.'

'A brief account, but quite concise, Tommy. Now, what about the missing link?'

Royle stared at Ferney impassively.

'Tommy, we worked together in Malaya for a long time. I'm not stupid. Your security involvement was as a member of the Secret Intelligence Service, was it not?'

Royle continued to look at his former comrade, lips so tightly closed they began to turn white. Force 136 and SOE were disbanded by Attlee's new government very soon after the war ended. Many operatives returned to their civilian jobs or back to their military careers, but some, like Royle, were transferred into the SIS, who wanted to learn all about espionage, sabotage and destabilisation techniques from the men and women who had been in the thick of it during the war.

'Would it help if I told you that it's written here in your file, in black and white, that you were fighting the Emergency as an officer of MI6?' Ferney spun the file around for Royle to read. He flipped the front cover. It was his SIS personnel file, and it certainly seemed genuine.

'Turn the page, Tommy. Li Pengfei is featured quite a lot. Tell me about Li Pengfei.'

YENAN, CHINA, OCTOBER 1944

Mao Tse-tung emerged from his well-lit cave house into the arid city that was his. Yenan had been the safe haven for him and his people and had become the communist army's headquarters in China almost a decade earlier. He was 50 years old and idolised by most of his comrades. Mao's will to win the forbidden city in Beijing, leading his country towards what he called democratic centralism – Chinese style communism – and world domination was fired by an inner force not quite madness.

He stood there wearing the same style standard heavy woven blue cotton fatigues that all his comrades wore. Mao looked around and squinted in the raw heat of the new day. This was a special day indeed. It could well herald a new beginning for the Chinese communists, for years holding a vicious rearguard action against Chiang Kai-shek's superior Kuomintang forces. This despite paying grudging lip service to a politically necessary United Front against the hated Japanese since 1936.

A surge of power flowed through him as he gazed at the land that was his – Yenan, as far as the eye could see, then further still. It was better than sex. It gave him a thrill of absolute power. All that was needed now was for the corrupt Chiang regime in Chongqing to be sidelined and for American dollars and weapons to become redirected to Mao in Yenan. Yenan was ideal for his plan, although it was not as accessible as he would have liked. Thousands had died on the Long March getting here. He was not about to relinquish it now. His Special Area, as it had been designated, was about 450 miles south west of the ancient Chinese capital Peiping, known better to the world as Peking. It would be renamed Beijing after Mao took his crown.

Mao shook himself from his reverie. He remembered that this day was to be a special day for the Special Area. Mao smiled to himself as he stood outside the curtained entrance to his cave house and surveyed his city; his Yenan. An autonomous city hewn into living rock, providing a unique defence against air raids and ground attack. He had made the city almost invulnerable.

'They are here, Comrade Chairman. The Americans and British have arrived.' A breathless figure shouted as he ran up the hill towards Mao.

Cap in hand to prevent it blowing off his closely cropped head in the rush, one of Mao's generals, Bin Lao, sprinted towards him and repeated the message as he stopped in front of his leader.

'Good,' said Mao. 'Is everything ready?'

'Everything,' said General Bin, replacing his cap and centring the bright red star to align with the middle of his brow. 'Banners and flags are everywhere. The whole city is festooned with them. The Nationalist flag is also prominently placed on all houses, alongside our own People's flag. That should make a good impression and show that we take the United Front seriously, unlike the nationalist dogs in Chongqing. This military mission will start to believe that we should be the faction to support for a stable China.

'I guarantee they will be eating out of our hands before they leave, but just to make sure I have organised some very convincing military drill displays and an exhibition of our captured Japanese weaponry. I will show them around the fields to prove we are not exploiting the land for opium, but for food to feed our growing anti-Japanese army. I will, of course, keep them well away from our poppy fields. I have arranged intermittent bouts of "spontaneous" applause for our honoured guests, and I have spoken to some of our more comely maidens to make themselves extremely friendly towards the foreigners.'

General Bin was a ruthless and ambitious member of Mao's inner circle. He added, 'We will also give sound applause and praise for Chiang and his fascist gang of …'

Bin stopped abruptly as Mao raised his hand for silence.

'Hsiao-hsin,' hissed Mao – 'be cautious.'

Mao side-stepped Bin, the same raised hand becoming a wave of welcome, his famous winning smile on his face.

Bin turned to see Major General Chou, Chiang Kai-shek's personal representative to Communist Yenan, walking up the hill towards them. He was wearing his tailor-made Kuomintang army uniform, the nationalist "sun" emblem on his smart peaked cap. Bin grimaced with distaste. All in Yenan hated Chou, Chiang's spy in the camp. Memories of the Long March and the nationalist mega-death air attacks against the communists were still fresh and raw. Under Mao's orders they had personally suffered his presence among them. It was yet another political gesture to the outside world that, as far as the communists were concerned, the United Front between Mao's rebel forces and Chiang's government forces was still in force and respected for the sake of the greater war effort.

'My dear general, I see you are already dressed and ready for the visit,' Mao Tse-tung said in his most conciliatory – some might say oily – manner.

'Indeed I am, sir. I am most interested to see how you, er, treat our western brothers.'

Mao suddenly clapped his hands together, and with a beatific smile announced: 'Kan-kuai – hurry now. It is time to meet our western military allies. We must make them feel at home, yes?'

Mao walked quickly to the meeting place, striding arm in arm with Bin Lao, leaving Chou in their wake.

'Lao, I have a special mission for you. I want you to be especially friendly to a young British officer arriving with the Americans and the others. He comes under instructions from Mountbatten to see for himself if we are useful to the war effort. The imperialist British are of little importance to us in the long run, but the more voices we have in our favour the better, and Mountbatten's is a very strong voice.'

'Very well, Comrade Chairman. Who is the British imperialist?'

'He has joined the mission at the last minute with a superior officer, also on Mountbatten's staff. But the man I want you to watch and be friendly with is called Lieutenant Thomas Royle, and according to our agent Li Pengfei, he is a British spy.'

Bin smiled conspiratorially. 'It will be as though we are best friends and brothers.'

*

The military mission had been reluctantly authorised by President Roosevelt and Prime Minister Churchill because the war in the Far East was going badly. Chiang-Kai-shek's forces had fought a rear-guard action against the Japanese since their brutal invasion of the Chinese mainland in July 1937. And now with the Americans involved in the war following the attack on Pearl Harbor, they had troops on the ground and flyers in the air to support the Chinese against the Japanese invaders, but still there seemed no significant progress. General Stilwell's troops and Brigadier General Frank Merrill's deep penetration guerrilla force nick-named the Marauders, were proving to be tough adversaries, and along with Claire Chennault's irregular air force, the Flying Tigers – the 1st American Volunteer Group later transformed into the US 14th Air Force – now had air supremacy. But troop and aircraft numbers were still deficient. By means of slow attrition the Allies were bit-by-bit losing the war in China.

This too concerned the British. Their troops in Burma relied on the vital supply route over a piece of friendly territory – the only piece in the area – still belonging to China, called by the airmen who traversed it "The Hump". Here Douglas DC3 Dakotas or their military version, the C47, flew over the lush mountain range to transport supplies to the jungle fighters. Their success or failure would impact on the outcome of the war in the Far East.

The Allied powers came to realise that the communist forces who were in all intents and purposes under siege in Yenan were seen as a potentially vital part of the war effort to defeat the Japanese – if they could be trusted.

Back in the United States, the Nationalist Chinese leader Chiang Kai-shek was hailed a hero, seen in much the way Churchill was during the dark days of the Blitz, before the Americans entered the fray. Chiang had risen to the top of the Kuomintang hierarchy and proclaimed himself the heir to the KMT's revolutionary founder, Sun Yat-sen. His Nationalist takeover of much of China had been greeted with approval in the United States. The old imperial order had been overthrown, opening a potentially lucrative door to US trade. Big business saw China as the land of the golden goose. To consolidate his position among the Americans, Chiang sent his glamorous wife on a number of official visits to the United States of America. Madame Chiang was beautiful, well spoken, and charmed the socks off everyone she came into contact with, from the ordinary man in the street to the biggest of businessmen and the highest of top level diplomats.

There were certain members of the US State Department who knew differently, however. They had received some very disturbing reports from their officers in the wartime Chinese capital Chongqing that Chiang Kai-shek was paying lip service to the United Front between the nationalists and communists, and was secretly wiping out communist enclaves. They knew he wanted to destroy once and for all the main communist stronghold in Yenan, but he dared not do so for fear of alienating his closest allies. Chiang had barely got away with his blockade of Yenan. General Stilwell too had little positive to say about the nationalist troops and was barely on speaking terms with Chiang. In all the operations he either oversaw or was advisor to, the KMT troops had always appeared ineffective and unmotivated. It was the American troops who were taking the brunt of every action, and he was suspicious of Chiang's motives.

The State Department had also been repeatedly warned of the widespread corruption taking place at the heart of the nationalist Chinese government. And there was mystery surrounding the whereabouts of the vast amounts of US money and weapons supplied to Chiang, which seemed to have inexplicably disappeared. Meanwhile, the KMT troops continued to use their old and obsolete weapons during engagements against the Japanese. The theory for this in the State Department was simple. Chiang was building up his arsenal in order to take on and annihilate the communists after the war, and that suited the US State Department just fine. Trouble was, if the KMT troops continued to be so poor, it would be the Japanese who would take over the country, and the golden goose would suddenly become a dead duck.

There had been a number of calls by the US State Department and the Department of War to send a military mission to the communist sector in China, so they could see for themselves what the communists had to offer. They were after all a strong fighting force who had been kept on the sidelines of the war because of a political squabble which, if left unchecked, could see the end of Chinese rule over their own land. US officials had watched with interest whenever the communists had engaged the Japanese invaders. And they were impressed by the determination, motivation and sheer good soldiering of Mao's army. What a waste that this resource was going unused simply because Chiang said they should not be trusted, they began to think.

The military mission arrived on horseback from the dusty airstrip where the long awaited mission's C47 aircraft had landed. Horse and mule were the most effective modes of transport in the inhospitable – and easy to defend – terrain. With them was their communist guide, General Wang Chen, who had told them on their arrival that they had the complete freedom of the communist city.

The western military officers were led, stiff and dusty from their long ride, into a large cavern, cut into the rock face. It was Mao's war room, containing a large conference table, maps and communications equipment. The officers were invited to be seated, and had tea and refreshments served. Popular music was being played on an old gramophone in one corner.

Gracefully and silently Mao entered the room. The music was stopped. Mao's arms were outstretched in a gesture of greeting, his winning smile rock steady on his cherubic face. Following close behind was Bin Lao, and Chiang Kai-shek's nationalist representative Chou. The communist guide Wang Chen stood bolt upright and with a single step was next to Mao, saying something in Mao's own Hunan dialect. Mao nodded and smiled again, walking over to the now standing observers, followed by Wang Chen. Mao also knew that the key to victory, first against the Japanese and then in the coming civil war against the nationalists, was regular shipments of guns and money from America.

'Gentlemen,' said Wang Chen, 'I am honoured to introduce you to our leader, Chairman Mao Tse-tung.'

Mao walked down the line of observers, shaking hands with each; Wang acted as interpreter. As each officer was introduced. Major-general Chou remained standing in the doorway, effectively ignored by the communists, but ever watchful and ever suspicious.

After the introductions Mao smiled once more and said, through Wang, 'I am available to you gentlemen at all times, either as a group or individually. Please feel at liberty to roam our city as you wish.' Mao bowed, then left.

Bin Lao made a beeline for Lt Royle and his superior officer Lieutenant-general Ernest Browne, and proceeded to lavish Royle with food and drink, and friendly banter. Popular music was being played on an old gramophone in one corner. Glenn Miller's "That Old Black Magic", "Brazil" by Xavier Cugat, Tommy Dorsey's "In the Blue of the Evening", and "Moonlight Becomes You" by Bing Crosby – all big American hits from the previous year, were played continuously at the reception.

Browne leaned over to whisper in Royle's ear. 'I think they know, old boy. Your cover has been blown.'

Royle nodded. 'I think you're right, sir. But how?'

*

In the days that followed the western observers, which included a delegation from the US Press Corps and two Russian journalists, were given guided tours of Yenan's collective farms – an experiment which Mao would in later years continue with disastrous consequences and the deaths of millions – manned by smiling and seemingly happy peasant men and women, diligently going about their agricultural labours with happy abandon. They often sang stirring songs as they worked, and in fact it wasn't just an act. They had joined the Red Army from villages throughout China as soon as they heard that it would save them from the yoke of corrupt warlords and landlords. Some had joined the communists as they wound their weary way through their villages on the Long March. And most found that life in Yenan was considerably better than the near-slave status they had experienced in their home villages. These people were peasant fighters. When fighting they wore their Red Army uniforms – the same drab outfit that Mao himself wore – and neither soldiers nor officers wore any form of insignia of rank. Only when working in the fields did they change their military caps with the distinctive red star in the centre, for the more traditional reed and bamboo conical sun hats.

The observers soon began to realise with some accuracy the lies they had been told in what they saw as an increasingly moribund Chongqing. They had been told by the nationalist officials that the communists in Yenan were living a hand-to-mouth existence and could be of no practical use in the war effort. As they looked around they saw the well-fed population of Yenan, the physically fit soldiers, the verdant fields and the spoils of the few communist engagements against the Japanese, proved beyond a shadow of doubt that an alliance with the communist force in Yenan could well be the key to victory over the Japanese in China. They had seen Mao's soldiers under the command of General Chu Teh go through vigorous military exercises which they realised the US Marine Corps would have been hard-pressed to improve on. Compared to these troops Chiang's nationalist army appeared amateurish. A large collection of captured Japanese weapons – and a contingent of Japanese prisoners now fighting on the side of the communists - added weight to their growing belief that the communist force must be given full support.

HULL, ENGLAND 1974

A uniformed police officer knocked on the door of the inspector's office and entered carrying a tray containing mugs of tea and a plate of digestive biscuits. The young policeman placed the tray on the desk and left.

'Go on,' said Ferney. 'What has this mission to China to do with you?'

'I was part of the observer mission to Yenan. Officially I was liaison to Ernest Browne. He was a lieutenant-general on Mountbatten's staff at South East Asia Command. Mountbatten was also very keen to discover how the China situation could be turned around. He had a lot of troops in Burma whose lives depended on a strong force in China.

'We spent a week in Yenan. The Americans were there for over a fortnight. Browne and I were the only British on the otherwise mostly-American mission. Our inclusion had been hastily arranged on the orders of Mountbatten himself, and Churchill. At the time I was still attached to SOE. In fact I was rather miffed at going on what I saw as a bit of a jaunt. I had been on standby for a drop into Malaya, which had to be cancelled.

'I met Li Pengfei on the second day in Yenan. He wore the uniform of Mao, but as soon as he spoke I was able to identify him as a native Malay.

'He told me he had been leading the fight against the Japanese in the jungles of Malaya since 1942. He was one of the leaders of the Malayan Communist Party and the Malayan People's Anti-Japanese Army fighting from jungle bases deep inside Perak. I was, of course, very interested in this. I considered him to be a valuable future ally. We forged an alliance there and then. Got on like a house on fire. It turned out he had a formidable force operating in the jungles of Malaya, which I had no idea about. He and his force had been trained by a former colonial officer and policeman, now also fighting from jungle bases in Malaya. But after meeting Li Pengfei I knew I would be able to take advantage of his men whenever I dropped in, as it were. On top of that I found him to be a charming, well-educated fellow, with a great sense of fun.'

'And after that,' Ferney prompted.

'We reached an agreement and I ran him as an unofficial intelligence agent. After that I left Yenan, for a look at Tonkin – that's North Vietnam in today's currency – and how the freedom fighters there were dealing with the Japanese. Very effectively, I realised. From there I was whisked away by submarine to Ceylon to personally debrief Mountbatten's staff.

'I'm not a diplomat or politician and I'd had enough of high level talks and seemingly endless negotiations with factions we may or may not be able to work with. I was frank with Browne, and he agreed to let me get back at the sharp end of the war. Two months later I was dropped into Malaya by Liberator, along with a shipment of food, reading materials and a portable radio. That's when I next met Li-Pengfei.'

'I suppose Li-Pengfei then helped you in the war effort behind enemy lines in Malaya,' said Ferney.

'Not just me,' Royle corrected. There were other Force 136 units operating in the bush. Li-Pengfei's communist force hid us, housed us, fed us and fought with us. We air-dropped weapons to make them a formidable fighting force. We disrupted Japanese supply lines, destroyed their military installations, ambushed their patrols. We had delivered a critical blow to the Japanese occupiers. All in readiness for the planned invasion as the war neared closure. Things didn't quite work out as planned. The Japanese surrendered before we could invade. It was one of our Force 136 units which took the unofficial surrender in Malaya. We policed the country with our communist allies and the Japanese until a regular force arrived, along with the new civil service.

'That's when Britain turned the tables on the communists. Our troops swooped on their units, who were all out in the open, and confiscated their armaments. Those arrested were later freed, and most of them returned to the jungle with their comrades to lick their wounds. It was from there they started planning their uprising.'

And Li-Pengfei?'

'He and his close entourage smuggled themselves out of the country to head for China or Russia. They returned with little more than renewed ideology. The Chinese were busy fighting their own revolution. The Malayan People's Anti-Japanese Army evolved almost overnight into the Malayan People's Anti-British Army. Their weapons were the ones we airlifted to them in the war and those taken off the Japanese. They were hidden in secret arms dumps buried inside the jungles.

'They soon started to ambush patrols again – this time British patrols. They used our weapons against us as well, once captured. A textbook guerrilla tactic, as used by the Chinese communists and in Vietnam – Indochina as was. Before we knew it we were in the middle of a full-blown war of our own.

'Li-Pengfei and his colleagues were inspired by the newly independent India and Pakistan and the Chinese Communist revolution. They were, of course, steeped in Soviet-style Marxism-Leninism, and while they had very little practical help from the Russians and Chinese, they had ideological support and a determination to take Malaya from the British.

'They had seen Mao do the same, only on a much larger scale. After the war Mao and his Chinese communists fought and beat the nationalist regime of Chiang Kai-shek. They had received no armaments from Russia, yet managed to defeat the largest standing army the world had ever seen. Inspirational, wouldn't you say?'

'Indeed,' said Ferney, pursing his lips. 'And what about the weapons promised by the observer mission in 1944?'

'It never happened,' said Royle. 'Roosevelt was in favour of ordering a large weapons drop in Yenan as the war against Japan was nearing its climax, but he procrastinated and delayed after receiving conflicting information from his State Department. His officials were hopelessly split on the matter. I believe he was about to give the order to send Mao his weapons, but sadly poor old FDR died before he could implement it, and Harry Truman certainly had no inclination to aid the communists. Besides it was all changing. The US now had two atomic bombs. Japan surrendered, and there was no longer a need for Chinese communist allies.'

Royle sighed, and pushed the empty tea mug away. He had no recollection of drinking the beverage.

'Li Pengfei was angry with the British for our duplicity. Seething would be a better word. But he still trusted me and I helped him get out of a few scrapes with our boys. He remained my man, but I just had no idea what to do with him as the war ended.'

Ferney drove Royle into the city centre, for lunch at a small Italian restaurant in Hull's Old Town. En route Royle made a telephone call to his sister's hotel from one of Kingston Upon Hull's white-painted public phone boxes. As they walked from the parked car to the restaurant a stiff breeze from the Humber estuary blasted them. It must have been at least three degrees cooler here, close to the docks, than the rest of the city. A stink of fish wafted across the air, emanating from the nearby fish docks, as one of the city's trawler fleet landed its catch of the day. They ate a light lunch washed down with a bottle of decent Valpolicella.

'By the way, your souvenir weapons are being kept at Cottingham police station until you can find a new place of safety for them,' said Ferney, as he called over the waiter and paid the bill.

Royle looked his old comrade in the eye. 'So, what now Bill?'

'Now? My job is done, old boy. As for you, you have a seat reserved on tomorrow's 0730 Intercity train to London, under the name Grafton. Here are your tickets.' Ferney handed them to Royle.

'Do I have a choice?'

'There's always a choice,' said Ferney. 'You had a choice back in 1940, when you signed up. You have the same choice now.'

'But it hardly compares to the war,' spluttered Royle, beginning to go red in the face and feeling Ferney was trying to emotionally blackmail him.

'Very true, but it's still king and country, old boy. Queen and country now. Don't give me all that crusty academic nonsense. I've been watching you while you've been talking. You have lost none of your tradecraft and you're still as wily as ever. I would warrant your bushcraft is still top notch too.

'We can smooth things over with the university authorities. It's a matter of national importance and we will make sure you will be able to return when the job is done. And don't worry about your sister. We are well aware that she and your son are your only living relatives. Your son is at boarding school, I understand. And your sister can stay at the hotel until your house is habitable again.

'In the meantime, we have a team looking for these responsible for the burglary and fire at your house. Did they get anything important?'

Royle looked glum. 'Only the draft of my manuscript. Everything else was either discarded or destroyed.' Royle decided not to mention the charred remains of the mysterious passports, no doubt being forensically tested at this moment.

'Very well. Get some rest, pack your bags and you will be met on the train. Got a business suit?' Royle shook his head, subconsciously looking down at his elbow-patched tweed jacket. Most of his clothes had been rendered unwearable by smoke damage from the fire.

Ferney brought out a bulging wallet and took out a wad of notes.

'Buy one. Wear it,' said Ferney. 'Other clothes too to supplement your smoke-logged wardrobe.'

'Five hundred quid, Bill? Pension money?'

'Merely a little slush fund for unforeseen circumstances. Expenses, that sort of thing.'

Royle looked at his old comrade with undisguised suspicion, but did not pursue the matter. 'Will I be seeing you again, Bill?'

'Unlikely. This is a one-time only job for me. I'm retired. Good luck, Tommy.'

*

Royle, now using his pseudonym Grafton, boarded the train to King's Cross at Hull's Paragon station. He found his reserved seat – the name Grafton was written in ink on a ticket sticking up from the seat. The seat beside him and the two seats opposite all had reserved tickets protruding from the top. His was a window seat, facing the direction the train was travelling.

Royle looked around the non-smoking carriage. It was gradually filling with passengers. He took off his suit jacket, neatly folded it and placed it in the luggage rack above his seat. There was a jolt, and the London-bound Intercity express began to slowly move off, right on time. His neighbouring passengers had not turned up. Nor had his contact. Royle sighed silently to himself and began to look around the carriage. Second-class, he observed, so his presence couldn't be that important. The train was not full, but it had stops to make at Doncaster and Peterborough before reaching King's Cross in about three hours' time.

The train sped south, out of Yorkshire and into Lincolnshire. The flat east coast countryside afforded wonderful views of an England Royle rarely saw or acknowledged. He had been caught up in the blinkered world of academia for the past fourteen years. He had only travelled to London once or twice every two years or so to visit the British Library or the Public Records Office to read historic files released annually from the UK National Archive. Royle was oblivious to the rest of the carriage as he stared out of the window.

They were approaching Newark when a voice called to him. 'Ah, there you are, Grafton. Glad you could make it. All set for the conference?' The man, in his early forties, Royle assessed, wore a dark grey business suit and a blue tie. His dark hair was slightly dishevelled and Royle thought it needed cutting. The sides slightly overhung the tops of the man's ears. He was carrying two plastic cups of steaming liquid. 'Damned horrible queue at the buffet car, but got there in the end.' The man slid into the window seat opposite Royle and handed him one of the cups. 'Tea, two sugars. Correct?'

Royle shook his head silently and took hold of the cup. The stranger took his own cup and smiled, then leaned towards Royle.

'Sorry about that, Dr Royle,' he said quietly, just audible above the clickety-clack of the train. 'Just a brief precaution, you understand.'

'I see. Of course,' said Royle, slightly bemused. 'I'm afraid I'm a little out of practice. I'm more of a bushcraft man than a tradecraft man.'

'Don't worry, doctor. We'll soon have you back up to speed. My name is Harrison. Donald Harrison. I'm your companion for this trip.' Harrison nodded at the two empty reserved seats. 'We'll be quite alone, those reservations are under false names.'

Royle nodded, but said nothing. He couldn't help thinking that matters were getting a little melodramatic. But then, he thought, there was nothing melodramatic about his house fire.

'Before we get to King's Cross, can you tell me about the time you saw Li Pengfei in the jungles of French Indo-China?'

What was this sudden, surreal, interest in Li Pengfei, a name from the past? But his house had been burgled and torched because of it. He had been given police protection. And he had been brought back into the security services – he still wasn't sure which one – all because of it.

'I suppose I recognised some of his handiwork when I was tasked to lead a patrol into the jungle north of Saigon back in 1945.'

'You were with the British Military Control Commission?'

'Yes, flown in under General Gracey's orders.'

'And Mountbatten?'

'Correct. I was still attached to Force 136, but my knowledge of bushcraft must have earmarked me for the job. I was sent in to help flush out Viet Minh guerrillas operating from the interior. They had been agitating ever since Gracey removed them from power in Saigon – and when they found out we were helping to re-install the French administration following the Japanese surrender. Viet Minh militias had started launching attacks on British and French installations. They had attacked targets in Saigon, where General Gracey was struggling to bring order to the country, in what was a dangerous power vacuum. Released French prisoners – mostly Vichy collaborators - had armed themselves and had gone into Cholon, massacring a lot of native Vietnamese. The Viet Minh retaliated in a French area of Saigon. There were a lot of tit-for-tat murders. The Japanese had surrendered, and under the terms of their surrender we ordered them to work for us. They were rearmed and acted as our police force. There were plenty of them and few of us, but they did a good job.

'Gracey's task was to install an administration to make ready for the return of the French. The trouble was the Viet Minh had seized power before our force arrived, and despite making friendly overtures to the British at first, they were spurned at every opportunity. Eventually they turned against us.

'There had been a particularly brutal attack on Vichy French prisoners held on a former rubber plantation to the north of Saigon. The Viet Minh had attacked in force. The British and Japanese guarding them were overrun. Some were killed, mostly Japanese, but eventually surrendered by force of numbers alone. No-one had expected the Viet Minh to be capable of commanding such a large force.

'The Vichy French prisoners were butchered. Then the guerrillas disappeared into the jungle as silently as they had appeared. That's when my small force was sent in to find them. Gracey was incandescent with rage that a secure facility could be breached so easily. He was deeply embarrassed that it had happened on his watch, not long before the Free French were to have taken over the administrative reins from the British.

'It was the Free French who demanded that the Viet Minh should be tracked down. General Le Clerc …'

'Ah, the Liberator of Paris …'

'The very same. Le Clerc made the request for a reconnaissance force to go in after the Viet Minh force. I was chosen as leader, I had two good

Gurkha soldiers and a dozen Japanese. All of us were armed. We also had a Free French officer as an observer.'

'That would be Captain Thierry?'

Royle stared at the younger man. 'Yes, you know the story, then?'

'Only some of it. Please continue ...'

Royle went on. 'We were ambushed. It was purely a diversionary ambush, to keep us busy while the Viet Minh force got away. It was very cleverly executed, and I later recognised it as being the work of Li Pengfei.

'We had worked together in the jungles of Malaya until the end of the war. He disappeared during the British return. Of course, at the time, although I recognised his work – he was an expert at booby-trap bombs – I did not consider that he would be involved with the Vietnamese nationalists.

'His bomb killed one of our Japanese contingent, and a firefight killed a few more. They were difficult to track, but nothing can move through the jungle without leaving a trail. You just need to look for signs: a leaf turned the wrong direction to the sunlight; a crushed tussock of grass; a twig broken by footfall. It was painstaking work. That night we made camp, and that night I met Li Pengfei.

*

Before nightfall Royle's unit made camp deep within the enemy triangle to the north-east of Saigon. They had carefully tracked the rebel force until they began to run out of daylight – meagre enough under the canopy.

The unit located a suitable spot and began to make camp. They brought out tarpaulin sheets from their packs, tied them to trees for shelter, then built two fires at each end of the camp to keep away undesirable predators that may come across their rest site, and also to provide light. The Japanese began a watch rota, all under the scrutinising gaze of the suspicious Gurkha tracker, Sgt Tenga. Tenga had no need for suspicion, however. The Japanese were powerless and demoralised. Even though they had been rearmed they would carry out the orders of their Imperial Command, which was to obey their subjugators without question. This they did with supreme efficiency.

By Royle's watch it was 2am, time for another rotation of the Japanese guard, when a hand gripped Royle's mouth and a blade was placed flat against his neck. Royle was instantly alert and aware that to move would be fatal. But he also knew the flat blade against the soft flesh of his neck was not an immediate threat, but more a warning to remain silent.

In the darkness, away from the flickering firelight, the strong hand muzzling his mouth smelled of earth and grime – the good, honest smell of a jungle hideaway. The blade at his neck felt broad and large. It was undoubtedly sharp and capable of either neatly severing his life-giving jugular vein, or with a little more effort simply decapitating the young special forces lieutenant.

Then came a whispered, rasping voice close to his ear. The man – this much Royle could now establish – had breath which smelled of chillies and rice. No hint of fish, which was so prevalent in Vietnamese cuisine.

'Ati-ati, Lt Royle, be careful.' The man was speaking Malay, but with a slight Cantonese accent. Royle felt shaken that the intruder knew his name.

Royle still failed to recognise the man in the dark, but remained still as the whispering intruder went on.

'Diam,' be quiet, the whispered voice rasped. 'Bangun,' get up.

He hauled Royle up by his shirt collar with a strong, lithe arm. The man still held the knife in his right hand. Royle was leant beside a tree, still beneath his tarpaulin shelter and mosquito net. He could see the outline of the figure before him, but he was still deep in shadow. Occasionally he caught the glint of fire glow in the intruder's black eyes.

'You know my name,' Royle said in a low voice. 'Should I know yours?'

There was a sharp, breathed laugh. 'Entah!' the voice said. Maybe. 'Perchaya,' trust me, he said. The man lit a match, illuminating his face.

'Li Pengfei,' smiled Royle. Li Pengfei appeared dirty and unkempt. His lean face was grime stained and his black hair matted with moss and fern. He wore a dark-coloured tunic and trousers. On a belt hung an empty scabbard for the broad knife still at Royle's throat, and a hand gun in a holster. Royle was unable to identify the make.

'Heran,' said Royle in a low voice. I'm surprised. The match went out and both were plunged into darkness again.

'Sa-pakut,' whispered Li Pengfei. I am here to collaborate with you. He slid his razor sharp kris silently into its scabbard and sat on his haunches watching Royle.

'You tried to kill us,' said Royle. It was your booby-trap which ambushed us. You killed my men.'

'I killed some Japanese, Lieutenant. But I had to make sure you kept on our trail. I fired the shot into the tree, which I expected you to trace back in this direction.'

'If you are fighting with the Viet Minh, why are you helping me?'

'I will explain this to you one day. We are comrades. We shall always be comrades, even though you may not realise it.'

Li Pengfei handed Royle a piece of folded paper. 'These are the coordinates of the fighters that you seek. They are very well hidden. Very well camouflaged. If you go to these coordinates you will see where they are. But you will need reinforcements. Do not engage them with the force you have here or you will be overwhelmed.'

Li Pengfei stood from his crouched position and said: 'Selamat tinggal, kawan.' Goodbye, friend. Then disappeared from beneath Royle's shelter.

At daybreak Royle summoned Captain Thierry, Sgt Tenga and the other Gurkha tracker, Corporal Hen-sing. He already had his map on the ground, weighed down by hefty boughs of wood at each corner, even though there was no breeze. He worked out the map reference points, which revealed the rebel fighters to be based in a jungle clearing twenty miles to the north.

'Sergeant, we will make for this point here,' Royle said, his finger pointing at a position on the map. 'We will reconnoitre and if we find the rebel base we will radio in for an attack. Mosquito fighter bombers from 684 Squadron should do it.' Royle looked at his sergeant. 'We seem to have a guardian angel, Sgt Tenga. An inside man who would like us to achieve our mission.'

*

The British Rail Intercity train had passed Stevenage and was near the end of its journey. King's Cross was less than 30 minutes away. Harrison was scribbling shorthand notes into a pocket-sized pad. Royle sat and watched as his companion's immaculate shorthand outlines curled and squirled across the short pages.

'Pitman's?' asked Royle, trying to make conversation. He had talked for most of the journey and the silence was now becoming a little uncomfortable.

'T-line actually. It's relatively new. Not quite as accurate as Pitman's, but a lot quicker to learn.' He flicked backwards and forwards through the pages, looking for a position he had marked during Royle's unusual debriefing. 'First time for everything,' he thought. 'Never debriefed anyone on a train before.'

'Now then, Dr Royle. I would like to go over a few things, if you please.' Royle nodded, resigned to going over a period in his personal history he thought best left forgotten.

'Li Pengfei said to you: "I am here to collaborate with you".'

'That's my translation of it. He spoke a single Malay word. In a situation like that you don't say ten words where one will do.'

'But the word was 'collaborate'?'

'Yes, he said 'collaborate'.'

Harrison flipped further through his notes. 'Li Pengfei said: 'I have been helping you since Yenan'?'

'Yes, he said that. I met Li Pengfei in Yenan in 1944 when I visited there as part of an American Observer Mission to Mao Tse Tung's stronghold. Li Pengfei and I met again when I was dropped into Malaya as part of Force 136.'

Harrison's notes again flipped a few pages. 'Li Pengfei said to you: 'We are comrades, we shall always be comrades'?'

'Yes. We worked together against the Japanese in Malaya.'

'I take it you called in an attack on the Viet Minh base?'

'Yes, it was destroyed. I observed from a hilltop. We called in Mosquito fighter bombers from Tan Son Nhut. There must have been a couple of hundred Viet Minh there, including women and children. The area was strafed and blanketed by bombs. I don't think many could have survived.'

'And Li Pengfei?'

'The next time I saw him was in Malaya. He was fighting with the communists, and I was fighting him.'

*

Harrison and Royle emerged from a black cab into the foyer of the Royal Embankment Hotel. Harrison carried Royle's small overnight bag through the smart and functional looking area, past the long reception desk and into the lift, pressing button number three on a panel which went up to five. Out of the lift they turned left down a corridor with rooms on either side. They rounded a corner and stopped at room 301, close to the stairs and the linen cupboard. Harrison knocked twice.

Momentarily a young man in a business suit opened the door, then stood to one side as Harrison and Royle stepped into the hotel room. The man nodded, gave the thumbs-up sign to Harrison, then left.

The room was comfortable, modern and clean, but not grand in any way. Taking up one wall were twin beds. The opposite wall held a dressing table, mirror and chair, and there was a small coffee table and two armchairs by the window. The view from the window was of another building, not the Thames, as Royle had absent-mindedly hoped. Royle scanned the room with a professional glance. The bathroom was located near the door, the wallpaper was a creamy beige containing a dark fleck, and there were two Impressionist prints on the wall above the beds, one was Monet's famous Waterloo Bridge scene, the second Royle was unable to recognise. The bedside lights were on and a television was on a TV table in a corner by the armchairs. There was a telephone on the dressing table.

Harrison placed the overnight bag on one of the beds and went to the far corner of the dressing table, where an electric kettle, cups and sachets of tea and coffee stood. He switched on the kettle and arranged the cups on a tray, then turned to Royle.

'Tea?'

Royle nodded: 'Milk, no sugar.' Royle smiled as he made it plain that the tea brought to him by Harrison on the train failed to have the correct combination of milk and sugar. A small yet subtle victory for him as he exposed a very minor gap in their personnel intelligence. Then he wandered over to the window, hefting the heavy curtains for a clear view of the office buildings behind the hotel. Raindrops had started to run down the glass.

It had just turned 11am when the kettle boiled and Harrison poured the tea. Elevenses. They sat in the armchairs and Harrison again produced his notepad, accompanied by a small tape recorder, which he placed on the table.

'Now then, where were we?'

'Malaya?' offered Royle.

*

'It was an Emergency, never a war. We managed to keep it tagged as an Emergency so the authorities in Malaya could completely control the lives of individuals there. There were countless decrees and regulations giving the British Government unprecedented powers in Malaya.

'In truth the almost dictatorial power the British authorities possessed was a consequence of the Emergency, not a pre-requisite. Rubber, tin and property were the reasons behind the semantics. Quite simply the British settlers were not covered for war with their insurance policies, so the authorities persisted in calling it an Emergency, and a purely internal affair.

'The Emergency broke out in June 1948 and we were desperate. It wasn't until about four years later when we began to get the upper hand against the CTs.'

'CTs?' interjected Harrison.

'That's what we called them. Communist terrorists, bandits. I suppose they would be insurgents today.' Harrison nodded and resumed his notations.

'I remained with my unit in India during its independence and partition in 1947. I was moved briefly to Palestine to fight the uprising there. Then I left the army in 1950 with the intention of returning to Malaya. The Emergency was causing untold problems over there. Civilians were being killed, plantation and tin mine owners murdered, our troops were being picked off and the country was on the verge of a Soviet inspired uprising.

'I was diverted by a call to Whitehall, to join the Colonial Service. Ostensibly I was recruited to the Secret Intelligence Service.

'After that I was posted to the staff of the High Commissioner in Kuala Lumpur. That was in 1951. For the next year or two we would still be taking heavy losses. But when I arrived we had reached a turning point in the uprising. We had a draconian resettlement policy to organise with the intention of starving the CTs into submission.'

MALAYA, NOVEMBER 1951

'This is one of the New Villages we've managed to set up. What do you think?' Bill Ferney appraised Tom Royle, who had just arrived to join the High Commissioner's team, although as head of Special Branch in that area of Malaya, Ferney suspected that Royle was also working in an MI6 role.

Captain Royle – he had been given the enhanced service rank after being posted to the High Commissioner's staff – disembarked from the Land Rover. At the edge of the jungle he saw a perimeter fence of barbed wire. Inside the fence were about three dozen newly built wooden huts. Fires were burning outside some of the huts and women were cooking over large pots. The men had not yet returned from their daily work.

'Looks like a concentration camp to me,' Royle said.

'Nonsense,' retorted Ferney. 'This is a master stroke in the fight against the CTs. Before we established the New Villages the CTs depended on squatter camps and kampongs on the edge of the jungle for their food supply. The villagers would have no choice but to comply with their demands, and hence the bandits remained well fed as they carried out their little war with us. These New Villages have changed all this. We truck the men into work and back every day, and we have a guard round the clock on the perimeter. Everyone is searched going in and coming out. The CTs can't get to the villagers. It's the start of our campaign to starve the commies out.'

Despite Royle's distaste for the desperate British tactic, he was forced to respect the thinking behind it. The villages were never short of food. The men were taken to work and brought home again each day. They were protected by armed British soldiers at all times. And the rebels were left without their main source of food. Yet, the villagers had been forcibly removed from their traditional homes and relocated into these prison camp conditions, having lost their freedom in the Imperial Power's fight to beat the communist rebellion once and for all. It was a brilliant plan, leaving Royle to wonder if the ends could justify the means. He knew there would be a price to pay for the treatment of these innocent villagers, and many others like them.

Royle and Ferney turned at the sound of military trucks roaring along the dusty track leading to the village. Two trucks came to a halt at the barbed wire gate to the village and a sentry inspected the papers of the passengers. Then a few minutes later the gate opened and the trucks roared into the compound. Malays disembarked from the rear of the trucks as soon as the vehicles had stopped and headed for their allocated huts.

'Fascinating,' said Royle.

'Don't knock it, old boy. It's to be Templer's grand strategy,' Ferney said. General Sir Gerald Templer was to be Churchill's choice of High Commissioner for the newly elected Conservative Government. His scheme was already being piloted in readiness for Templer taking up his new appointment.

'I had heard about it,' said Royle. 'But I didn't expect it to be so much like a prison camp.'

'Price of freedom,' replied Ferney, climbing back into the Land Rover's driving seat. Royle sighed at the irony of Ferney's remark, then climbed into the passenger seat. The Special Branch man started the vehicle and headed back down the track towards Kuala Lumpur and headquarters.

*

Royle and Ferney were sipping fresh lemonade on the verandah of Lieutenant-Colonel Miles Buchanan's house in the hills above Kuala Lumpur. Buchanan was a senior advisor to the Malay High Commission and had been a major player in SOE's Force 136 during the war. As such he had been glad to see Royle again as an old comrade.

'I hear you have just visited one of our New Villages, Captain Royle. I won't ask you what you think of them, suffice to say it is a vital project to weaken the insurgents.'

'I don't think Captain Royle was too impressed, Colonel,' said Ferney, grinning at the young officer he was about to send into some of the most dangerous jungle territories anywhere in the world. Royle looked down at the floor, inexplicably embarrassed by Ferney's honesty.

'I just thought it reminded me of a prison camp, sir,' said Royle, looking Buchanan straight in the eye.

'Indeed it does at first sight,' said Buchanan. 'Would it surprise you to learn that the vast majority of villagers are actually beginning to opt to settle in our New Villages in return for the protection we can give them? In the past many of these ethnic Chinese villages on the edges of the jungle have suffered brutal repression from CTs. Villagers who refused to co-operate with the rebels were often beaten. Some were murdered. Villages have been burned to the ground. We offer these people armed protection and security.

'As you know the CTs are mostly ethnic Chinese guerrillas. They expected help from the ethnic Chinese villagers such as the ones you saw today. Cut off the food supply, and at the same time protect the villagers who would have become victims, and we will have the terrorists on the run in no time.

'The grand thing about this is that the CTs can't easily blend into the main population. They are ethnic Chinese for the most part, and therefore stick out like a sore thumb if they break cover into the Malay majority. Their ethnic kin are protected behind barbed wire and armed garrisons, therefore we have them. Believe me, it is the turning point.

'We have plans for villages like this to house between 50 and 13,000 people – we won't destroy the community life. The whole village will simply be transplanted to one of our New Villages. So far they are rather basic, a prototype, but all will have better sanitation and facilities after Templar has a look at them and makes them actual policy. In the larger relocation centres there will even be leisure facilities.

'We've only had a few villages unwilling to move. Unfortunately we have had to force them into their New Village, but on the whole it has been voluntary. Once they realise it's all for their own good they are quite happy to be moved.

'Most of these people were living in squalid conditions as squatters near mines or plantations. We give them a better life and keep them away from bad influences.' Buchanan laughed and took another sip of lemonade.

'Templar has plans to relocate 450,000 people as part of the New Villages Policy. We may extend it to other non-ethnic Chinese villages if the guerrillas become forced to prey on them as their food supply lines run short,' explained Buchanan. The former special forces officer did not mention plans to incorporate a further 13,000 Malay villagers into the controversial, yet effective, New Villages programme. 'But enough of that. What of your old friend Li Pengfei?'

'My information,' said Royle, 'Is that Li Pengfei is running the guerrilla operation, at least on the Peninsula. I'm preparing to head in-jungle imminently to see what I can discover.'

The day's rains had just stopped, but the rainforest canopy was still dripping like a waterfall. Royle trudged through the trees and foliage feeling clammy in his army issue rubberised rain cape. Beneath it his backpack carried enough rations for three days. If he was any longer than that he would have to live off the land.

As the temperature rose steam began to rise, and rain droplets evaporated off the bracken strewn ground and the leaves above his head. Royle had always found the high humidity the most challenging aspect of conditions in the jungle. His shirt and trousers were already soaked with sweat, even after he had removed the rubberised waterproof cape that had kept him dry from the rain, at least on the outside.

But Royle was back in familiar territory and he felt strangely elated that he was again spending time in the one place he felt most at home – the rainforests of Malaya.

Royle had entered the jungle close to one of the old kampongs – an ethnic Chinese village that had been recently evacuated by the British authorities. Blackened embers from the village huts still smouldered slightly after the village had been torched by the authorities. Not a vindictive tactic by the British, but a ruthless scorched earth strategy to prevent insurgents from using any resources from the deserted villages. Although this strategy was purely another means of starving out the terrorists through lack of food and materials, it was watched with anger and resentment by the kampong populations. It was to be one of the most difficult of ideological rapprochements when Templer eventually arrived to implement his policy of winning the hearts and minds of the whole country, and therefore pulling the rug from under the very feet of the communist insurgents.

Royle was here because it was where one of the latest sightings had been of the insurgents heading back into the rainforest. His plan was to track them as far as possible. He carried three weapons, tools really; a 9mm pistol and a large machete, and some gardeners' shears, secateurs.

The pistol was mainly for self-defence against hungry or angry jungle creatures and the machete was to help him cut his way through the most inaccessible sections of the rainforest if he needed to move quickly. Both were to be used in emergencies only. Royle preferred to make his way through the undergrowth quietly and stealthily, making as few tracks as possible, and that's why he used the secateurs. These small shears could cut through the strongest thin vines that clogged up the most used jungle paths. And they were silent.

In the gloom of the forest it was difficult to track, and it took some time for Royle's eyesight to become accustomed to the half-light. This was as light as it was going to get in the jungle, and Royle knew it could take the best part of a day for him to become completely at ease and able to track properly. It was always the same as one entered the trees below the rainforest canopy. You go from brilliant sunlight into immediate gloom. Had there not been time constraints on Royle he would have entered the jungle just as dawn was breaking, therefore walking into the trees with eyesight already adjusted to the semi-darkness. But Royle had to pursue a band of insurgents after a tip-off from a double agent. A few of these double agents were starting to come to the fore now the food was getting scarce. RAF bombers were dropping propaganda leaflets on CT positions, offering fabulous rewards to any terrorist who betrayed their leaders. The New Villages policy was starting to work against the CTs at last. The CTs were becoming dispirited and there were more and more cases of bandits betraying their comrades. Royle just hoped the resettled villagers would be able to forgive the British for destroying their traditional homes when the communists were finally defeated.

Royle stooped to the ground and could hardly believe his luck. A footprint in a muddy spot close to a tree. A footprint. Never in all his years tracking and during his wartime collaboration with the communists had he ever seen any of these fearsome guerrillas leave so much as a broken branch behind them in the jungle. But a footprint? Either the bandits were getting careless or desperate or maybe both, thought Royle. He looked around. There were more footprints heading in a northerly direction, petering out eventually in a carpet of rotting leaves, pieces of tree bark and soft twigs and branches. But by now Royle had a direction to follow, and the tell-tale signs of broken leaves from bushes and crushed blades of grass. It was like following a road map, thought Royle.

It was mid-afternoon and the sound of the living jungle was all around him. How he had missed it. The Malay rainforests were some of the most inhospitable places on the planet, but he loved being beneath the canopy – and walking out again in one piece.

The trail seemed to have been made by about four or five bandits. It was difficult to be specific in this environment, despite their carelessness. Lucky for him though, thought Royle. Looking for the start of a trail could take days unless a tracker knew where to look. This had been unusually easy. He soon discovered why.

In a clearing, normally the easiest type of area in a rainforest in which to analyse tracks, the trail suddenly and inexplicably disappeared. Royle stopped short, puzzled by the lack of a trail previously so easy to follow. He had been able to follow the trail while walking. He didn't even need to stoop or stop. Now he stooped, on all fours as he looked closely at the ground desperate to regain his advantage.

There was a rustle in the trees and one, two, then three bandits emerged to his right. A fourth then appeared to his left. All were armed with Second World War Japanese Imperial Army rifles, aimed at him. Without a word, Royle raised his hands. A voice came from behind Royle. He spun round, and in that second mused on the fact that he had heard nothing emerging from the trees he had just walked out of.

'Very sensible, Thomas,' came the voice in English, with a thick Cantonese accent. 'But please, lower your hands. You won't be shot, unless you try to shoot us first.'

A smile came over Royle's face, despite being effectively captured by rebels.

'Li Pengfei, I should have known. But I thought you were up near the Siamese border.'

'One has to move around in these uncertain times, Thomas. Your relocation programme is hurting us somewhat.'

'They won't let you persecute the kampongs anymore, old friend. They know that's your weakness, so they have cut off your supply lines. You will be forced to live off the jungle, and that's not very easy or efficient. You will be spending all your time surviving instead of doing what you set out to do, and that's to get rid of us British.

'You know, Li Pengfei, we have a plan in force to pull out of Malaya and your country will be independent, a true sovereign nation. It has some of the richest natural resources in the whole of South East Asia. Why are you people trying to disrupt this?'

'Oh, Thomas, you British should never have returned in 1945. Six years ago our people took control of the country and kept law and order, only for you British to return and remove us from our positions of power. All for a letter of thanks from Lord Mountbatten, a campaign medal and a few Malay dollars in money as a one-off pension.

'You did to us what you did to the Viet Minh in Indo-China. The people wanted them and you threw them out of power so the French could return to take their possessions.

'And you say you want to give power back to the Malays? You refer to the Malay Union plan. This will never succeed, the Sultans will see to that. It will give all races in Malaya an equal say, and the native Malays will never allow that. They want to keep the Chinese and Indian races under their thumb. They intend to rule after you British have left. They have no intention of sharing power, except with themselves. And that is why the Malay Communist Party has moved to take power from the landed elite and eject the imperial power that has kept us subjugated for centuries.'

Li Pengfei was by this time shouting and red in the face.

Royle moved close to the terrorist leader and said in a low voice: 'I've never heard you talk like this before.'

Li Pengfei smiled. 'You have to say these things to the capitalist dogs when the foot soldiers are listening.'

Royle's smile half vanished until it appeared as only a part grimace and a frown. What on earth was Li Pengfei's game? His memory flashed back to the jungles of Indochina. Then Li Pengfei had run with the revolutionary Viet Minh, and Li Pengfei had given them to Royle and his force. Li Pengfei and I were allied once. My Man; my agent, delivering intelligence which I acted on for SOE. Could he have been turned? Was he a double agent?

Royle looked at his old comrade. Yes, Li Pengfei could once again be my man. If I could run him again, this time for SIS, perhaps he could become Britain's most valuable spy in the communist camp. God knew, we needed something. The CTs were running our forces ragged and making impossible gains.

*

They spent the night in the clearing beneath tarpaulin shelters, sleeping off the ground in hammocks. It wasn't the rainforest's crawling things that worried them; it was the poisonous crawling things, which they knew would definitely ruin their day, given the chance.

The next morning they quickly broke camp without taking the time to either wash or break their fast, and headed further into the jungle interior. All they had to refresh themselves was water.

Royle soon noticed that one of the communist bandits was missing, presumably an advance guard to give the CT base they were heading towards warning of his impending arrival.

The small group of terrorists and Royle plodded through the jungle for another hour and a half before Li Pengfei raised his hand in silence to indicate a halt. The guerrilla leader placed his hands to his mouth and emitted a shrill, bird-like whistle of the Oriental Cuckoo. It was a Viet Minh recognition call, Royle recalled.

A few minutes passed before leaves in the undergrowth began to move and out stepped a communist guerrilla Royle not seen before.

Li Pengfei moved quickly to the man and both embraced, smiling broadly. When they moved apart they were speaking to each other in Mandarin, which Royle could not completely understand. All Royle was able to glean from the conversation at the distance he was standing from them was that the other was named Chin.

Chin walked towards Royle and, still speaking in quickfire Mandarin, gesticulated in Royle's direction.

Li Pengfei came up and said: 'He wants your revolver, Thomas. And your machete.'

'Of course. I understand completely. What now?' said Royle, handing over his weapons to Chin. One of Li Pengfei's men took them from Chin and stashed the gun inside a backpack and hung the machete from his belt.

Chin then indicated that Royle should be blindfolded and then led further into the jungle for another hour, assisted on either side by Li Pengfei's men.

In time they all stopped. There was the smell and crackle of a wood fire burning, and the bubbling of food stewing in a pot. Royle was unable to identify the smell, but it reminded him of something from his wartime days in the Malay jungle with Li Pengfei.

Royle's blindfold was removed, and he was disappointed when he realised he was not at the guerilla base, but at a small camp containing half a dozen British Army issue tents, the aforementioned camp fire, and a stew bubbling above it.

Li Pengfei whispered in Royle's ear. 'Today's dish of the day is monkey stew accompanied by coconut and ginger rice. You won't find it in any of the finest restaurants of Penang or Kuala Lumpur,' Li Pengfei laughed, and walked into one of the tents.

Royle stood where he was. It appeared he was now definitely a prisoner of the CTs, and he had heard how they treated British prisoners. Royle had also heard horror stories about how the CTs treated kampongs which refused to help them, especially now that they were becoming increasingly rare because of the New Villages policy. A cold shiver ran down his spine as he recalled a story Buchanan had related to him the day before he had left for his solo jungle excursion. An uncooperative kampong head man had been brutally killed by having two young and malleable trees bent towards each other, then having his arms and legs tied to each tree, to be slowly pulled apart as the trees returned to their natural position. This was now one of the scenarios flashing through Royle's mind as he looked around the camp in a desperate bid to find an escape route. But even if he did escape he had no way of knowing which direction to head for once away from the CT camp.

Royle decided to wait and see. In any event, at the moment there was no chance of escape as he was being watched like a hawk by a dozen CT guerrillas armed with either old Japanese or British rifles, presumably dropped during the war and hastily hidden when the CTs decided they had to go underground again after the post-war British reoccupation.

Royle walked over to the large pot of bubbling food and sniffed. Monkey stew, he thought. Well, he'd had worse. He didn't like to think about some of the things he had eaten during his Force 136 guerrilla days.

Li Pengfei came up to the pot and ladled a large dollop of the meaty stew onto a deep tin plate, piled some rice on top and then walked into one of the tents. Moments later he emerged and sat down in front of the fire indicating Royle to do likewise. Soon Chin emerged from his tent, the one Li Pengfei had taken food into, and sat on the other side of Royle. Other men then joined them in a circle around the fire, with two men left to patrol the camp perimeter. One of the guerrillas took on the task of ladling food onto tin plates and handing them to the seated men. Then when all the plates had been passed around they began to eat.

Royle couldn't help thinking that this could be his last supper, but at the same time wondered at how civilised the CTs were being in an increasingly untenable situation. Royle realised this show of food was all a message that the communist guerrillas were not starving and could survive perfectly well on bush food. It was like a flashback to Mao Tse-tung's Yenan in '44, although not on such a grand scale. Unfortunately for the guerrillas, Royle was perfectly aware of the time and effort wasted in hunting and cooking enough bush food to keep a guerrilla army on the go. He looked around. Chin and Li Pengfei looked well fed, but their men appeared to be distinctly malnourished. And, thought Royle, if they wanted to send this message to an important member of the security service, they would presumably wish for Royle to spread the news and therefore they intended to release him. He hoped.

When they had finished their meal, in relative silence, two of the men went over to relieve the guards, who then helped themselves to the remainder of the stew. The others rose from their mealtime crouch and went about their various duties. Then Chin turned to Royle and said something in Mandarin, again too quick for Royle to catch. Li Pengfei translated: 'Chin said, 'I hope your sister likes monkey stew'.'

Royle jumped, as if kicked. The mention of his sister jolted him to full alertness. What did these devils know of his sister? Then he looked at his old wartime comrade. Li Pengfei knew he had a sister, but how could he know Amelia had returned to Malaya after the war to help look after the family rubber estate? Both she and Royle were the sole surviving beneficiaries of the estate after the Japanese withdrawal. While Royle remained part owner of the estate his security work meant he had had little or nothing to do with its running. Amelia had returned from England to take over and had married plantation manager Sam Harper a little over six months ago. During the war Harper had been interned by the Japanese, but returned to his old job on his release, after two months of recuperation. He had been as devastated by the death of Royle's uncle, who had owned the rubber plantation before the war, as Tom and Amelia had been themselves. A simple marriage ceremony sealed the inevitable, and all the British in the community came to see it.

Li Pengfei motioned Royle towards Chin's tent. 'This way, Thomas.' Li Pengfei ducked through the tent flap. Royle followed him through.

In the semi-darkness a woman sat on a simple wooden chair, bound and gagged. At her feet was a deep tin plate with the remains of monkey stew and rice. It was Amelia.

Royle gave Li Pengfei a murderous look as his old fighting comrade removed the gag from Amelia's mouth.

His sister's red lipstick was a little smudged from the cloth that had prevented her from shouting out. Li Pengfei then cut her bonds and brother and sister embraced. Royle held Amelia at arm's length to see if any harm had come to her. Her blond hair was ruffled and strands of it hung unkempt across her handsome face. She was wearing a light cotton floral dress – and a pair of battered British Army boots. Apart from that, she appeared to be in good health.

She smiled and said: 'I'm all right Tommy, don't fret.'

Then Li Pengfei said, 'We have taken good care of her, Thomas. We had to remove her shoes when we took her because she would be unable to walk here in them. We went to great pains to find her a pair of boots that fit. There aren't many size-six British Army boots, but we managed to find a pair. And of course, the soldier who owned them won't be needing them anymore.'

A look of shock flashed across Amelia's face and her eyes moistened. Royle gave Li Pengfei and Chin a look of utter hatred. These monsters had murdered a young British soldier – a National Service conscript, probably – just for his boots. Just so they could make a point to the British rulers, via Tom Royle.

'You can share this tent with your sister tonight,' said Li Pengfei. 'Tomorrow we take you back. You both have safe passage. Goodnight.'

With that the guerrillas disappeared through the tent flap, leaving Royle and his sister alone. Silhouetted through the canvas, by the light of the still blazing camp fire, stood two armed men on guard outside their tent.

LONDON, OCTOBER 1974

It was going dusk in the room at the Royal Embankment Hotel. Harrison rose from one of the easy chairs near the window to switch on the wall lights.

They realised they had missed lunch and both felt famished.

'I'll ring room service for some sandwiches to be sent up, if that's all right Dr Royle?'

'By all means,' said Royle, sipping bottled water from the room's mini-bar.

Half an hour later the sandwiches arrived, along with two large jugs of coffee.

They ate for a while and sipped at the fresh coffee, which revived them both after the long debriefing session. Royle looked at the younger man and wondered how long this was going to take.

As if reading his mind, Harrison said, 'Not much longer now, Dr Royle. Next I want us to go back to Malaya, to the end of the Emergency. What contact did you have with Li Pengfei at this stage?'

MALAYA, JULY 1957

'The communist terrorists were losing badly by mid-1957,' said Royle. 'They had never recovered properly from the New Villages policy, which by this time was completely in place. One thing that Li Pengfei had predicted, the failure of Britain's Malayan Union plan, was quickly realised. He was right that the Sultans would not entertain a process of equality between the races. It would for a start mean a serious loss of power to themselves.'

'How so, if the British ruled?' asked Harrison.

'No, the Sultans ruled the majority Malay people. It was through their consent and acquiescence that they allowed the British to take control of the running of the country and profit from the vast mineral wealth of the place, but it was the Sultans who ruled their own territories within the Malay States, and took their own cut from the British operations.

'After the Sultans refused to work with the Malay Union plan it was dead in the water. It was replaced by a system which favoured the Malays and guaranteed them power in perpetuity. A new political party was formed, the United Malays National Organisation, or UMNO. In 1957 its leader, Tunku Abdul Rahman, was in charge of the largest party in Malaya, consisting of the majority of Malays, and he was preparing for full independence, scheduled for the last day of August.

'Negotiations had gone well and London wanted to finally put an end to the CT insurgencies. They had by this time reduced considerably, but they were still a danger. They still made increasingly desperate raids on plantations and mines, targeting British site managers and workers. They had to go to more dangerous lengths to steal food, and in general their situation was looking more and more untenable.

'The Malayan Communist Party had been making a number of approaches to suggest a truce. The British had a new strategy that was defeating them slowly and surely. Helicopter troop drops in the jungles wiped out CT bases. They were no longer safe in the bush. Propaganda raids intensified, with leaflet drops on known CT sites, towns and villages, offering huge rewards for guerrillas who turned in their leaders.

I witnessed one such collaboration, when a guerrilla came into one of our HQs and presented the CO with a canvas bag. Inside was the head of that man's guerrilla leader. The man was now one of us, he led a platoon back to his base, which was destroyed. He returned to a nice big cash windfall and lived a normal life for the first time.'

Harrison flipped through Royle's now reactivated file, sliding his finger down an appropriate page until it came to the year 1957.

'I see by this time you had been promoted to the rank of Lieutenant-Colonel.'

Royle nodded. 'I was engaged in quite a bit of political work by this time. Shmoozing the Sultans, you could say. I also kept in regular touch with Li Pengfei, through dead letter boxes in some of the larger towns and cities. But London wanted peace, so the next time the MCP offered a truce we invited them to talks. It was decided to meet at our remaining family estate at Baling, in Kedah, which we inherited from our uncle and aunt. We had sold our estate in Singapore to one of the big multinationals by then. Li Pengfei was leading the peace negotiations on behalf of the MCP.'

*

Lt-Col Tom Royle, dressed in a white open-necked shirt and light coloured shorts, socks and polished black shoes, waited at the edge of the jungle with a platoon of soldiers, led by a major. It was dawn. Beneath their feet was the wealth that was the Royle-Harper rubber plantation. Waiting in the family home nearby was the governor-general, ready to meet the communist terrorist leaders who had become a spent force, but were still a damned nuisance, especially with Malayan independence celebrations only a month away. With them was a Gaumont newsreel team, ready to record for posterity and show in news theatres back in Britain what they had undoubtedly been told could be an historic moment – the surrender of the communist terrorists in Malaya.

They had been waiting half an hour when they heard the undisguised sound of footfall in the jungle undergrowth.

Two ethnic Chinese guerrillas emerged from the trees, carrying British issue rifles, British issue pistols were slung from their belts, and British issue ammunition was hung across their red-coloured shirts. A few paces behind them emerged Li Pengfei, a Webley revolver holstered in his belt. Royle gave an involuntary half-smile at the gesture; a last weak and inconsequential piece of bravado to show the ruling British that they were still capable of liberating valuable weapons from their European capitalist overlords.

Lights bathed the area, even though the sunshine was quite bright in itself. Royle heard the whir of a Gaumont Empire News film camera as it started to roll.

Royle walked across to Li Pengfei and shook hands, then began to walk with him and the major towards the house, just a half mile down the track. The two guerrillas followed, and behind them all was a platoon of soldiers, marching two by two.

The Gaumont commentator's voice could be heard over the marching and the pleasantries.

As they walked slowly up the hill towards the Royle-Harper house, Lt-Col Tom Royle came to realise that this could be a make or break moment in the Emergency. His years of secret communications with Li Pengfei may yet pay off. And as he was thinking this the voice of the Gaumont Empire News reporter drifted his way as he began to make his recording: 'And here we see the Communists, escorted by Lt-Col Thomas Royle, the famous Force 136 guerrilla leader and former colleague of Li Pengfei during the Japanese occupation. All necks crane for a glimpse of the number one terrorist in Malaya – and there he is. That's him, Li Pengfei, the man responsible for a brutal seven-year campaign of murder and terrorism against the ordinary people of Malaya …'

The commentator's voice diminished into the distance as they continued their progress towards the house. Li Pengfei pretended not to have heard the commentary and Royle realised that this platoon of British soldiers armed to the teeth must have found it strange not to have shot these terrorists on sight the moment they emerged from the trees. He looked across and saw that the same emotion was on the faces of Li Pengfei's small entourage.

Royle looked at Li Pengfei as they walked. His shoulders were stooped, but he appeared to be well fed. He was much bulkier and heavier than Royle remembered, and he seemed to have aged beyond his years. His skin was pale and sallow through spending years surviving under the rainforest canopy, where sunlight was filtered out by the density of trees. Even though over the years he had left the forest briefly for his secret meetings with Royle, Li Pengfei still looked a ghostly pale figure.

Royle said to his former comrade: 'Are you keeping well, old friend? Although we have communicated regularly over the years we have rarely met in person.'

Li Pengfei started to speak, to say he was fit and well, but he caught his tongue. *Everything today must be truth*, he thought to himself, so began his reply again. 'Thomas, I have lived in the jungle many years. The sunlight has been a blessing whenever I came out for our rare contacts, but then I had to return into the gloom. Food has been short, thanks to your ingenious closing down of our supply lines. And I have been ill for some time with beri-beri. I am, however, more than capable of negotiating our peace with whoever is willing to listen.'

'The governor-general is waiting in the house as we speak,' Royle smiled reassuringly. But inside he was worried about his ex-comrade. Beri-beri had killed his father while he had been incarcerated in Changi Prison by the Japanese. Royle looked at Li Pengfei again. Yes, he is desperately ill. He realised now that Li Pengfei's bulkiness must have been caused by the oedema that the disease produces. And Li Pengfei had it bad.

Li Pengfei said: 'How is your sister, Thomas? I hope she is well. I very much regret the events of a few years ago when we had to kidnap her in order to persuade you and the British that we could survive well in the jungle, and that we could get our hands on anyone we wished.'

'That was six years ago, old friend. You made sure she was treated decently, didn't you?'

'I did, Thomas. Your friendship has always been valuable to me, even when we have fought on opposing sides.'

'I could have killed you that day, Li Pengfei. You know that, don't you?'

'Of course, it would not have been natural for you to have thought otherwise. I would have expected no less.'

'And what of your Mr Chin?' asked Royle, as the big Royle-Harper house came into sight.

'Ah, he was a representative of the Chinese Communist Party from Beijing.'

'I'm surprised. I didn't know China was taking such an interest in our little war.'

Li Pengfei looked up at Royle and smiled broadly. His uneven teeth, made loose after years of a poor jungle diet, did not detract from the jolliness Li Pengfei suddenly ensued. 'There are many things you do not know. Chairman Mao took a great interest in our struggle. You remember him, of course, from 1944. He was the great manipulator. He manipulated the Americans then and he's manipulating the world now. Chin stayed with us for some time. He proved to be surprisingly resilient and rarely complained about our conditions. It was his idea to kidnap your sister as a propaganda coup. The coup failed, of course.'

'And Mr Chin returned to Beijing afterwards, I take it?'

'Oh no,' said Li Pengfei, as they approached the steps to the house's wide verandah. 'He is still in the jungle. Under six feet of earth.'

'Jungle fever?' asked Royle.

'Shovel,' said Li Pengfei with a gleam in his eye. 'To the back of the neck.'

*

Harrison put his shorthand pad down and stopped the tape recorder.

The sandwiches and coffee had been polished off in between Royle's stories.

'So what happened at the talks?' asked Harrison, placing a new tape cassette into the machine, and turning a page on his pad to start his notes again.

'Well, we all knew Li Pengfei had turned up for the talks with a particularly weak hand. The communists were desperate for a negotiated peace. They offered to stand down their forces throughout Malaya in return for a legitimate place within the new political process. The Malayan Communist Party was a proscribed organisation, and had been before the Second World War. They offered to fight on our side against the Japanese because their country was at stake and they saw the British as being better wartime bedfellows than the Japanese. At the end of the war we thanked them, then left them out of the post-war reorganisation of the country. They didn't like it, kicked up a fuss, caused trouble and were banned again.

'The governor-general was on the phone to Tunku Abdul Rahman as soon as Li Pengfei made his offer. The line had been left open during the talks because the Tunku had refused to negotiate in person with the terrorists. The talks had been going on for hours, and by this time it was mid-afternoon.

'The Tunku's response was a definitive "no". He demanded immediate unconditional surrender.

'Li Pengfei was in some considerable discomfort from his illness, but he stood up to make a dignified bow to the governor-general and everyone else in the room, and slowly walked out of the house, where he linked up with his two bodyguards, who to be perfectly honest would have proved completely useless in the face of the overwhelming lethal force we had at our disposal.

'It was extremely brave of Li Pengfei to walk into the lion's den so disarmed, and he was not about to agree to absolute surrender. As he walked out of the door one of the governor-general's aides picked up a telephone and quietly spoke a single code word, then replaced the telephone on the hook.

'Half the platoon of soldiers headed back down the path towards the jungle while the other half escorted the MCP party from behind. The major in charge of the unit marched with the men in the rear. I'm afraid I rushed out, pushed passed the rearguard and caught up with Li Pengfei, still walking slowly, shoulders more stooped than ever. The talks seem to have really taken it out of him.

'I walked close to him. Even had my arm round him for some time as we walked down the track towards the trees. You see, I knew they were going to murder all three of the terrorist envoys as soon as they reached the trees. The journalists and the crowds had dispersed as the talks dragged on, but none were allowed back down the track to the jungle. The code word was the giveaway.'

'What was the word?' asked Harrison.

'Magnolia.'

'And was that a word used commonly for assassination?'

'It was a word used by the communist fighters when they fought with me during the war. It was their code word for "attack". Ironic, don't you think?'

'And do you think Li Pengfei heard the code word as he was leaving the house?'

'He didn't need to. He could tell by the demeanour of the soldiers that it wasn't going to end well for him.'

'So what happened?'

'I walked with him all the way back to the jungle, laughing, joking, and talking about old times. We had reached his departure point before we knew it. The advance guard had positioned themselves in lines on either side of the path. We heard them cock their rifles as we approached. The platoon's normal commander, a lieutenant, had taken his revolver from his Sam Brown belt and was holding it in his hand, pointing towards the ground. I told Li Pengfei's men to walk in front of us and I continued to stay close to Li Pengfei. I was taking the risk that they would not open fire if there was a chance that I may be hit. There would definitely be a hail of bullets and we would have been left dead with more holes in us than gruyere cheese.

'As it turned out I was right. None of the soldiers moved as we approached. I saw the young lieutenant look enquiringly at the major, who had caught up with us from behind. He shook his head and Li Pengfei and his escort disappeared into the jungle, never to be seen again.

'As an added precaution, I stood at the entrance to the jungle and started to leisurely light my pipe, ensuring none of the soldiers went into the jungle to hunt Li Pengfei down. I must have stood there smoking for half an hour until I set off back up the hill to the house.

'As I smoked the major certainly smouldered – with rage.'

'So you prevented our forces from getting rid of one Malaya's most notorious terrorist leaders, thus ending the Emergency at a stroke. Why ever would you do something like that, Dr Royle?'

'Because there was more to Li Pengfei than a terrorist. He was working for us. It was very complicated.'

'Ah,' said Harrison, in a tone suggesting that they had finally reached a point he had been heading towards all the time.

'Fancy a nightcap, doctor? A quick one in the bar downstairs, before we turn in for the night. I fear we may have a long day ahead of us.'

*

The next day the two men returned from breakfast at 8.30am and settled down in their chairs. A new pile of tapes had appeared by Harrison's cassette tape recorder, along with a new notepad and spare pencils, which had not been there when the two had gone downstairs for their morning meal.

Both had shared the room overnight. Royle decided that Harrison was under orders not to let the Force 136 veteran out of his sight.

Harrison placed a new tape in the cassette recorder, opened his new note pad, wrote the date and time in long hand, then said: 'Very well Dr Royle. Shall we continue?' Royle sat back in his chair and nodded.

'Dr Royle, last night as we were concluded our talk, you said Li Pengfei was working for us. Were you running him?'

Royle looked at the younger man. His questioning had become more aggressive than yesterday. He appeared to be working to a deadline. 'In a sense, I was,' answered Royle, ambiguously.

'Please, doctor. Be specific.'

'I'll be as specific as I can,' said Royle. 'Li Pengfei was a double. He ran the terrorists in that part of Malaya, but he also provided us with information, through me. On more than one occasion a terrorist operation was thwarted because of information Li Pengfei had passed to me. You must understand. We rarely met. We used dead letter boxes to communicate. We may have met once a year, and then only briefly. I neither saw nor heard of him again after the talks at the Royle-Harper house. Our link was cut off forever.

'To the extent that he was my agent, yes he was when it suited him. He was a constant help to me. Smoothed my career path no end. My promotions were undoubtedly a result of his information. The only condition on his part was that he should remain anonymous as my source. My people knew him by my code name for him – Cuckoo.'

'Very apt, doctor.'

'You must realise this is the first time I have identified Cuckoo. I presume he died shortly after our so-called peace talks.'

'No, doctor. He didn't die.'

'Then this information must never get out. If he can be linked as the betrayer of some of the communists' most spectacular terror operations during the Emergency, then his life is worth nothing.'

'Of course, it will of course need to go into the registry. They do so love putting names to code names in the admin section.'

'Can they be trusted?'

'All fully vetted. All entirely trustworthy.'

Royle nodded, realising at the same time this charming man had suddenly become more alert when the code name Cuckoo was revealed.

Royle looked at Harrison again. 'If he didn't die, and you know he didn't die, do you know where he is now?'

Harrison smiled, but said nothing.

The younger man said: 'Did something happen soon after Malayan independence? A personal tragedy?'

Royle flushed slightly. 'Yes, you obviously know it did. A few days after independence was declared at the end of August 1957 my brother-in-law was murdered in a CT raid on the Royle-Harper house. He had just returned from town in his car after carrying out some business when he was ambushed as he approached the house. His car was an armoured Armstrong Siddeley Sapphire, built like a tank. A lot of planters and mine owners had had their cars armour plated since the early 1950s to give them a better chance in an attack. They all carried weapons of some description. Sam carried a Thompson sub-machine gun and a 9mm automatic pistol. Neither the car nor the weapons were of any use to him because the CTs had mined the entrance to the house. As his car went in he was blown to pieces. Amelia never got over it, even to this day. That's why she moved to England.

'We found out later that the CTs who killed Sam had targeted the house because of the planned double-cross by our people against Li Pengfei.'

'Very sad. Do you believe Li Pengfei had something to do with this?'

'At first I did, then I got to thinking why should he? He knows me. He knows Amelia. He knew the relationship we both had with Sam. And he knows I saved him and his pals from being shot full of holes after the peace talks. Who knows who did it?'

Harrison stood up to gaze at the boring scene outside the window. 'I can tell you who was responsible for your brother-in-law's death. It was Li Pengfei.'

Royle sat stiffly in his chair, his knuckles turning white as his fingers tightened over the chair arms.

Harrison returned to his seat. 'I'm afraid Li Pengfei ordered the killing for two reasons. The first, and most important reason, was that Li Pengfei had identified Sam Harper as a secret member of the Comintern. Harper had been giving information about his fellow colonials to the communists for years. Li Pengfei discovered this from your Mr Chin, or as we know him, Colonel Chin Le-fuong of the Chinese People's Liberation Army. Harper was Chin's man. I'm afraid your brother-in-law was a traitor who had caused the deaths of many British and Malays over the years. It took him so long to act because of your sister.'

'Amelia? How?'

'Li Pengfei was in love with your sister. They were having an affair, didn't you know? Li Pengfei warned your sister about what he knew. She didn't believe Li Pengfei at first, but her suspicions were aroused and eventually Harper's behaviour led her to believe the worst. To test the Harper theory Li Pengfei offered information to Amelia, who then mentioned it as gossip to Sam Harper. The first couple of times, the information was genuine, and there was some serious loss of life. Then they began feeding Harper false information. Again the information was acted on, but without such dire effects this time. This clinched matters, and both Li Pengfei and Amelia realised that Harper would have to be liquidated.

'Amelia w-was involved?' stuttered Royle.

'She tipped Li Pengfei off when Harper went into town. The trap was set for when he returned.'

'But Amelia was devastated when Sam was killed. Even now she can't talk about it.'

'Yes, guilt is a powerful emotion. Sadly Li Pengfei and your sister never met again. He was forced to go deeper into the jungle and simply disappeared – until now.'

'So you do know where he is.'

'Yes indeed, Doctor Royle. He's in South Vietnam, and we want you to bring him out.'

SAIGON, DECEMBER 1974

The US Air Force C-124 transporter circled erratically as it approached Tan Son Nhut airport. Tan Son Nhut was South Vietnam's main airport and flew a constant stream of visitors and freight in and out of the South Vietnamese capital. During the height of the war Tan Son Nhut had become the busiest airport in the world. These days, since the peace treaty and the American withdrawal, it was much quieter.

Flights by American liveried aircraft had become increasingly rare since the peace treaty was signed between Hanoi and Washington in January 1973. These had at first been carried out in secret in Paris, and later when progress began to be made, both sides agreed to public announcements. Agreement was reached and President Nixon announced the suspension of all US offensive action in Vietnam after a series of heavy bombing raids on the North, in particular Hanoi. The Paris Agreement was signed, and American prisoners of war were released by Hanoi. That year the US withdrew all its troops from South Vietnam, apart from 16,000 remaining advisors and administrators, and a high number of CIA operatives.

It had been a brutal and bloody affair, much of it conducted on television and given wide coverage in the world's newspapers. More than 58,000 Americans had died. Two million civilians were killed in the war, along with 1.1 million North Vietnamese and Viet Cong.

But in October 1974, despite the peace accord, the Politburo of the North Vietnam government in Hanoi devised a plan to win back the rest of the country. They decided that 1975 would be the year when the two countries became one, under communist control. Hanoi's invasion of South Vietnam was to begin in December 1974 and would intensify until the whole of the south was under communist control.

In August of 1974 the US government was in disarray. Impeachment proceedings against President Nixon after the Watergate scandal were well under way when Nixon resigned from office. His Vice President, Gerald Ford, took over at the White House, becoming the sixth incumbent who had to cope with the impossible problem that was

Vietnam, and a stubborn senate that had decided that no more American dollars would be spent on what had become a war-torn backwater, at least in their eyes.

As Tom Royle flew into Tan Son Nhut, Hanoi was already violating the Paris treaty by launching an attack on the southern province of Phuoc Long. Hanoi knew the route was open to Saigon when President Ford limited the US response to just diplomatic protests – the US senate had blocked his appeal for financial aid and arms to allow the South to fight back effectively.

That was the green light for the Politburo in Hanoi. Secret plans for a full-scale invasion of the south were finalised. It was a plan for final victory, knowing that the Americans would not intervene, and that the corrupt government in the south was a spent force.

*

The C-124 was continuing to spiral down to the runway, now releasing flares from its tail – just in case there were Viet Cong missiles tracking them from the airport perimeter. There weren't.

As the aircraft lurched, yawed, climbed and dropped in its evasive approach Royle looked around him. He was holding on to a network of strong webbing in the hold of the giant plane. This part had been converted for passengers and there were half a dozen other men, all officers in US Army uniform, in the passenger compartment. All the passengers sat on hard seats and were buckled in for the final approach. In the cargo hold were a number of anonymous crates, all destined for US facilities in Saigon, including the embassy.

Royle had spent years enduring rough flights, parachute drops, covert submarine landings and dangerous races overland from one battle zone to the next. The danger no longer worried him. He was fatalistic about it. Royle had no choice but to place his faith in whoever was in command of the vehicle he was in. He had no control over his life for those few relatively short hours or minutes of danger, but he had no choice but to be philosophical about it. The chances of survival were good, but he also knew the chances of fatal failure were higher than normal. As such, Royle now hung on to the cargo webbing in the plummeting aircraft and considered his actions once he landed on South Vietnamese soil.

The engines whined as the aircraft descended, then seemingly at the last minute, the transport plane levelled out and immediately landed on the tarmac, screeching and bumping its way to the terminal at Tan Son Nhut. As they taxied to their berth Royle recalled his first visit to this airport. He had flown in with the British Army's 20th Indian Division in 1945 to impose control over Saigon and eject the Viet Minh from its seat of government, seized in the power vacuum immediately after the Japanese had surrendered. Royle couldn't help wondering that if his force had left the Viet Minh in power all these years of conflict may never have happened. The Vietnamese had been fighting for their freedom since 1945 – hell, long before that, against the French, then against the Japanese, then against the British during their short post-war tenure, then against the French again, and latterly, after the French had finally withdrawn in 1954, against the Americans.

*

Wearing khaki shirt and trousers and strong boots on his feet, Royle hefted his rucksack and walked towards the terminal building with his fellow passengers. They were undoubtedly advisors on a new tour of duty in Saigon, but the American force there was non-existent. They were there to give the final desperate instructions to an increasingly demoralised and under-equipped South Vietnamese army.

Royle walked into the building – it hadn't been like this in '45, or in '64 when he had last set foot in Vietnam. A lot of money had been spent on the airport since then. American money. It had also been hugely expanded and strengthened, to enable a constant traffic of heavy transporters to take off and land around the clock.

At the terminal door was his contact. Dressed in a light tropical suit, white shirt and black tie was Charles Kravitz, military liaison officer at the US Embassy. Royle knew him better as his CIA contact in Saigon. Both men had met in 1944, up in the North. Kravitz was in the OSS, the Second World War US espionage outfit which later evolved into the Central Intelligence Agency. Royle had crossed into Vietnam from China to assess the strength of the Japanese and Vichy French forces in the country, after his illuminating meeting with Li Pengfei and Mao Tse-tung in Yenan. Kravitz had been Royle's guide and had introduced him to a wiry, bright-eyed Vietnamese leader he later discovered to be Ho Chi Minh. At the time Ho was working with the OSS and had been anxious to foster links with the British too. Royle remembered being impressed by the man who was later to inspire the North Vietnamese to take up arms against the French and the Americans, and their southern brothers.

Royle stretched out his arm as he approached his old friend and both men shook hands warmly.

CHONGQING, EARLY NOVEMBER 1944

Royle had made the arduous journey by horse, road, military aircraft, rail and road again from Mao's Communist stronghold in Yenan to the temporary wartime capital of China, Chongqing, in Szechuan province.

He left Browne to fly back to Ceylon and report back to Mountbatten, while Royle had more overland travelling to do.

Royle checked in to the Imperial Hotel for a long bath and a good meal before continuing his mission – a meeting with some of the American officers and foreign service diplomats just arriving back from Yenan. Royle and Browne had left the communist stronghold early, hence the arduous journey to Chongqing. The military mission had a more comfortable return, in an American C-47 transport plane. The Browne-Royle delegation to Mao Tse-tung had been arranged with the help of the Americans for Britain to have a taste of the communist fighting force and their observations of how they thought the Chinese communists could help in the fight against the Japanese invaders. Then it would be on with his journey to Indochina. His next job was to determine Japanese and Vichy French strengths in the north of the country as invasion plans were being drawn up for liberation.

His mission was to make contact with an American OSS operative who had been in and out of Indochina over the past year.

Chongqing was a mix of colonial structures and bombed out ruins. As China's wartime capital the city had been heavily blitzed by the Japanese air force, only recently blocked by Chennault's 14th. And still there were occasional air raid warnings as Chiang Kai-shek's nationalist government hunkered down with its mainly US allies as Japan's advances finally became rarer. It was thanks to Stilwell's military genius as deputy Supreme Allied Commander under Mountbatten at South East Asia Command, and Chennault's Flying Tigers that had stopped the seemingly unstoppable Japanese from moving ever closer to complete domination in China. Stilwell loved China and was a China expert. As a colonel Joseph Stilwell had been a service attaché to US Ambassador Nelson Johnson as the embassy evacuated first from Peking and then

Nanking before the arrival of the invading Japanese in 1938. Now, as a disillusioned general directing Chiang Kai-shek's land armies Stilwell had suffered the wrath of the Kuomintang's leader, and by extension the Pentagon. He had uncovered the embezzlement of millions of US dollars in military aid being siphoned into private bank accounts by Chiang and his high level government colleagues. His reports to the US Secretary of State and his bosses at the Pentagon were not politically welcomed and a bitter Stilwell earned himself the epithet "Vinegar Joe".

So it was in an atmosphere of graft, corruption and suspicion that Royle arrived in the provisional capital.

Standing on his hotel balcony overlooking the Yangtse River, it was coming dusk, and the blackout had already been imposed. Buildings across the river were dark silhouettes and the wide, fast-flowing Yangtse was a black track still used dangerously by unlit shipping.

The next morning Royle met a harassed looking US Foreign Service officer in the hotel lobby. John Davidson had worked for the US State Department since before the war and had been born in the Middle Kingdom, being educated privately as a child by a talented governess, then shipped off to Harvard before joining the service. Davidson was in every aspect what the Americans called an "old China hand".

Royle soon understood the reasons for Davidson's stress. He had half a dozen reports to write up to be encrypted and fired off to Washington DC for his masters to read.

Davidson had been impressed with his visit to Yenan. There had been a positive can-do atmosphere among not only the communist leadership, but also among the population and soldiers of the communist Eighth Route Army.

'Good to see you again, John. How was the rest of the visit?'

'Couldn't have been better, couldn't have been better. All my reports will have this message – the communist forces are our best hope in China.'

Royle cocked an eyebrow at that. 'Is that the view of you all?'

'Most of us, Tom. They were amazing, from the high echelons down. They had captured Japanese weapons, they have proven battle wins, and they aren't corrupt.'

Royle couldn't help himself and looked around the room to make sure no KMT spies were around to listen to that remark.'

'You must have seen for yourself how things were over there, despite all the privations they have been suffering. No matter what Chiang Kai-shek says, the communists are still blockaded by a crack nationalist army group at Sian,' said Davidson, his eyes bright with fervour. He believed he had found the lost secret that could win the Sino-Japanese war for the Allies.

'They have great generals, fantastic motivation, and captured weapons that they have used with devastating effect against the Japanese,' added Davidson.

'Yes, I saw all that, John,' said Royle, frowning. 'But don't you think it was all a little bit staged?'

'I wouldn't say staged exactly. More like everyone was keeping to the Party line. And that was to welcome important guests and allies.'

'With the even more important prospect of receiving regular consignments of good all-American weapons …'

'Exactly Tom, and we think … I think … they should receive those weapons. Look what the KMT have done. They have kept what weapons we have given them and locked them away. And their theft of US currency is surely the crime of the century.'

'Both sides are stockpiling weapons for after the war, when they will have their own showdown,' said Royle.

'That's probably so, but Potomac rules apply here,' said the State Department officer. 'And those rules say give them the means with which to defeat our common enemy, and then we worry about any further consequences afterwards.'

Royle smiled at that. 'Sounds like Whitehall rules too,' putting on his HM Diplomatic Service cover.

'So John, what else can you tell me about your time after we left?'

'Well, as you know we were a rather mixed group at Dixie – that was our code name for the communist so-called "special area". We had our own State Department delegation, members of a military mission, and Theodore White, a journalist for Time in attendance.

'By the way, Stilwell's been relieved. Chiang has had his way at last.'

At that Royle shook his head in dismay. Stilwell's genius had halted the Japanese in their tracks.

'At our allotted cave house I was sharing a room with an OSS officer. He was on the lookout for any immediate tactical advantage that could be had. Nice enough chap, if a little intense. It was all fairly comfortable, given the circumstances. As you know, they all live in caves in Yenan, although ours wasn't an actual cave. Special treatment for the guests I expect.

'We were looked after by Eighth Route Army orderlies, or chao tai yuan, which literally translated means "entertain-the-guests-officer".

'While we were there we had a private conflab about where we stood following Stilwell's downfall. But then it was down to the business in hand. We had a number of meetings with Dixie's commander-in-chief, General Chu Teh, and Mao's number two, Chou En-lai. We had most of our conferences at what was termed the Reception House, where there were all manner of delegates, from Mao Tse-tung himself and other high ranking communists, to two KMT delegates, who were continuously and disparagingly referred to as "spies". In addition there were a number of other foreign correspondents, mostly from the States, plus two scruffy-looking Russians from Tass, the Soviet news agency. Colonel David Barrett was in charge of our mission.

'One night Chou En-lai invited us to his house. It was guarded and had five or six rooms, but it was still a cave. His wife poured us tea and then Mao himself arrived to join us. We talked frankly for about three hours, then Chu Teh came in. All veterans of the Long March, and very impressive. No decisions were made, but the overwhelming impression I got was that they are calmly confident in their own growing strength – and patient.'

'You know, Tom. We weren't there just to assess the Dixie factor in the war. We had future plans too for afterwards. Think about the possibilities of a US-Chinese Communist military alliance. That would go a long way to prevent a Soviet takeover of northern China when Russia finally decides to join the war against Japan. Think about that for a minute.'

Davidson was starting to get a little angered by what he saw as Royle's dismissive attitude to an apparently won-over US delegation.

'Please, John. I'm just a little tired. Don't forget we didn't have the luxury of a flight back to Chongqing. I apologise if I appear a little distant, but I am all ears. It's a fascinating story, and Yenan is a fascinating place. I honestly didn't want to leave. It's a much more refreshing place than Chongqing. Please go on,' smiled Royle, remembering that Davidson was first and foremost a US Foreign Service officer who had taken the time out of a busy schedule to talk to him about his experiences at Dixie after he had left.

Davidson nodded, took a deep breath, then continued his story.

'I really think these are people we can do business with, Tom. They are conscientious and able. I'm sure they did make things a little special for us for our visit – they had been waiting for us to do something official for quite a long time. But I felt the welcome we received was genuine. They want what we have, and we may let them have it because they have what we want – true grit and an unbeatable spirit.'

Davidson stretched his long legs in the comfortable armchair and looked at the thickly-carpeted floor for a moment before continuing. A note of embarrassment was lightly etched on his face.

'There was one somewhat disturbing sight.' Davidson looked up at Royle, who leaned forward to hear as Davidson's voice was lowered to a near whisper.

'There were a number of Japanese prisoners of war. We didn't really think much of it, seeing as they were Japanese. But one of our officers had the task of studying the Japanese order of battle, and Chu Teh's adjutant, General Yeh, organised a continuous visitation of Japanese prisoners to him. All wore the Eighth Route Army uniform of the communists and had evidently been re-educated to the communist way of thinking.

'The new prisoners who remained unconvinced of the new order were always accompanied by a Japanese soldier now fighting with the Chinese communists, who had by all accounts seen the light, as persuaded by the Reds.'

'Are you saying they had been brainwashed? All of them?'

'All of them, apart from the newer prisoners, who were apparently being worked upon.'

'That's a little worrying, John.'

'Yes, it was,' said Davidson. 'But they are the enemy after all.'

'What if we were the enemy, John?'

'Not a chance. We are their great hope.'

'You know, John. On our way out, we were on horseback. We "accidentally" strayed off our designated route. We weren't accompanied by the Reds, they were still fully engaged with you and the main delegation of observers. We passed though some of the communist-held farms, and they seemed completely derelict and uninhabitable. Then we rode through fields and fields of poppies. Opium poppies. Literally, their opium of the masses, as Marx once called religion.

'Do you think they are financing their war by selling opium for the dens of Chongqing?'

Davidson shrugged, looked at his wristwatch then got up from his chair. Shaking hands with Royle, Davidson said, 'I'm sure you British know more about opium wars in China than we do.' Then with a nod, he walked through the front door of the hotel to make his reports to the State Department.

Royle walked back to his room to pack.

SAIGON, DECEMBER 1974

'Charles, it's great to see you. It's been thirty years. And you're still here and in this game?'

Kravitz laughed and led Royle through lines of South Vietnamese soldiers, passport control and customs simply by waving his CIA credentials.

'Not all the time, Tommy. I've only been here for the past six years. Worst six years of my life, old pal. If I'd known our ally back in '44 would turn out to be Uncle Ho who caused all this shit I would have shot him there and then up in the mountains of the north. Anyway, you're still in the game too, I see.'

'Only for the last few weeks, Charles. I was a mere teacher before then.'

'You, a teacher? Not easy to believe, my friend.'

'But true. Taught South East Asian history to spotty undergraduates. Very popular subject recently in actual fact, thanks to you Americans.'

'Well it would certainly be nice to know what's going to happen here. The reds have been rattling a few sabres on the border. There have been a few incidents, and now there's been an all-out attack on Phuoc Long province. I'm waiting to see if the President orders retaliation. This airport could be getting pretty busy again if we end up moving back in.'

They climbed into an open-topped US Army jeep, with Kravitz at the wheel, and gunned the engine so that a cloud of gravel and dust was all that remained in the space they had occupied seconds earlier, heading towards the heavily fortified US Embassy building in Saigon.

As they drove through open countryside towards the city they watched people working the rice fields, sometimes knee deep in water. It seemed for a short moment idyllic, then as they turned a bend they had to pull in to allow a convoy of Southern army trucks through, on their way to the airport.

Kravitz indicated them with a wave of the head as they drove passed: 'Heading to Phuoc Long. It seems the attack by the north wasn't merely a border skirmish, but an incursion in force.'

'So you're saying that despite the treaty the north is flouting it and continuing its attacks?'

'Come on, Tommy. You're the professor. We've all broken the treaty hundreds of times since it was signed. Us, them, I wouldn't like to say which side has broken it most times. But it has always been a limited breach and matters have always gone back to normal again soon after.

'This time it seems different, so that's why we can't take the scenic route back to the embassy. I need to find out what's going on up there.'

Kravitz put his foot down and the jeep roared on towards the city.

As the high wrought iron embassy gates clanged shut behind them, Kravitz gunned the jeep at high speed towards the back of the building. The vehicle skidded to a halt and both men leapt out and walked quickly through a rear door, guarded by two battle-dressed US Marines.

Kravitz signed Royle in, showed him through to a comfortable common room, used by the embassy's intelligence staff, then ran up a flight of stairs, disappearing through an anonymous wooden door.

In the common room the air conditioning was on, keeping the temperature a refreshing and relatively cool 70 degrees Fahrenheit. Royle walked over to what seemed to be a constantly topped up coffee percolator, poured himself a cup of the steaming liquid, decided to take it black to keep him alert after his flight, then settled down to read a magazine – National Geographic – in a comfortable armchair. The fact that there was no-one else in the room was an indicator that there was indeed some sort of flap on and all the CIA staffers at the embassy were occupied by it.

Despite the stronger than average coffee – a blend reserved for the US Marine Corps but often used by other US government intelligence departments – it had failed to keep Royle awake. Royle was jolted into wakefulness by Kravitz and another man, similarly attired. It was like a CIA uniform, Royle thought to himself with a smile.

'Dr Thomas Royle, may I present Joe Guardino, acting deputy station chief,' Kravitz said with a smile, though Royle noted a hint of tension about his American friend.

'Glad to know you, doctor. I've heard a lot about you. And I'd like to know even more,' said Guardino.

The two men shook hands and Royle was immediately wary of the CIA boss. 'I'll help in any way I can, of course,' said Royle.

The two men continued to look at each other unblinking, until Kravitz finally broke the tension.

'Great. That's great, let's go up to my office so you can both get acquainted. Hell, I need to get re-acquainted, too.'

They walked up the bleak staircase and through the door Kravitz had earlier run through. It led to a wide corridor lined with offices. None had an outward looking window, but all were comfortably air-conditioned. They walked quickly through double doors, across a stair well, through another set of double doors and into another identical corridor. Kravitz opened a door to his left and all three men entered.

All three settled down in comfortable office chairs, Guardino taking occupation of Kravitz's desk. Kravitz sauntered over to his own personal coffee percolator and poured out three cups.

'So, Dr Royle, Chuck tells me you and he go back a long way.'

'We do, and it all started here. Well, a few hundred miles further north as a matter of fact.'

'Tell me,' Guardino almost ordered.

'Of course,' said Royle, taking a leisurely sip of the almost too-strong blend. 'I was in the SOE during the war. I was brought up in Malaya, but left to enlist when war was declared. While I was away the Japanese invaded South East Asia and attacked Pearl Harbor. Because of my jungle experience I was recruited into the Special Operations Executive as a member of their Force 136, which operated in the Far East.'

'He was like us in the OSS, Joe,' explained Kravitz. 'Except we had more money and resources.' The veteran former OSS agent laughed out loud, and Royle joined in. Guardino, however, remained stony faced.

'Go on,' said the acting deputy station chief. By now Royle realised that Kravitz and Guardino were by no means best buddies.

'We met up north in '44. Charles was my guide as I tried to infiltrate to assess Japanese forces in Indochina.'

'Hell, yeah. We had a good few months up in the hills and further in-country. Had a great native guide. You may have heard of him, name of Ho Chi Minh.' Kravitz let out a huge bellow of laughter.

Guardino snorted with contempt. 'You should've shot the fucker when you had the chance.'

'Hey, he was one of the good guys then. In those days beggars couldn't be choosers. Let me tell you something, old Uncle Ho was so important to us then that we recruited him into OSS.'

Guardino looked at Kravitz from behind Kravitz's untidy desk. He snorted again.

Knowing he had baited the younger man, Kravitz then began to pull in the line. 'Sure, he was one of us back then. Ho Chi Minh even had a designation. He was OSS Agent 19 back then. He knew the country backwards and had an extraordinary network operating throughout the country.'

'Pity this great intelligence network didn't get the Brits in the moment the Japs surrendered then,' Guardino observed, sourly.

'Oh, we did. I was in the first wave. Unfortunately Ho and his Viet Minh got into position first. And the rest is history,' Royle observed.

'Which gets us back to you Dr Royle. Why is MI6 sending a history teacher out here?' asked Guardino.

'I believe I'm here to tie up a few loose ends, Mr Guardino.'

The acting deputy station chief impulsively stood up and walked towards the door. He turned to Royle. 'Just don't get in the way. We may have a situation on the border and we're all very busy.' When Guardino said 'all' he glanced at Kravitz. Guardino's message was clear. Royle could not rely on any help from the CIA.

'It was good to meet you, Dr Royle.' With that Guardino disappeared out of the door.

'Did you have to antagonise him, Charles?'

'Hell, Guardino's an asshole. He thinks us old timers ain't worth jack shit. Tommy, I've seen things here that would make your hair curl – even from our days way back then. That little bureaucrat has only been here 18 months, and I don't think he's even left the embassy compound in all that time.'

'Ah well, where does that leave me?' asked Royle

'I've arranged for transport to take you to the British Embassy. I only brought you here because Guardino said he wanted to meet you.'

'But I go off duty at six. I'll meet you in the Caravelle Hotel bar then.'

'Thanks Charles, or should I say Chuck?'

'Listen to me, you lame Limey. You're the only person I know who still calls me Charles. Not even my dear departed mother called me

Charles. Everyone has always called me Chuck, ever since I can remember. But if ever I hear you call me Chuck again I'll have you thrown out of the next helicopter headed north – at 3,000 feet.'

'Charles it is then,' laughed Royle.

*

The bar at the Caravelle was a large affair. At the height of the war it was regularly frequented by the world's Press corps, CIA, old French stay-behind ex-colonials and senior US military officers. Surprisingly lacking in those days was a presence by the infamous Saigon prostitutes, who plied their trade in all the other bars and hotels of the city. The Caravelle had standards.

Now Royle sat at a table in the Caravelle bar, sipping his third martini. It was 8pm and Charles Kravitz had still not turned up for their rendezvous. And for the sixth time Royle had had to politely say 'no' to girls who had now taken up residence in the bar. He hoped they now had received the message that he did not wish to be bothered by them. Times must be hard. The Americans had all left Saigon and the bar was almost empty. During the war it had always been hard to get a seat. Obviously the no prostitution policy had been abandoned. And despite being relatively empty, most of the girls were getting lucky with the men who walked into the bar. Mostly, he noticed, high ranking members of the South Vietnam armed forces.

Earlier a US military jeep had taken Royle from the US Embassy compound to the British Embassy, where Royle was first introduced to the British Military Attaché, Major Fred Conti, who was ostensibly the link between the embassy and the Secret Intelligence Service, and then shown the small room where Royle would be accommodated during his stay in Vietnam.

Conti introduced him to the new ambassador, John Bushell, who had only arrived in post that year. A Scotsman with an Italian father, Conti turned out to be a fairly down to earth fellow, aged in his mid-thirties, who offered Royle a tour of the city, in his words 'before it's too late.' Conti had laughed at this. The British had refused to fight alongside their American cousins in Vietnam, despite pressure and even bullying on the part of President Johnson back in the mid-60s. Now it looked like the British had been right not to get involved, although they had provided secret advisors and liaisons with the Americans throughout the conflict.

It was never talked about, but SAS units had been active with American and Australian special forces deep in-country, and Britain had secretly provided naval and aerial logistical support to the Americans. Conti had done his homework on Royle and was impressed to realise that Royle had been one such advisor.

Royle had in 1960 decided to leave the jungles behind and concentrate on a career in education, now the Emergency in Malaya had been declared over. He pursued a degree at Cambridge, emerging with a First in South East Asian history. A Master's degree followed and he was assured of a lectureship after taking part in some unique Saigon-based research, intended to be for a doctoral thesis.

But Royle was still active as an SIS officer, and it was in this capacity that he landed in Saigon's Tan Son Nhut airport in September 1965 for an advisory role with the Americans. On landing, he knew enough about the situation to secure a good doctoral thesis, and with his MI6 hat on, he set about advising the Americans about jungle warfare, and how to win the hearts and minds of the locals, Malay-style.

He lectured them about the success of the New Villages programme in Malaya, then explained why he didn't think such a plan would work in Vietnam. In Malaya the vast majority of kampongs brought into the New Villages programme were ethnic Chinese villages. These were the villages the mostly ethnic Chinese communist terrorists targeted for supplies and intelligence. Other ethnic Malay kampongs were largely ignored by the communists, and so did not need to be inducted into the programme. This was mainly because of the racial differences of the Chinese and the Malays.

In Vietnam the situation was completely different. All the forces now fighting the Americans and the Southern armies consisted of the North Vietnamese Liberation Army and their southern sympathisers the Viet Cong. All were Vietnamese, as were all the villages. In order to make the American version of the New Villages programme work, the Americans would have to secure every single village in Vietnam to reach their goal of cutting off the copious supply lines to the ever increasing VC forces.

The Americans were intent on pursuing this course of action, however, and as Royle had predicted, failed miserably.

Royle also advised on the use of helicopters in jungle warfare, and this was a policy that was a major success. Helicopter drops were first used as a mainstream battle plan by the British in the jungles of Malaya. They flew troops in to drop zones, later picking them up when their mission was over. It proved to be a quick and simple solution to getting a large force on the ground where they were needed in a very short time. The Americans used this tactic throughout the war in Korea, and later in Vietnam, with great success, and even adapted it most valuably with the use of helicopter medivacs. These were responsible for saving the lives of thousands of US soldiers who may otherwise have died from battle wounds had not skilled medics flown in to stabilise their condition before choppering them out again to the nearest mobile army hospital.

*

Meg had come into his life the previous year, and they were soon married. Meg – her Malay name was Mugintha, but Royle called her Meg – travelled with Royle to South Vietnam as he toured the country lecturing US Army officers on the Malay Emergency and how the lessons learned there by the British could be adapted by the Americans in Vietnam. She stayed in secure US military compounds while he gave open air talks on the New Villages and helicopter warfare. He told them about guerrilla warfare and tactics and how best a regular army could defeat them. As a Malay, Meg was looked on in the compounds with some suspicion. On many occasions she was the only female there. Sometimes there were nurses from local MASH units who she could befriend, but for most of her time in South Vietnam it was a lonely existence.

*

Mugintha was the daughter of one of Tunku Abdul Rahman's closest aides and had first met Tom Royle at a reception in Kuala Lumpur in 1960, when she was 25 and Royle was coming up to 40. Meg's mother had died in an attack by communist terrorist insurgents early on in the Emergency and Meg had been her father's official consort since she had turned 21. As a result she had attended many government functions over the years.

Meg had been excited about her new role at first, but after a year of fixed smiles, polite conversation and over indulgence at banquets she had begun to tire of the official life and longed to go into the classroom to teach. She had a university degree in Chemistry and it was Meg's ambition to pass on her knowledge to children in Kuala Lumpur so that they could become scientists for the future benefit of the country. It was a lofty ideal which Meg never came to realise.

Instead she was attending another boring reception, the reason for which she had no idea, nor did she care. She had long ago stopped taking note of the reasons for a function. She just did her duty and went along with her father.

This event at the Istana Negara, the National Palace, seemed different, however. The majestic, white-domed palace was home to the current king of Malaya. As she entered the palace's luxurious East Wing on the arm of her father Meg noted the large room was filled with very high ranking British military officers and some very influential civilians. She later learned that the Tunku himself was expected to attend, as was the British High Commissioner. And the guest of honour, she noted, was a British officer who was clearly the centre of attention within the small group of people in attendance. Her father told her the man responsible for this small yet exclusive gathering was Lt-Col Thomas Royle, the famed Force 136 officer who in later years had played a major role in defeating the communist terrorists during the Emergency, which was now all but over. Royle wore his beloved, bemedalled 20th Indian Division dress uniform for this, his retirement party. Meg looked at Royle with a kind of wonder. All this for one man. So many important people. She started to look more closely at Royle. He seemed slightly bemused and embarrassed at his send-off. He had been in uniform, literally as well as figuratively, for 20 years, and now he was embarking on a new way of life.

Meg manoeuvred her way to speak to Royle. He stood straight and tall. His hair was thick and dark and his tanned, craggy face looked down at this attractive young woman as she stood before him, and he beamed a huge smile in her direction.

That was the moment both remembered as the instant when their stars crossed. They danced, she better than him, and Royle found himself seriously courting her. They married the following year and spent a short honeymoon in Penang and Singapore before Royle embarked on his university degree, specialising in South East Asian history and completing his dissertation on the Malayan Emergency.

Royle and his wife travelled to South Vietnam in his advisory role in 1965, passing his jungle fighting knowledge on to American and Australian so-called advisors.

QUY NHON, SOUTH VIETNAM, SEPTEMBER 1965

Royle was lecturing a company of US Rangers from a makeshift outdoor classroom close to a joint US-Australian base a few klicks from a dense canopied jungle. The base, on the coast of central Vietnam, had its own cinema, stores, bars, a swimming pool of sorts, and rows and rows of green army-issue tents where the troops would sleep, but that's all. The base was nicknamed The Ark by the troops; a double meaning because of its shape – an arc – and because it was a haven for the fighting men who had come to this country to save it from itself.

It was surrounded by electrified razor wire, a ditch filled with petroleum that would ignite at the flick of a switch, and if the enemy managed to get through all of that, a second razor wire perimeter fence that was booby-trapped with mines to explode if touched.

Inside the base was also a large parade ground and a small airstrip, a relic of the Japanese from the Second World War, capable of allowing fixed wing reconnaissance planes to take off and land, and close to that a large helicopter LZ, or landing zone, a fuel store and ammunition dump. Inside was also the FSB – fire support base – an artillery battery that was a lifeline for troops facing a strong enemy.

It was early morning and Royle was giving the Rangers coordinates for the jungle, where they would all take part in a practical exercise in silent recce and passage.

At 25 Celsius the sun was already hot on the men listening intently to what their English mentor was saying. It was destined to rise to a high of 28 degrees, and there was a good chance of rain. And when it rained it Vietnam it was like nothing rookie soldiers had ever witnessed back home. All of the men, including Royle, wore drab green fatigues, boots and a bush hat. Only Royle was devoid of any command insignia, yet his authority remained unquestioned. Here was a guy who had done it all, first against the Japanese and later against the commies, all within hardship posts lasting years in the jungles of Malaya.

Royle could only feel bemused by their attitude towards him, which he realised uncomfortably bordered on hero worship. They had listened intently at his theory classes on jungle warfare – which all the so-called grunts and officers alike realised was widely different to the training they had received at home before being deployed here. This was a man passing down priceless experience on how to survive in the jungle. Not just that, but how to walk through thick undergrowth soundlessly, how to navigate in the dark when no stars were visible, how to track a company of "gooks", the Americans' derogatory term for the Viet Cong, or as the Australians called them, "nogs". He taught them how to find food when times were desperate, how to lighten their heavy packs as much as possible during long range missions in-country, and showed them the best way to lay an ambush on a jungle trail. Now the theory lessons were over and it was time for the practical.

Royle dismissed the men, who rushed off to collect their already stuffed packs and their AR-15 Armalite rifles, the lightweight 5.56mm weapon of choice for the US Army, and later for Australian soldiers. Royle sauntered into the officers' mess where the commanding officer Colonel Joseph 'Homerun' Hollister was waiting.

Hollister had picked up his nickname in Korea after heroic hand-to-hand fighting which lasted two full days. Hollister was commander of a signals platoon with orders to capture, keep hold of and establish a signals intelligence array on a strategic hill in an area that would become the demilitarised zone between the two Koreas when peace finally came. It was a battle of total attrition, with heavy losses on all sides. Ammunition was running low for the Americans, and then the advancing Chinese started to lob grenades into the American defences. It was a bitter sweet moment, the signal that the Chinese too were running low on firepower and were resorting to explosives to remove the Signals unit. One high frequency mast had already been badly damaged, but two more remained, providing vital sigint. A message had already been sent for reinforcements, but it would be a long wait, Hollister realised, and time was not something they had a surfeit of. What the Chinese didn't know was that Hollister had been a major league baseball star back home in New Jersey. Hollister had the idea that if he could hit a baseball out of the park, he could do the same with a grenade. So while his remaining men put up a determined wall of fire with what ammo was left, Hollister picked up a dead soldier's rifle, checked it was empty of bullets, gripped the barrel and proceeded to knock grenades left and right, away from his own men and back into the Chinese lines, halting their advance. When reinforcements arrived, in this case a British company of Glosters, the surviving Chinese scattered and medics treated a bullet wound to Hollister's side, which he had hitherto failed to notice, such was the flow of adrenaline through his rapidly tiring body. His baseball hits had saved the day and he was forever more nick-named 'Homerun' Hollister. He also received a purple heart and the Congressional Medal of Honour.

'A very interesting briefing Colonel Royle,' said Hollister, sliding a coffee mug across the bar towards the British officer.

'Thank you colonel, but the next bit will be most telling,' smiled Royle. 'See who was listening.' Both men looked through the mess window as the Rangers marched out through the gates, heavy packs on their backs, towards the grid reference Royle had given them. It was only about two kilometres to the jungle's edge, but in this heat and with those packs on their backs it would be a difficult march that would get more difficult once they entered the bush. And when they were operating in the height of summer, the temperatures could get extremely uncomfortable indeed.

'You know, Tom. I had to smile when you told them that your preferred method of cutting a path through a jungle was not a machete or knife, but a pair of hand-held garden shears.' Hollister laughed a booming laugh. 'That's what my mom and dad use to keep our back yard flowers tidy back home.'

'Most people do, Joe,' smiled Royle. 'But think about it. The object is stealth and silence. If you go around slashing at jungle vines and branches with a machete, no matter how sharp, Uncle Ho himself would be able to hear the racket all the way in Hanoi. Secateurs are small. They easily fit in a pocket – ideal for an overloaded soldier. And most importantly they cut through the jungle quietly.'

'It's ok, colonel, I'm sold. It's an inspiration, that's what it is, Tom. You all ready to go?'

'Ready, Joe.'

Royle picked up his own pack and marched off to the waiting Sikorsky helicopter that would fly him to the jungle's edge, where he would give the Rangers their final lesson in jungle survival. He would leave the warfare bit up to them. And tomorrow, Royle thought as he walked toward the chopper, it would be the turn of the Australians. They had a recon unit that needed special attention and had already been given a dose of SAS training. A couple of weeks with them, and then fly home with Meg to start his new life. He couldn't remember the last time he'd had a quiet life.

*

Meg – strong, extremely wilful, intelligent and beautiful – had been heavily pregnant when the couple arrived.

She began to go into early labour while Tom was out of contact – deep in the jungle with an Australian reconnaissance company. US Army doctors at Quy Nhon took her into the base hospital, a surprisingly well equipped facility that was capable of providing medical treatment for most soldierly complaints ranging from foot-rot to serious battle wounds. The hospital was not geared up for childbirth, however. Even more disastrous for Meg was that she was haemorrhaging badly and both she and the doctor in charge knew that the only way to save the baby would be to perform an emergency caesarean, from which she was unlikely to survive. Mugintha told the duty doctor to get on with it, which they did, with heavy heart, knowing full well that she would be lucky to survive long enough to see her new-born child.

Meg died in childbirth at the US compound in early October 1965.

The child, a boy, survived. She lived long enough to see her son, which the nurses laid on her breast for a first and last time. They placed the child in a makeshift incubator when Meg died. Thomas named the child Adiputera, meaning first child, or prince.

Royle's mission in Vietnam had been coming to an end and Meg announced she had fallen pregnant in February that same year, after a period of R & R at the family home in Malaya. Still she agreed to travel back to Vietnam with Royle to complete his advisory role, then both looked forward to travelling to England for Royle to start his academic career in Kingston upon Hull, where a position as lecturer in South East Asian studies awaited him.

After Meg's death Royle took Adi to England and set up home in the village of Cottingham, close to the university. He was joined by his sister Amelia who took on the task of surrogate mother while Tom threw himself into his academic work, achieved his doctorate and commenced to lead a subdued and insular existence. Twenty years of blood, death and jungles lay behind him. His exploits were unknown to his students.

As the years passed he became known as an unassailable authority on his subject, specialising in the country that had become Malaysia. He was respected as a knowledgeable tutor, a hard but fair marker, and a man who cared about his students' progress. Yet he remained aloof from colleagues and students alike. His life had revolved around his work, his continuing research, his sister and his son.

For a small stipend Royle was happy to act as a volunteer talent-spotter for the Service, and he had arranged a number of behind the scenes recruitments with graduate students, but this was the full extent of his dealings with the secret world.

He published academic papers and books on his subject, which became required reading for students throughout the country. As his son grew he was enrolled at a local private preparatory boarding school. Now at age nine Adi was quick to make friends, and was bright and keen to study. He proved to be good at sport, particularly rugby, football and cricket. He wasn't bad on the athletics track either, nor in the classroom, proving himself as good with a pen as on the sports field. Tom could see Meg in him, with Adi's fine Eurasian looks.

*

Royle gave up waiting for Kravitz in the Caravelle bar and walked back to the British Embassy, through the sweating crowds of Saigon locals, the rickshaws, cyclos, scooters and cars, mostly of French and American manufacture. Military vehicles of the Army of the Republic of Vietnam – the ARVN – regularly thundered through the main streets in either direction, leaving choking clouds of blue exhaust fumes in their wake. Everyone knew to keep out of their way. They would stop for nothing, or no-one, as they rumbled to their next battle. Things were really not looking good for the South.

Royle walked through the embassy gates and into the building, saluted by two uniformed Royal Marines as he entered.

Royle found Fred Conti in his office. Late though it was, the near panic that had been almost physical over in the US Embassy was starting to infect Conti, the eyes and ears in Saigon for the British SIS.

Conti put down a lengthy print-out and smiled up at Royle. 'I'm guessing it's the start of an invasion by the North,' he said casually.

Royle looked at him steadily. 'Phuoc Long?'

'You heard?' asked Conti.

'Charles Kravitz vaguely mentioned it earlier,' said Royle. 'I long ago realised that when Charles was being vague about something it was usually something of utmost importance.'

'Well, it looks like this could be it. The North Vietnamese Liberation Army had been massing across the border and have attacked positions in Phuoc Long in force. Large numbers of troops, heavy artillery and main battle tanks. The South Vietnamese army is in disarray and in full retreat. It's a rout.'

'So when will we know if this is an invasion or another border skirmish?'

'Probably in the next few hours,' said Conti. 'But the commies are using an awful lot of firepower for a quick in-and-out cross-border raid.'

'This must account for Kravitz's no-show this evening.' Royle recounted his plans to meet Kravitz at the Hotel Caravelle.

'Well, we should have a few hours before we know for sure,' said Conti. 'What say we step out for a drink and a chat?'

*

They sat near the entrance in a noisy bar close to the British Embassy. Eric Clapton was singing his version of Bob Marley's "I Shot the Sheriff" through the tiny speaker of a tinny transistor radio at the back of the counter. A classic-style jukebox remained dark and silent in one corner, clearly broken and unmended. Conti had clipped his pager to his trousers belt in case matters started to go very bad, very quickly, although this was regarded as being quite unlikely.

'I was brought back to Saigon by Sir Robert Thompson. I had met him in Malaya during the Emergency and we worked closely together during that time,' Royle stopped speaking to sip his fourth martini of the night. Not a patch on the Caravelle ones, he thought, then realised that four martinis were enough for one night. He was already starting to feel their effect on his travel fatigued body.

He continued, 'Thompson had been a senior civil servant in Malaya during the Emergency. After 1960 the troubles were over in Malaya and we went our separate ways. I took the academic path, Thompson continued his rise to the top of the civil service tree. Next I heard from him must have been in '64. I had just gained my Master's degree and he contacted me. He smoothed the path for a lectureship and my doctorate, on the condition that I would join him in Saigon. Naturally, I was intrigued and agreed. Now, Thompson wasn't your stereotypical civil servant. He was a doer and a troubleshooter. When I arrived in Saigon later in '64 he told me that he had been tasked to form a mission to serve in Vietnam. Thompson's mission was to be composed mainly of former ranking British police officers who had served in Malaya. There were some special forces involved as well, often serving with the Australian and New Zealand forces, but also with US units in-country.'

'And if you were involved, spooks as well, it seems,' smiled Conti, sipping a very cold Red Stripe beer. Both men were dripping wet in the high humidity of the December evening.

'As far as I am aware, just the one spook – me,' laughed Royle. 'Although, there were a number of ex-Special Branch there too. And I was involved in Malaya militarily, in the war and during the Emergency – right up to my neck.

'Anyway, it was Thompson who got me involved as an advisor. It was Thompson's mission that oversaw the US hamlets programme – their version of the New Villages we pioneered in Malaya back in the '50s. As I said, I was in a purely advisory role and only stayed about a year.'

Royle deliberately failed to mention his reason for leaving Vietnam and the grief that still stung after all these years.

'Fascinating, Dr Royle, simply fascinating,' said Conti, sipping his beer again. 'So, how can I help you today?'

'Has London told you anything about me or my visit?'

'Just that you would be arriving and that I should show you every courtesy and provide you with whatever help I can.'

'Very well,' said Royle, pushing his unfinished drink away and calling a waiter over to order a cola. 'I have been sent here to find someone and bring him out.'

'An agent?' asked Conti, conspiratorially.

'Sort of. It's a man called Li Pengfei. An old … comrade of mine, you could say.'

'Never heard of him, Dr Royle …,'

'Please, call me Tom.'

'Of course, you must call me Fred. Hate it myself, but there it is.'

Royle's cola arrived, and the waiter left the bill in an empty glass in the centre of the table, along with the bill for the drinks.

'Li Pengfei,' mused Conti. 'I'll put the word out discretely. See if anyone knows his whereabouts. But what's he doing here?'

'That's anyone's guess, but I suspect he's doing what he does best – playing one side against the other.'

'Very well, Tom. As long as he hasn't changed his name, or dead, I'll try to find him for you. In the meantime ...' Conti raised a fistful of US dollars at the waiter, who bustled over to their table to take payment. The men rose to leave. 'I had better attend to our little crisis in the North.'

There was a knock on Royle's bedroom door. Conti entered with two cups of morning tea. The military attaché set the cups down on a bedside table and opened curtains at a window that looked out on to the ambassador's garden below. It was 5am on 14 December, and the low sun was rising, spreading a golden-pinky glow around the room.

'Good morning, Tom. Hope you slept well. Drink up, we've got a lot on today.'

Royle rubbed his eyes and sat up, picking up his cup and sipping its contents. He had a slight headache from the drinks he had consumed the previous night, and continued to sip his tea as Conti delivered the day's news.

'It looks like the much feared invasion has already started, and that 13 December 1974 could go down in history as the day the balance of power tipped towards the North in this war.'

'Phuoc Long?'

'Correct. Northern troops launched an invasion of Phuoc Long Province from Cambodia yesterday. A number of villages were overrun by the communists, but the main battle took place at Phuoc Long City – that's just 100km from Saigon. General Tran Van Tra is leading the campaign for the communists. Regular forces of the Vietnam People's Army have joined up with Viet Cong units. There are 30,000 of them against just 5-6,000 South Vietnamese troops. The good guys seem to be hopelessly outnumbered.

'The town of Tay Ninh has already been taken. That's significant. It's the home of the Cao Dai religion – a very powerful and influential body of people. But the South Vietnamese Army up there are a tough bunch. My information is that they have made a bloody stand against the Northern forces, which includes part of the North's crack 205th

Regiment. The Tay Ninh garrison are hardened warriors and have had a good record fighting back Northern regulars. Not this time, it seems.'

'What happened?'

'It appears there were supply problems. The South Vietnamese air force were kept at bay by the North's use of SA-7s. These are highly effective shoulder launched anti-aircraft missiles. They effectively prevented the garrison from being re-supplied, and also forced South Vietnamese fighter bombers to fly at too high an altitude, therefore rendering them virtually ineffective. Similar tactic to that used against the French at Dien Bien Phu in '54, but with more modern weaponry. Long story short; the garrison was overrun. There have been similar stories in Binh Tuy and Long Khanh, where Viet Cong fighters joined regular forces from the North. It seems these attacks were merely diversionary, however.'

Royle was out of bed and getting dressed at this point.

'Anything else?' asked Royle.

'Reports are still coming in, but we believe there are elements of the North's 301st Corps and the 7th Division. We also think there is a newly formed 3rd Division involved. The main attack seems to be supported by an artillery regiment and an anti-aircraft regiment, and importantly, a tank regiment. Probably Russian T-54s.'

'As you say sounds like a full-scale attack,' said Royle. 'Can the Southern forces turn it back?'

'One can only hope, Tom. Hope and pray.'

Conti was no defeatist, but he knew the forces of South Vietnam had been fatally weakened by being cut-off by Washington, both financially and militarily.

*

By 5.20am Royle was washed, shaved and dressed, and being driven down town by Conti in a plain-looking brown Cadillac that had seen better days.

They pulled up outside a wreck of a building in a Saigon suburb. The wall of the building had the unmistakable peppering of gunfire, the windows were shuttered, with the glass obviously broken, and the roof of the two-storey building was warped and broken, yet mostly intact.

'This was at one time a CIA safe house, later an interrogation centre,' said Conti as they stepped out of the car. 'No use for it these days, of course, until now.'

Inside the house the still rising sun spread rays of light through the slatted shutters on the windows. The wooden floor creaked as they walked around.

'Is this a good time to ask you what's going on?' asked Royle, reaching a state of tension and alertness he hadn't felt since Malaya. The feeling was bordering on uncertainty and fear, and decisive readiness for action. Anthropologists would call it the caveman syndrome – the urge to flee when danger called. It was an urge Royle had felt many times in his life, and he knew that fear would not be the dominant emotion. He always knew that this was an emotion that should not be ignored.

'Let's just say you're here to meet a friend of yours who knows a friend of yours.'

'Cryptic,' snorted Royle.

'Indeed,' said Conti, as they both walked in semi-darkness towards a light flowing out from beneath a door at the back of the house.

Conti knocked softly on the wooden door – a single rap, followed by three more in quick succession. From the other side of the door came the sound of a chair scraping on the wooden floor, then the door opened.

It was Kravitz, dressed in the uniform of a Captain in the US Marine Corps. His uniform was dishevelled, dirty, and on closer inspection, bloody.

'My God, Charles, what's happened to you?' was all Royle could utter. Then he looked past his old CIA friend and saw a man tied to a chair. His face was bleeding and his head hung forward. The prisoner, a Vietnamese, was breathing heavily.

'Excuse the appearance, Tommy.' Kravitz turned his attention to Conti and nodded. 'Just got back from Phuoc Long. Damn, I'm getting too old for this.'

'Is it as bad as our intel suggests?' asked Conti.

'Maybe worse. Too soon to say just yet. But that's not why we're here.' Kravitz dragged his chair back and sat down beside the Vietnamese. Kravitz indicated two more chairs – wooden, European kitchen style chairs of French design – and Conti and Royle sat down across the kitchen table.

The Vietnamese was still breathing heavily, obviously in pain, when Kravitz gesticulated exaggeratedly towards the man in mock polite introduction.

'Gentlemen,' said Kravitz. 'I am pleased to introduce Mr Nguyen Le Quoc.' Kravitz smiled at Royle. 'No relation to our friend of forty years ago, Tommy.' Kravitz grabbed the Vietnamese by the hair and lifted his head up for his visitors to see. The man's head was battered and bruised. His eyes were almost closed and what could be seen of his pupils seemed to be filled with blood. Blood was trickling from his ears and flooding from his mouth. Broken teeth were littering the wooden kitchen floor in a pool of sticky blood. It looked like one of his cheek bones had been fractured.

Royle looked at Conti, who just shrugged. 'This is the way of things over here, Tom.' Royle knew that these were the actions of desperate men.

Kravitz continued, 'Mr Nguyen here is quite an important man in these here parts, Tommy. I think you may want to speak to him.'

'Really, Charles. About what?' said Royle.

'I would guess he knows where to find your friend,' said Conti. 'Li Pengfei, right?'

'Right,' answered Royle in a low voice. Conti knew more than he was telling.

'London sent the information through last night, coded of course. I got in touch with Kravitz, with some difficulty I might add. Should have known he'd be up north in the thick of things,' said Conti.

'Hell, it's the only way to find anything out these days. The South Vietnamese just lie about things to twist the intel. They still hope they'll get more dollars from Uncle Sam if they put a good spin on things. As for our guys, they lie too. They're desperate that Langley doesn't find out too much about what goes on over here. And that means covering up and sending false intel. CIA has been doing it since the first day it went operational. But I needed to know exactly what was happening on the ground up there, so I caught a flight up to Phuoc Long with some of the meanest looking South Vietnamese sons of bitches you've ever seen. They are tough soldiers who could show our own Green Berets a thing or two.

'Anyways, back to our Mr Nguyen. He says he knows where your guy is and he's about to give you the skinny,' Kravitz turned to the exhausted Vietnamese, 'Ain't that right, Mr Nguyen?' The Vietnamese failed to answer through his bloodied mouth, so Kravitz slapped him across the head lightly. Light as the blow was, in the man's weakened state his head flew forwards again, causing Kravitz to grab his hair and pull it back again.

Kravitz smiled at Nguyen. 'Now then, Mr Nguyen, I want you tell my friend here what you told me earlier.'

The Vietnamese grunted and shook his head. Kravitz tutted, then asked again. Once more the Vietnamese shook his head. 'Very sad, Mr Nguyen. I asked politely but you refuse.' Kravitz smiled at the man again, then looked at Royle. 'Mr Nguyen here is a member of one of the VC cadres right here in Saigon. Your pal, Mr Li Pengfei, leads that cadre.' Kravitz turned his attention to the Vietnamese again. 'Now, Mr Nguyen please tell my friend where he can find Li Pengfei. It's quite important, so I would be obliged if you could help us please.'

Again, the Vietnamese shook his head.

'Shame,' said Kravitz. 'Ok Tommy, before he got so stubborn, I persuaded Mr Nguyen to reveal where Li Pengfei would be, and he was quite happy to tell me all. I can't think what has gotten into him.

'All right, Tommy. Li Pengfei will be at Su's bar in Cholon at mid-day today. You're welcome,' smiled Kravitz, pulling out a hunting knife from his combat belt. The two British men left and did not witness the execution.

*

Cholon was a mainly Cantonese-speaking town about 30 miles west of Saigon, bustling with outdoor food sellers and other merchants. The noise of people going about their daily business on small motorcycles and motor scooters was deafening as Royle was driven by Conti into the hubbub of the Chinese quarter. The streets were dusty and dirty, with empty, abandoned buildings lining the main road. Burnt-out vehicles lay motionless in the town that had once been a major trading centre. But despite the area's downturn since the departure of US forces, life seemed to be going on as normal, as if there was no invasion force 100km away.

Su's Bar was down a gloomy side street. The street was made dark by the narrowness of the alleyway it was in and by overhanging roofs, even though it was now mid-day.

Conti had said nothing about Kravitz's interrogation of the VC cadre leader, even after they had earlier stopped at a small Saigon café for breakfast. It had been a brutal meeting, yet both men felt famished and finished a huge American breakfast and two large cups of coffee, again taken black and strong by Royle. After that they had returned to the embassy where Royle accompanied Conti to the comms room. The teletype machines were deafening as they entered and Conti immediately went over to the embassy's communications officer to see what the latest news on the cross-border attack was.

'Captain Roger Saxby, this is Dr Thomas Royle, our distinguished guest from London. He still holds the rank of lieutenant-colonel and has the highest security clearance,' said Conti with a smile, as he introduced the two men. Royle and Saxby shook hands, and Saxby got back to monitoring events further north. Saxby was the embassy's senior intelligence analyst. Royle looked at the young army captain and realised he had been working all night to keep tabs on the invasion force. Saxby looked exhausted.

Conti placed his hand on Saxby's shoulder in a comradely manner, telling him without saying so that he knew he had been working on the intelligence from the north without rest, and that it was appreciated. Both knew it was also going to be a long day of intelligence gathering before they would have a good idea just how serious the invasion was going to be. If there was a chance the invaders could reach Saigon any time soon the embassy's contingency plan for evacuation would have to be implemented.

'So, what have we got, Roger?' asked Major Conti.

'Well, sir, the northern forces are still making a slow advance through the villages of Phuoc Long, but southern forces are digging their heels in. There was some fierce fighting overnight, but so far it's really a stalemate, with the north slightly out-manoeuvring southern forces.'

Conti told Saxby the information Kravitz had brought back from the front line, then said, 'All right, thanks Roger, and keep up the good work. Why not get one of your junior officers to take over for a while so you can snatch a bit of shut-eye? I reckon you'll be needed bright-eyed and bushy-tailed before the day is over.'

'No thanks, major. I think I'll just stay here for a while. If things start to quieten down I'll have a kip, but in the meantime I need to remain so I can deliver a good sit-rep to the Yanks for the Follies.'

'Very well, I'll have some more coffee brought in,' Conti promised as he and Royle left the comms room.

'Follies?' asked Royle.

'Yes, alas not the Follies of old. These were the regular US war updates delivered to the Press Corps at 5pm every evening. When the war was at its height they were nick-named the 'Five o'clock Follies' by hacks covering the war, as bad news followed bad news in reports back home. The officers who led them always had some good news spin to deliver to the Press, who all knew better after having seen first-hand how bad things were getting in-country. Hence, the Follies. US involvement is now virtually non-existent, of course, and there is only a handful of Press Corps still in Saigon. The rest were pulled out to cover other world events last year, as soon as the peace agreement was signed and the US withdrew its forces. However, the Five o'clock Follies remain, though only in name. These are now regular briefing meetings between the US, the South Vietnamese, and their allies, whether they be official or unofficial. We still contribute to these intelligence briefings and Saxby will be toddling along later with our version of events up in Phuoc Long. Sadly the Press are no longer invited,' Conti laughed as he and Royle headed back to their battered old Caddy for the 30-mile drive to Cholon.

*

Su's Bar was dark and deserted, apart from a barman, Su, presumably. Chairs were still stacked atop tables from the night before. Su looked up from reading his newspaper as the men approached.

'Yes, gentlemen?' the bar owner asked in heavily Cantonese-accented English.

'Two beers,' ordered Conti as they sat down on bar stools. Su drew two cold beers into clear glass tumblers and placed them down on paper coasters in front of the two men. Su then moved away to the end of the bar and continued reading his newspaper.

Neither heard the man dressed in ordinary Vietnamese work clothes walk silently up behind them. Royle was speaking to Conti when he saw Conti stiffen and slowly place both hands on the bar.

Then a voice said softly in Royle's ear, 'Salah jalan, Thomas?' Have you taken a wrong road?

Royle smiled on hearing the Malay language and turned to come face to face with Li Pengfei. Li Pengfei was holding a revolver into Conti's back, and prodded him painfully as he asked Royle, 'Who is your friend, Thomas?'

'This is Major Fred Conti, military attaché at the British Embassy. Fred, this is the man we came to meet here, Li Pengfei.'

Conti grimaced as the barrel of the gun continued to press into his kidneys. 'Pleased to meet you, I'm sure,' he grimaced.

After a few silent seconds Li Pengfei emitted a loud guffaw and sat down beside Conti, with the gun resting on the bar, still pointing at him.

'Well, you have now met me. What now?' asked Li Pengfei, with a friendly smile on his face. It was a smile Royle knew of old, and it was the most dangerous smile he had ever encountered. Often it had proved to be a smile of death when he served with Li Pengfei in the jungles of Malaya during the Second World War.

'Shall we sit?' Li Pengfei indicated one of the tables over in a far corner. They took the chairs down from the table tops and seated themselves. Without being asked Su brought Li Pengfei tea. Both British men still had their beers.

Then Li Pengfei barked at Su in Cantonese, 'Hsien yu pei chi ko hsiao tieh tzu.' Prepare some assorted appetizers. 'Mo-liao hai yao ho chia-fei.' At the end we shall want to drink coffee.

Su disappeared into a back room and began shouting in quick-fire Cantonese, then returned to his station behind the bar. He was watching the group now, suspicious that this member of the Viet Cong, whom he sympathised with greatly, was speaking with two foreign devils who should by rights be immediately killed.

But Su also knew that Li Pengfei was the wisest of men and had many ways of dealing with the westerners, who were now finally about to be tipped into the Mekong and the East Sea after long years of the bitterest fighting. So Su just kept his post and watched, even when customers came in. He served them in the surly manner that was seemingly expected of him, then continued his watch on this most extraordinary of events.

First food arrived, steaming straight from the wok in five separate bowls. The appetizers Li Pengfei had ordered. The woman serving them was obviously also the cook, judging by her food-stained apron and her sweat-stained blouse. A younger girl brought bowls and chopsticks for the three men.

Li Pengfei picked up his chopsticks and indicated to his companions that they should start to eat. Li Pengfei started to eat first out of politeness, to show that the food was not drugged or poisoned.

Conti and Royle followed suit. Despite the grubbiness of the bar, and presumably the kitchen, the food was excellent.

After swallowing a few mouthfuls of food Royle turned to Li Pengfei. 'Until a few days ago, I thought you were dead.'

Li Pengfei smiled and nodded. 'As far as Britain is concerned, I am, Thomas.'

'I came here to find you and bring you in,' said Royle.

Li Pengfei continued eating, nodding as Royle spoke. 'I was told to invoke your old codename – Cuckoo. Nothing's changed, has it?'

Li Pengfei put his chopsticks in his bowl and wiped his mouth on a napkin. 'Nothing has changed, Thomas. I am still the man I always was.'

'You look much better than the last time I saw you, old friend.'

'I am fully recovered and fighting fit again, Thomas.'

'What the devil are you doing here?' Royle banged his fist on the table, unable to contain his frustration any longer. Su looked up from his newspaper and reached under the bar for something Royle was sure would turn out to be a Kalashnikov.

Li Pengfei raised his hand at Su and shook his head. Su returned to his pseudo relaxed position at the corner of the bar, but this time he didn't even pretend to look at his newspaper.

Then Li Pengfei looked at Conti. 'This man does not have clearance,' he said in a low voice. 'He must leave us to talk alone.'

'Tom, this man is a terrorist. I'm not leaving you alone in this mantrap,' whispered Conti.

'I won't be alone, Fred. We are old comrades, Li Pengfei and I.'

'Christ, I thought you had been sent to settle an old score. To kill him and get him out of everyone's hair,' Conti was speaking too loudly again and Su the bar owner was at full alert again, although he did not reach for whatever weapon he had hidden behind the bar this time.

'It's not like that, Fred.'

'Major Conti, you are free to leave. I grant you safe passage, out of this bar and out of Cholon. But you must leave Thomas here so we can speak together.'

Royle nodded at Conti and said, 'This is why I came Fred. You have to go. I'll see you later, I'm sure of it.'

Li Pengfei barked an order to Su – 'Hu-sung,' pointing at Conti – Escort and protect him.

Su nodded and beckoned towards the door. Two men came into the bar and stood on either side of Conti. Li Pengfei looked at the Scotsman. 'Take your car and drive back to Saigon. Your business here is over. These two men will escort you out of Cholon with my guarantee of safe passage. If you come back, however, I cannot be responsible for the consequences.'

'Is that a threat?' said an exasperated Major Conti.

'No, major. It is a statement of fact.'

Royle nodded at Conti and said, 'Thanks Fred. We may yet meet again, but I have a job to do here.' Conti grunted with derision, rose from the table and was led out.

Royle turned to Li Pengfei. 'He will be all right, won't he?'

'You have my word,' said Li Pengfei.

'Very well. Let's get down to business.'

'First I have an assignment to complete. Come,' said Li Pengfei, rising and indicating for Royle to follow.

'What assignment?'

'You will see,' said Li Pengfei, that dangerous smile back on his prematurely wrinkled face.

They went over to Su behind the bar, and the bar keeper reached under the bar and handed a brown paper package to Li Pengfei. The package was approximately six inches square and tied with parcel string. Su then reached below for a small backpack, and Li Pengfei carefully placed the package inside then indicated for Royle to follow him out.

They trudged through fields and undergrowth outside the town, until they came to a dusty straight road. It was in good condition and fully metalled, and only covered in dust from the fields on either side. It was wide enough for two-way traffic.

Li Pengfei indicated for Royle to go under cover in a ditch beside the road. Then the Malay walked 50 metres up the road towards a rock. He hefted the rock up and into the ditch, then placed the package in the hole the rock had been resting in. With a small gardening trowel Li Pengfei then covered the package up with soil and dust from the ditch. He then led a wire from the package back down the ditch towards where Royle was still crouching.

'Who are we going to blow up?' asked Royle, trying to keep his voice calm.

'That will be apparent very soon,' answered Li Pengfei as he connected the wire to the terminals on a small control box containing a simple nine-volt battery and an activation switch. It was clearly home-made, yet ingenious.

Li Pengfei looked at his American-issue GI wristwatch. It showed 15:04 hours. Li Pengfei scanned the road until a faint column of dust could be seen on the horizon.

'The Americans built this road,' said Li Pengfei. It's a very good road for military vehicles, but it is also a quite good trap.'

'Who are we trapping?' asked Royle.

'It is a supply column with military escort, driving up to Phuoc Long, where as you know there is a major skirmish taking place. The South Vietnamese forces are running low on supplies and ammunition. They can't be dropped by air because of heavy anti-aircraft activity. We are just going to focus their minds a little closer to home in the next ten minutes or so.'

It took the slow moving convoy 16 minutes to reach the point where Li Pengfei's booby trap bomb had been buried. The Malay's thumb hovered over the firing switch as the vehicles rumbled up and passed the ambush point.

First came two American-made armoured cars, followed by an armoured personnel carrier. Then came two heavy lorries, two more armoured cars, then half a dozen more heavy lorries.

As the first lorry came level with the booby trap device, Li Pengfei flipped the switch and there was a huge flash followed by a deafening explosion and then a fierce blast. The lorry was torn apart, but a millisecond later it disintegrated in a huge series of explosions.

'As expected,' shouted Li Pengfei in Royle's ear. 'They sent the ammunition truck first. Let's go.'

Royle and Li Pengfei ran at a crouch along the ditch, away from the mayhem they had left behind. They heard the sound of gunfire and rocket launchers then, followed by more explosions and heavy return fire.

Still running along the ditch Li Pengfei shouted to Royle, 'I neglected to mention, I had a Viet Cong unit lying in wait. The booby trap was merely the signal to attack. Of course the road is now blocked and will be for many hours. That supply column will not make it to Phuoc Long.'

They ran along the ditch for another half mile, then cut across a field, lush with maize, until they reached a village. They walked into the village and entered one of the huts. Li Pengfei made green tea for them both, then sat cross-legged on the raffia matting floor.

'Is that how you killed Sam Harper, Peng?' said Royle, glaring straight into Li Pengfei's face.

'He was the enemy, working against the British and about to jeopardise my operations in Malaya. He had to die.'

'It's time to talk,' said Royle.

*

'I know about Amelia,' said Royle. It was dark now. And quiet. Only women, their children, and the head man were left in the village. Li Pengfei had told Royle that all the men had left with the Viet Cong. They wouldn't be able to stay long and would have to move on at dawn.

'I wanted to tell you, Thomas, but Amelia said I shouldn't.'

'When did it start, Peng?' asked Royle.

'It began long ago, Thomas. Just after we kidnapped her that time. I would never hurt her, Thomas. I loved her from afar after she moved back and took over at the plantation. Even when she married that traitor, I had her watched and protected.

'Then when that Chinese Communist Party commissar came to visit and suggested kidnapping someone at random, I immediately thought of Amelia. I am ashamed to say it was a way to get close to her.

'Even then I believed she could never be mine. When we took her, I swear we took good care of her.

'After you had seen her and had returned Colonel Chin ordered Amelia to be executed and her head taken to Kuala Lumpur to be displayed somewhere public. I knew the plan was a poor one from the start, but I just wanted to be close to Amelia. It was an unforgivable lapse in self-discipline.

'I killed Chin personally and we buried him in the depths of the jungle. We sent a message back to his bosses in Beijing to say that he had succumbed to a rare form of malaria and had died a brave man's death.

'But Chin had told me about Harper. He was working for the communists and taking orders from Beijing. He passed intelligence on to our fighters about targets, both hard and soft.

'Harper had to be disposed of. Amelia reluctantly went along with our deception, and when the information she gave him resulted in attacks on plantations and mines in the region she finally realised the extent of Harper's betrayal.

'We became lovers, Thomas. In secret. As I escorted her out of the forest following her kidnapping. It would not be seemly for a Malay of Chinese extraction who is also a communist fighter to be seen as the lover of a wealthy English woman who owned a rubber plantation. We started an affair, and her guilty love became real love for me, and a slowly burning hatred for her husband. I produced enough evidence to prove that Harper was a traitor. He had been drinking heavily and treating her badly by this time; his own guilt, no doubt.

'She eventually agreed to let me know when Harper was away from the plantation and she made it possible for our people to rig a booby trap device to destroy Harper's car – much like the one we just planted against the Southern convoy, although a lot less powerful. It was enough to blow Harper's car to pieces, and to instantly take out a traitor. My people were told that Harper was a member of the Special Branch who had been responsible for the death of 100 of our freedom fighters. A lie of course, but one they believed completely.

'Amelia and I continued our affair in the strictest secrecy – after all I was Public Enemy Number One at the time in Malaya. But it could not last. Guilt eventually led Amelia to sell the plantation to one of the big corporations and move to England.

'Ironic, Thomas, isn't it. The British had pulled out all the stops to kill me, yet I was working for them all the time.'

DECEMBER 21 1974, HULL, ENGLAND

Detective Constable Redpath knocked on the door of Amelia Harper's room at the Paragon Hotel, the Hull city centre hotel that adjoined the city's railway station. It was time for breakfast and Redpath was routinely to accompany the woman down for the first meal of the day for the umpteenth time since her brother Thomas Royle had been called away with some Whitehall top brass. It was an assignment Redpath had come to enjoy. It gave him a pleasant room, a very nice dinner each night and a bar bill that would be paid for by the Humberside Constabulary, or perhaps even the Home Office, he didn't care which. Redpath's initial disdain for this nurse-maid assignment had become a relaxed enjoyment, and he was determined to get the best out of it. Who knows what horrors his next job could bring up?

Redpath knocked again. Still there was no reply. He called out Amelia's name – 'Mrs Harper, time for breakfast. Mrs Harper?' Silence.

The policeman returned to his room further down the hall, phoned reception and ordered a porter to come up immediately with a spare key to Amelia Harper's room, then strode back to wait outside the woman's door. Minutes later the porter arrived with the appropriate key. He put the key in the lock and turned it. As the lock clicked open Redpath gently pushed the porter out of the way and turned the handle. The door opened. The room was tidy, the wardrobe was filled with Amelia's clothes, but there was no Amelia.

'Perhaps she went to breakfast without you, sir,' said the porter.

Damn, thought Redpath. Never thought of that. Redpath pushed past the porter and ran down the stairs to the breakfast room. Still no Amelia Harper. He checked with the head waiter and at reception. Mrs Harper had not been down to breakfast.

Fantastic, thought Redpath. My first, and now probably only cushy assignment was over and this flouncy old bird has outwitted me.

*

The first thing Redpath did was to telephone his Inspector to tell him the situation as he knew it. Redpath held the earpiece a few inches from his ear as his superior unleashed a torrent of verbal abuse at him. Then the line went silent for a while and the Detective Chief Superintendent came on the line. This was Redpath's boss of bosses. Even the Chief Constable listened to the advice he gave. The DCS spoke to Redpath in a low, distasteful tone, as if Redpath was something he had trodden in on the street. It was unexpected bad luck that Redpath had to grovel to the Detective Chief Super as well as to the Detective Inspector. Clearly they had been in a meeting together when Redpath phoned. Typical poor timing for Redpath, he thought.

'Go back to headquarters in Hull and await instructions', Redpath was ordered. *Oh well*, he thought, *at least I may get to do some real police work for a change. Cushy number as this was, being a nursemaid to some middle-aged toff was not my idea of CID work. Shame though.*

*

Amelia Harper was consumed with guilt.

Her past was catching up with her, and she was determined to tell her brother the truth.

It was a truth that had re-emerged since the fire at the house and since she was given a police minder in this city centre hotel. So long forgotten, and now it seemed like only yesterday.

And that night Amelia had thought of – dreamed of – Li Pengfei, her secret lover all those many years ago.

It was a passionate and lucid dream. She was in Li Pengfei's eager embrace, making love in a guest house in some anonymous kampong just inside the jungle. He was gentle with her, and at the same time urgent in the sweltering heat of the steaming Malay jungle.

Psychiatrists would later describe it as Stockholm syndrome, where the victim of a kidnapping would join forces with the kidnappers and even fall in love with the leader of the gang.

But Amelia was convinced this was no Stockholm syndrome. She had seen Li Pengfei with her brother a few times, and had always admired his bearing, his happy demeanour, his well-built body and his ready laughter. She also admired Li Pengfei's politics, and his determination and belief that he would eventually achieve an historic victory. She knew Li Pengfei was a communist. She also knew he was a friend of her brother's. Both did not make sense, but she didn't care. When Li Pengfei came with his men to take her to their jungle hideout, she didn't know what to expect. She at first thought it could mean death, but Li Pengfei immediately began to put her mind at rest. Despite the danger, she felt safe with Li Pengfei around.

Amelia's marriage was also in trouble. Sam had begun drinking heavily during the daytime. He would go out and treat his plantation workers with scorn and with cruelty. He said he was under pressure from the big rubber companies to produce more rubber from the plantation he was by now co-owner of, through his marriage to Amelia. He would beat workers who failed to make their quota, which he set artificially high. Workers on the plantation were treated like slaves, and they endured it because there was nowhere else for many of them to find work.

At first Amelia put Sam's behaviour down to his imprisonment by the Japanese during the war, and the cruel treatment that had been meted out to him. But when she witnessed his drunken attacks on plantation workers who had been working until they dropped in fear of their master, she began to re-appraise Sam as a person and as her husband. They became distant.

It was on her return from the jungle encampment, after her brother had been brought into the camp and then later left, that Li Pengfei accompanied her back home. Before leaving the camp she had witnessed Li Pengfei having a furious argument with Colonel Chin, the Chinese Red Guard officer sent from Beijing as an advisor to the Malay National Liberation Army and billeted with Li Pengfei's men. Both went into the trees, she presumed to settle a point. The argument could be heard becoming fainter as both men walked further into the forest, and then there was a long period of silence. Peng had returned alone, soil and bracken sticking to his trousers. Then they set off back to the plantation.

It was at a small kampong just as they would have emerged from the jungle when both Amelia and Li Pengfei first made love. It was a sudden, urgent joining for them both, and it took both of them by surprise as they revealed their nakedness to each other in that small wooden guest house. It was a night of complete joy and sexual commitment. As their muffled sounds of love making slowly melted into the humid night air, the heights of ecstasy both had experienced would remain a powerful memory for the rest of their lives.

At that first love-making Amelia confessed that she loved Li Pengfei, and Pengfei returned the compliment.

Amelia knew after that first night with Li Pengfei that she loved the terrorist leader. It would prove to be a difficult relationship. Li Pengfei was a wanted man. He had become Public Enemy Number One and was pursued by the majority of the British Army in Malaya. Including her brother. Tom Royle had been tasked with catching the communist leader, despite his friendship with the man he had been in league with during the big war. After every liaison together, Li Pengfei would have to vanish back into the jungle. The leaving tore both lovers apart, but there was no alternative.

They would meet in secret very occasionally, whenever it was safe for Li Pengfei to leave his jungle hideout. She knew he had posted a secret guard on her, to ensure no harm would come to Amelia Harper. These were dangerous times, and British women had been killed as well as British men during the communist insurgency. But Li Pengfei had become Amelia's guardian angel as well as her lover.

He left messages for her to meet in cities throughout the Malay Peninsula. Amelia had no reason to know that these meetings would take place after Li Pengfei had held secret meetings with her brother, who was one of the leading fighters against the communist rebellion. Either that, or when Li Pengfei had delivered a message in a mutually agreed location for her brother – a dead letter box.

Li Pengfei had always arrived in some sort of disguise at a small room or hotel they had rented for the day, or night. He could be dressed as a wealthy businessman, or a common coolie, but it would always be the dashing jungle fighter, Li Pengfei, who emerged as Amelia's passionate lover. They were both devoted to each other. They knew each would die for the other, and their love would last until death.

*

Amelia Harper had left the Hull city centre hotel carrying a light bag shortly after supper the previous night. She caught the last train to London King's Cross, caught a taxi to Heathrow Airport and bought a ticket for the first available flight out. Its destination was Paris Charles De Gaulle. From there she managed to board a red-eye flight out to Bangkok. So far luck was with Amelia Harper. She had managed to evade the police and was now out of almost everyone's jurisdiction. She had paid for both air tickets in cash, after cashing cheques from her private account earlier that morning, while Detective Constable Redpath had been making his daily report. She had the freedom to roam wherever she wished in Hull, and only returned to the hotel for meals and bed. She knew she would have to obtain air tickets on standby rather than book them covertly via a travel agent, but the cash would have to be obtained from her bank once it opened. She also withdrew a tidy sum of cash which she would need to survive in the Far East. Unfortunately she would have to use an unofficial bureau de change in Bangkok when she landed, no doubt losing out with an exorbitant exchange rate. But that could not be helped. To obtain Thai baht from a bank or travel agent would have meant identifying herself and having her passport details recorded. This was much better in order to stay under the authorities' radar. For the flight tickets she used false names. She knew there would be no security check linking tickets and passports. With enough money to hand one could simply disappear using the world's airlines.

MONDAY 23 DECEMBER 1974, DON LUAN, SOUTH VIETNAM

Royle and Li Pengfei could hear the artillery booming in the distance and it seemed to be getting nearer.

The temptation had been to head for nearby Song Be airfield and take a flight on one of the C-130 transports back to Saigon, after it had disgorged its cargo of South Vietnamese troops and equipment. But both could tell the fighting was heading in that direction and Song Be would be a prime target. Li Pengfei seemed to have inside information too that this was so, although he remained silent about any foreknowledge of the battle plan.

Word came through that day that Song Be had indeed been captured by the North Vietnamese. Each day was turning into a disaster for the South Vietnamese forces. The Duc Phong, Bo Duc and Buard districts had been overrun by the communist Vietnam People's Army nine days earlier. So far they knew they were safe in Don Luan, at least for now. The area was protected by the 341st Regional Force Battalion. The 341st had repeatedly thrown back Northern assaults. But Song Be had been protected by the 340th Regional Force Battalion, together with three reconnaissance companies and a lot of extra ordnance. Li Pengfei, here in Don Luan keeping his head down in a South Vietnamese stronghold on an ever-moving front line in the new Northern assault, and Tom Royle knew that it was only a matter of time before Don Luan too would be taken. Royle felt a pang of regret about Song Be. Kravitz had been billeted there immediately after the episode with the VC cadre member who revealed the whereabouts of Li Pengfei. Kravitz would surely be put to death if still there when the communists took that strategic area. The airfield had been so important that South Vietnamese parachutists had launched an airborne assault to retake it, capturing a number of Chinese advisors in the process. But they were forced to retreat from the area after North Vietnamese heavy artillery began pounding their positions. This was another big disaster for the Southern forces. The South

Vietnamese army units still fighting in the area could now not be evacuated or regrouped.

'Why did you bring me here?' asked Royle. Li Pengfei and he were atop a hill beneath a shady tree trying to determine the way events would unfold over the next few hours. The heat was oppressive and both were bathed in perspiration.

'I wanted to take you to Bo Duc to meet someone, but that is now impossible.' Bo Duc had been taken by the North Vietnamese on 14th December as part of their big push to take the strategically important province of Phuoc Long.

'Who?' demanded Royle.

'Someone who would be able to confirm a somewhat fantastic story, Thomas. A story I was involved in back in 1969. I can't talk about it myself until we find someone to confirm it. You would simply not believe it, my friend.'

Gun and artillery fire could be heard from the hilltop. The 341st had sent out units to keep the communists at bay, but with Song Be taken there was now little chance of reinforcements or of ordnance replenishment.

'My job was to make contact with you and bring you home.' Royle looked at Li Pengfei and shook his head. 'You always were a bad influence on me, Pengfei.'

Li Pengfei smiled. 'I have also been your guardian angel on a number of occasions, Thomas.'

'And I yours, Pengfei.' Both smiled and looked into the distance. Then Royle looked Li Pengfei in the eye. 'Seriously, it is time to return. Right now. This was always going to end badly for the good guys – I'm referring to the South Vietnamese.' Li Pengfei laughed. He had always considered the North Vietnamese the good guys.

'We need to get hold of a Jeep and head back to Saigon. The Embassy will arrange transport out and we'll be in London before the week is out. And then you can tell me your fantastic story. I take nothing for granted where you're concerned, Pengfei. Believable or not, I will want to know.'

Royle placed a comradely arm around Li Pengfei as they slowly descended the hill. 'When we get to London I'll arrange for Amelia to come down to see you. I think you may both have a lot of catching up to do.'

Just then a shout came from the crest of the hill, ordering the two men to halt. 'Ngung!' ordered a Vietnamese dressed in black. He held them in the sights of his Kalashnikov assault rifle.

Royle and Li Pengfei held their hands up to show they were unarmed and willing to comply with the order the soldier – a Viet Cong irregular – had barked at them.

Turning to Li Pengfei, Royle said in a whisper, 'You need to get away from me right away. If I manage to escape I will meet you at Su's Bar in two days.'

Li Pengfei looked at his old colleague and just nodded. The Viet Cong guerrilla began to walk down the hill towards them, the AK47 rifle continuing to point in their direction.

'Dung ban,' said Li Pengfei in Vietnamese, do not shoot. 'Toi dien tu Don Luan,' I am from Don Luan. 'Toi dang co gang dat duoc an toan.' I am trying to reach safety.

The Viet Cong soldier sneered, then looked at Royle. 'Va nguoi ban My cua ban?' And your American friend? The guerrilla shifted position, moving closer so the gun now pointed straight at Royle's chest.

'Ong la tieng Anh.' He is English, explained Li Pengfei in Vietnamese, moving closer to the freedom fighter.

The guerrilla looked sharply at Li Pengfei, then looked to his rear. He appeared to be expecting reinforcements.

Just then Li Pengfei struck. He sprang forward, driving into the VC fighter, using his right arm to force the rifle off target, and the palm of his left hand to drive up into the soldier's chin, forcing his head back and causing the man in black to fall to the ground. At the same time the fighter's finger spasmed on the trigger, sending a hail of white hot rounds into the clear ground.

'Go!' shouted Royle, and Li Pengfei sprinted down the hill, on to a rubble-strewn road and out of sight. The guerrilla got up from the ground, dazed, and picked his gun up from beside him on the grassy hillside. He cocked the gun as if ready to shoot Royle. At the same time Royle heard a vehicle in the distance rev into life and speed off. Royle breathed with relief realising it was probably Li Pengfei on his way to

Saigon. Now Royle had to think fast. He hadn't had time to get away with Li Pengfei.

The furious guerrilla fighter aimed the gun at Royle's chest.

'Wait!' called Royle. He understood little Vietnamese, but repeated the call in Mandarin, keeping his hands high and in sight.

'I am British, a civilian. Not part of your war. A journalist,' lied the spy.

Keeping one hand in the air, Royle slowly and carefully reached into his shirt pocket and retrieved his British passport, holding it out for the soldier to see.

'British. Journalist,' repeated Royle. Then in Mandarin, 'Yingguo ren. Jizhe!'

Royle knew the North Vietnamese had a high regard for western journalists and did all they could to keep them from harm, which wasn't always easy or possible in battle situations. But he was aware of the unspoken truce between the North Vietnamese Army and journalists covering the war. Hanoi believed it was important to win the propaganda war as well as the physical and political war, and western journalists were one means to that end. He was now gambling that these unofficial rules of engagement had reached the Viet Cong, particularly this Viet Cong soldier who was bleeding from the mouth after Li Pengfei's attack and still pointing his gun at Royle.

'Nha bao?' repeated the guerrilla. Journalist?

Royle nodded, 'Vang,' he said, using one of the few Vietnamese words he was familiar with. Yes.

The guerrilla fighter held his free hand out and said 'Giay to!'

Royle frowned and shook his head, not understanding.

The Vietnamese used his free hand to point at the passport and beckoned Royle to hand it over.

'Giay to, giay to!' he demanded in a louder voice.

'Ah, passport. Of course.' Royle handed the passport to the VC cadre member and resumed waiting with his hands up.

'Nguoi Anh?' said the fighter, then in broken English, 'Bri-tish?'

Royle nodded and smiled. 'Yes.'

'Ban cua ban?' asked the guerrilla. Your friend? Clearly wondering what this Briton's link was with the man who had attacked him. The fighter then pointed down the hill towards where Li Pengfei had fled.

Royle nodded. Then in Mandarin he said, 'Ji huai nanren,' Very bad man. 'Xingshi. Wo shi renzhi.' Criminal. I was hostage.

Just then two other VC fighters cleared the top of the hill and descended towards the fighter, peering intently at Royle.

The fighter looked at the two men and said, 'Nha bao tu Anh.' Journalist from Britain, he said, indicating Royle with a wave of his Kalashnikov.

He handed Royle the passport and pointed down the hill.

'Ban di ngay bay gio.' You go now, he said to Royle. 'No la rat nguy hiem o day.' It is very dangerous here.

Royle bowed slightly, taking hold of his passport, said thank you in Vietnamese, 'Cam on', then walked slowly down the hill.

TUESDAY 24 DECEMBER 1974, BANGKOK, THAILAND

Amelia Harper replaced the telephone on its hook in her room at the five-star Peninsula Hotel on the Bangkok waterfront. She swore under her breath.

She walked over to her seventh-floor balcony and gazed out across the river, lost in thought for a few moments. It was mid-morning and the temperature was gradually rising for another hot day in Thailand's capital city. The noise of the city – car engines, horns, shouts - drifted upwards towards her, amid the growing smog that hung below.

Amelia Harper straightened her back, which had become stooped with worry and strain, smoothed down her light floral dress, and walked back inside the room. She turned the air conditioning up, sat on the bed and picked up the telephone again. There was a click and the hotel reception desk came on the line.

'How can we be of service, Mrs Smith?' crackled a helpful female voice at the other end of the line. Amelia had been exhausted when she arrived at the Peninsula late on the 23rd, and Smith was the first false name that popped into her head. She had left the hotel in Hull in a hurry, knowing she needed to confront her brother. Things had already gone too far, she had realised. And she had called her nephew's boarding school to explain that there had been a family crisis, which meant that Adi would need to spend Christmas at school. She felt sad about that, too.

'Good morning,' said Amelia. 'I would like you to put a call through to the British Embassy in Saigon please.'

'Very well Mrs Smith. Please remain by the telephone. We will call back when we have a connection.'

TUESDAY DECEMBER 24 1974, SAIGON

Royle managed to steal an abandoned army Jeep after his escape from the VC at Don Luan and rendezvoused as arranged at the dreary Cholon bar owned by the sullen Su. Both Royle and Li Pengfei then drove to the British Embassy in Saigon as it was going dusk after a long, difficult, uncomfortable, and at times dangerous drive back from Don Luan.

They left the jeep Royle had stolen inside the embassy compound, and walked into the building through the front door. Two Royal Marines saluted as they walked through the door, and watched them with suspicious eyes as Royle led Li Pengfei to the comms room.

As Royle had expected, Conti was there, as was Captain Saxby, still monitoring the intel as it came in, his eyes dark rimmed with exhaustion.

Conti looked up as Royle entered, and a smile of joy transformed his face. This changed to a look of bemusement as Li Pengfei entered in Royle's wake.

'Tom, glad you're back in one piece,' Conti said, shaking Royle's hand. As he did so the Major never took his eyes off Li Pengfei. Royle noted the tension.

Royle smiled. 'It's all right, Fred. Li Pengfei is one of us. Please afford him all the courtesy you would to a man in from the field after a long absence and presumed dead.'

Conti looked at the man. A Chinese from Malaya. One of us?

'It's true Fred,' said Royle. 'Li Pengfei has saved my life many times over the years. We go back a long way. I trust this man completely.'

'Even so, sir,' said Conti, suddenly becoming formal with Royle, his superior officer. 'That he may be, but what about his security clearance? I can't let him stay in here.'

Royle fixed Conti with a glare. 'Major, I haven't known you long, but I have come to regard you as a valued colleague and a friend. But I must tell you this. Li Pengfei has been working with the British Secret Intelligence Service since Malaya. Before that he was allied to SOE when we fought the Japanese in the jungles of Malaya. His intel has been more than valuable to us. And it still is, especially now.'

'You mean the incursion by the North Vietnamese army?'

'You know as well as I that this is more than an incursion. We need a flight to London as soon as possible. And as for security clearance ... Li Pengfei probably has a higher security rating than I.'

Conti looked at Royle and Li Pengfei, his mouth slightly agape, then seemed to suddenly pull himself together. 'Of course, Tom. I'll make the arrangements right away.'

Royle and Li Pengfei sat lounging in armchairs in one of the embassy common rooms, still covered in dust and grime from their long drive, when Conti walked in.

'I've secured you a couple of seats on the next C-130 out of Tan Son Nhut. Destination Hong Kong. From there you will need to contact the Governor's people on arrival and they will arrange transport to London.'

'Thank you, Fred.'

'You have half an hour to get to the airport. I'll get a driver to take you. Best get your things packed. He'll meet you at the gate.'

Conti strode to the door on his way back to the comms room. 'By the way, Mmerry Christmas.'

*

The C-130 transport plane took off on time from Saigon's main airport. The place was buzzing with activity and much busier than when he arrived. Aircraft of all types were taking off one after the other, most of them heading to the new war zone near the Cambodian border. But from what Royle and Li Pengfei had seen earlier that day, the South Vietnamese forces were quickly running out of airfields from which to receive supplies and reinforcements.

The increased activity, however, meant that take-offs and landings were minutely controlled from the tower and their aircraft promptly hoisted itself into the air en route to Hong Kong.

The aircraft was unmarked apart from the usual camouflage paint job. It appeared to have no country of origin. It climbed to 20,000 feet surrounded on all sides by the dark night. After about ten minutes the aircraft banked to the right as it turned in a long arc. A few moments later a man emerged from the cabin and approached the large aircraft's only two passengers. He shook hands with both, yet kept his gaze fixed on Li Pengfei, knowing the man's role fighting alongside the Viet Cong.

'Colonel Royle,' said the man in what Royle supposed was an accent from the south of the United States, perhaps Alabama. The man, who introduced himself as the captain of this particular flight, but did not volunteer his name or actual rank, was dressed in faded blue Levi jeans, leather cowboy boots and a neatly ironed drab olive tee-shirt. 'There has been a change of plan. Hong Kong is no longer our destination. We've been requested to change course for an airfield in Thailand. There will be further explanation when we land.'

After the captain returned to the flight deck Li Pengfei pointed a thumb in his direction. 'CIA,' said the professional guerilla fighter.

'Yes, I expect you're right,' said Royle.

'This is an Air America flight. These people are a law unto themselves.'

'Air America?'

'Yes,' said Li Pengfei. 'A CIA front organisation made up of civilian aircraft carrying out a dirty cross-border war.'

'I see. Well, I expect the flight to Thailand won't be as long as we had anticipated.'

Two hours later the C-130 began its descent. The two passengers looked out at their destination. It seemed to be a large military base – a small military city – lit up without fear of attack. In the background was laid out a well-lit runway. Thailand officially remained neutral in the Vietnam War, but was concerned that the communist movements slowly taking over neighbouring Laos and Cambodia, and threatening within Thailand itself, could one day remove the ruling monarchy. Thailand had therefore given itself over to American protection and had allowed the USA to establish military bases on its sovereign territory.

The large aircraft landed smoothly on the tarmac and they taxied slowly towards a reception building close to two large radar installations.

The rear of the aircraft lowered and the two men descended, to be met by an American party of military police.

'Colonel Royle and … friend?' said one of the three MPs. Royle nodded. 'Sgt Bakerson, 720th Military Police Battalion, sir. Welcome to Korat air base, gentlemen. I need to escort you to the officer's mess in Camp Friendship, sir.'

'I see,' said Royle, slightly bewildered, as the MP saluted crisply to both men. There didn't seem to be any animosity towards Li Pengfei this time, which surprised Royle.

The visitors and their military escort were led to a brown-coloured Lincoln Continental, which drove smoothly away from the air base, which was crowded with US military planes, including more C-130s and C-124s as well as New Zealand and Australian military aircraft and unmarked planes, presumably more from Air America. On the edges were some Royal Thai Air Force aircraft.

They drove towards the adjoining military base.

Royle could see while driving through the base that it was largely made up of US engineers. They passed fast food joints, American-style bars, soda shops and a huge baseball field that could almost be classed as a stadium. Beyond that was a PX depot and in the distance a secured armoury and munitions dump. In the other direction was a refinery-like fuel facility.

The car pulled up outside a low, long wooden building with a gently sloping roof. A sign outside read: Mai Pen Rai Lounge. Above was written 'The Good Life'. It was the Camp Friendship Officers Club, and lights blazed from the windows. Sgt Bakerson opened the door and led the two men and their escort into the club. As the door opened they were assaulted by a wall of raucous noise. Shouting, singing and Christmas music on the juke box blasted their ears.

Sgt Bakerson led them through the happy crowd, many in uniform, many not, past the crowded bar and through a door into a back room.

'Gentlemen, please make yourselves comfortable. Would you like me to get you both a drink?'

Royle asked for a cold beer. Li Pengfei wanted coffee. One of the MPs in the escort party strode off to the bar to get their drinks. He returned with them in less than a minute.

'If I can ask for your continued patience a little while longer,' said Bakerson, 'the camp commander will be along shortly to speak to you. In the meantime please remain here. Thank you.'

Without waiting for a reply the military policemen left. No doubt off to their own Christmas Eve party and a little peeved that they had been called on to look after these two people who weren't even Americans.

*

Both Royle and Li Pengfei were falling asleep sat on their uncomfortable wooden chairs in the room, which was by the look of things used for late night poker games, and still stank of cigarette and cigar smoke from the previous night's game. It had been an arduous day, first escaping from the Phuoc Long area before the situation got worse, then the long and dangerous drive back to Saigon by stolen jeep, and the flight to Hong Kong, which was diverted soon after take-off for this US base at Korat in Thailand.

Half an hour after their arrival at the Mai Pen Rai Lounge the camp commander walked in. Colonel Spencer Clark was a tall, gaunt man in his early 50s and was dressed in military fatigues, ironed and pressed to within an inch of their life. Clearly Christmas meant little to this man.

'Colonel Royle, Mr Li. Welcome to Camp Friendship. I apologise for keeping you waiting and for your, er, unexpected arrival.'

'I'm getting used to the unexpected, Colonel,' said Royle. 'But an explanation would be welcomed.'

'Of course. But by way of an explanation, please just give me a second.' Clark turned towards the door and bellowed: 'Sergeant!'

The door opened immediately, letting in the festive din again. Sgt Bakerson poked his head into the room. 'Yes sir?'

'Are things ready, sergeant?'

'Yes sir, Turner and Ramirez are at the back door now.' The sergeant closed the door again.

Colonel Clark opened the back door and indicated towards the two other MPs, then held the door open as he stood to one side.

Into the room walked Amelia Harper.

Li Pengfei's jaw dropped in total surprise, hanging open for a few seconds until he recovered some of his seriously dented composure.

Royle too was stunned. 'Mel? What the devil are you doing here?'

Royle's elder sister smiled a sad smile. She wore heavy boots, khaki trousers and a matching shirt. Men's clothes, so unlike Amelia. Her hair was pinned up and she wore a US army fatigues cap on her head. Her tanned face was subtly made-up, however, with pale lipstick and slightly smudged eye shadow. Royle guessed correctly that his sister had been crying.

'I believe I may have a confession to make,' said the woman, with an edge of steel to her voice that neither Li Pengfei nor Tom Royle had ever noticed before. 'To both of you.'

CHRISTMAS MORNING 1974, CAMP FRIENDSHIP, THAILAND

All three had been left alone in the back room of the Officers Club. It was early morning on Christmas Day and sunshine flooded through the room's two windows, looking out on to an empty parade ground. In the distance was a huge, rusting, water tower, built by the Americans ten years ago to service the ever growing military city that Korat had become. Nearer was a structure which they later discovered to be a friendship tribute wall, built by the Thai government in thanks to the US forces manning Camp Friendship. Dated 11 December 1968 the inscription on the whitewashed wall, with a protrusion on its right in the likeness of an eternal flame, read: 'To acknowledge the close relationship between the US and Thai military forces working together with the National Security Command for the benefit of the people of Thailand'. It had been presented to the camp by the Thai Prime Minister, Field Marshal Thanom Kittikachorn, and his name was inscribed on the wall in large black letters.

The three sat at the table, a breakfast of scrambled eggs, fried ham, pancakes, maple syrup and coffee had been brought in for them an hour ago. It remained cold and uneaten.

Amelia Harper sat upright, her hands clasped on the table in front of her.

'I managed to give the Hull police the slip, Tommy. I flew to Bangkok and contacted the Saigon Embassy from my hotel. But they told me you had left.

'Major Conti was put on the line and he explained you were with Pengfei,' Amelia looked at her erstwhile lover and her eyes began to glisten with tears. 'I managed to convince Major Conti that my meeting you was a matter of life and death. He seemed to know something about me, and he co-operated. I thought it would have been much harder. Getting to see you here was easier than I expected, Tommy. He arranged for your flight to be diverted here and he managed to find me passage on a military flight. I arrived just a few hours before you did.'

Royle smiled at his sister. 'So what was such a matter of life and death that you had to fly half way round the world to tell me?'

'I am not the person you think I am,' said the woman. Her lips pursed slightly as she prepared to tell the two men she loved most in the world her terrible, guilty secret.

*

'I was recruited into the Communist Party in 1939. I may have been only 14 years old, but I was idealistic and it felt so romantic. I fell in love with a Russian intelligence officer when I was just a girl. An infatuation really. Nothing physical, you understand. Not at first, anyway. It was a heady time. We were at war against the fascists in Europe and Asia, and I was too young to do much about it, though I wanted to desperately. I fell madly in love, or so I thought. But I fell more in love with Marxism Leninism.

'In 1939 Russia was still looked on with suspicion, after their treaty with Hitler. But they were not combatants and Peter – that was the name he gave me – showed me a way to fight the war politically. Peter introduced me to several Chinese members of the Party, which was a true shock to me. These people were plantation workers and servants, yet they held Communist Party meetings in secret, knowing that one day it would lead to revolution.

'I was the posh girl in the group, and they were suspicious of me at first, but Peter made sure I was made welcome and I was given the best of political indoctrinations.

'I rejected our wealth and imperial ambitions for the socialist ideal. But Mother and Father found out and sent me to England. What they didn't realise was that England was a hot-bed of radicalism, and I started to attend meetings of the British Communist Party. They were Stalinist and held him up as a saviour. Lenin's heir. The man who could bring about world Socialism. I fell under the spell again.

'For years I took Stalinist doctrine to heart, secretly learning all I could about the Soviet system in the USSR.

'By the time you arrived in Manchester, Tommy, I was attending meetings in the city centre every week, every Tuesday. I told you it was Red Cross training. It wasn't – just Red training.

'Not much was known about the Chinese Communists back then in England, so I became useful to the local party, offering them information about our comrades in the Far East. As the war progressed the communists in Malaya had become the main arm of opposition against the Japanese invaders. I knew some of the leaders. I knew they were committed in the anti-Japanese struggle.

'Somehow that information – that I was that rare beast, an English girl member of the Chinese Communist Party of Malaya – reached the Soviet Comintern and I was invited to Moscow to speak to some senior Soviet intelligence people. I gladly gave up what information I had out of a sense of duty. I told our aunt and uncle I was going to a Red Cross conference in Glasgow for a week. I told school the same story and both were happy to let me go.

'I told the Comintern all about the British comrades and the comrades I knew of in Malaya.

'It didn't strike me at first, but it was only then – after I had told this tissue of lies – I realised how easily and believably I was able to lie.

'I had been due to return home to Malaya for 1940 – presumably our parents had thought my communist leanings would have been smothered by my introduction to the Old Country – but the continuing war made that impossible. I was stuck in Manchester with our dear aunt and uncle, unable to pass on the Soviet messages I had been given to our comrades in Malaya.

'I was so happy when you came over, Tommy. You looked so dashing in your uniform of the Manchester Regiment, but then you too disappeared. Tommy, I had no-one. No-one to talk to. No-one to confide in.

'After the war I came back to Malaya. God, the place was such a mess. Our family was dead. We inherited the rubber plantations of our parents and Uncle Jim's in Kedah, then you disappeared again Tommy. Alone again.'

She smiled and squeezed Royle's hand lightly.

'After Mao Tse-tung was victorious in 1949, I tried to make contact with Peter. He had disappeared and I never heard from him again. I tried to make contact with some of my Chinese Communist Party comrades, but it turns out they had all been killed in the civil war fighting with Mao's forces. Such a bitter end for them after their successes against the Japanese. I offered my services and was invited to spend some time at the Whampoa military academy just across China's border. I went. I was indoctrinated back into the Chinese Communist Party. I was introduced to some very senior party members on a trip to Peking, including Chou En-lai and Bin Lao. I was something of a celebrity. An ex-imperialist English woman from Malaya who was now a committed communist at a time when the Malayan Communist Party was already flexing its muscles against the British.

'At Whampoa I was trained in intelligence gathering and tradecraft. I returned to Malaya and made contact with the Malayan Communist Party. With you, Pengfei.' Amelia now held Li Pengfei's hand in hers.

'Our love grew after the kidnapping and our fight against the British imperialists began to reap victories. But all this time I was taking my orders from Peking.'

Li Pengfei laughed. 'And I was taking my orders from London.'

Royle rose and walked over to the window. 'And the lion lay with the dragon,' he murmured. Amelia looked at him with a hurt expression on her suddenly care-worn face.

It was getting hot. Soldiers were out and about carrying on with their duties, but they seemed slack and relaxed. Full of the Christmas spirit, he thought. Royle did not feel at all Christmassy. His sister had just revealed that she had been a communist agent during the Emergency. A time when it was his job to eradicate the Malayan communist rebellion. Li Pengfei's, too. He felt flat and depressed. She and Sam Harper must have been a great team in place for the communists. Royle turned to his sister, still holding hands with Li Pengfei.

'So I take it you and Sam were the communist party's star Quislings in Malaya.'

Amelia looked taken aback, then looked at her brother.

'Oh, Tommy. Sam was never a communist. He was a hard-working man who ran the plantation well at first. We managed to accrue a small fortune. Unlike the bigger plantations reliant on shareholders in London, we ran our business directly from our house on the estate. We sold the Royle estate in Singapore, and the money from that went into a family trust fund for all of us. We carried on the operation at Uncle Jim's rubber estate, which we renamed the Royle-Harper estate in Baling. Sam didn't treat the workers too well by this time. He too had lost his family in the war and when we got together we sort of connected. The locals hadn't helped us during the Japanese occupation. The workers turned their

155

backs on our family, Tommy. They turned their backs on the Harpers too. Sam never really got over that. Before the war Sam treated the workforce well. He never beat the plantation workers. Afterwards he was a changed man. His incarceration was a painful experience, and he had to scrabble for survival almost every day. He survived, but endured with a deep and lasting hatred of the Japanese and the Malay plantation workers.

'But I never loved Sam, Tommy. It was suggested that I marry him so I would be in place to help the MCP.'

Now Li Pengfei moved his hand away and stared at the woman he loved.

'But my information was that he was a traitor and in the pay of the communists.'

Amelia shook her head. 'I was the traitor, not Sam. Peking knew you were a double agent. They fed that information to you because Sam Harper was a man of great influence and was helping to turn the tide against the communists in Malaya. He ran self-help committees, advised home guard units, had the ear of the Governor-general. They needed to get rid of him. You too, Pengfei.'

Li Pengfei shook his head sadly. 'You were the traitor. The information I gave you to feed to Sam was in fact fed to the communists by you for the sole purpose of putting your own husband in the frame as a traitor. After that it was relatively simple to get my people to take him out of the equation.'

'I had grown to despise Sam,' said Amelia. 'He was a brute and a drunk. He was a casualty of war.'

'You had to make yourself untouchable,' murmured Royle.

'Yes,' said Amelia.

'But the communists began to start losing the war. Pengfei here was a very valuable double agent and his information led to many communist operations being fatally compromised,' said Royle, struggling to understand fully what his sister was telling him.

'Yes,' said Amelia. 'Pengfei was next on the list. After the peace talks failed and he disappeared into the jungle I convinced my masters that I had arranged for his death. I told them it would be carried out by his own men deep in the jungle. They believed me.' Amelia looked at Li Pengfei.

'And thanks to you doing such a convincing disappearing act. I saved your life, Pengfei.'

'Why are you telling us this now?' asked Royle. Now he was seething with barely disguised anger.

'Because it was I who set you on this course to find Li Pengfei. I was responsible for the faked break-in at the house. I was responsible for the fire. My masters in Peking told me of your little agreement with Pengfei, that he was a double who reported to you. They came to the house one day. Said they were under cover as Moonies, teaching the religion of that idiotic Korean. They had been true to their cover and had been to virtually every house in Cottingham espousing the glory of the crazy Reverend Moon. There were two of them, a man and a woman, youngish, probably early thirties. The man wore a dark suit and tie, she wore a woollen dress with matching jacket. Both looked quite the part, carrying with them an attaché case of religious information. Unfortunately they hadn't realized the amount of distaste for such groups, especially in such a middle class and well informed suburb such as Cottingham. One woman had threatened to call the police if they didn't leave straight away.' Amelia laughed at the memory. 'Anyway, they came to my door, gave a password I hadn't heard for years, and then went straight into their instructions for me, all the time smiling their inane, beatific smiles. They handed me what looked like one of their religious leaflets, which was in fact coded contact instructions for when the plan was executed. It was fairly clear that they believed Li Pengfei was still alive, and that became my primary interest too. I realized Pengfei was still active. It was also obvious that the only way to find him would be through you, Tommy, and your MI6 contacts.

'I re-established contact with my comrades in Beijing through the embassy in London. I told them I would do what they wanted. I still had my code name and the necessary code words. With Li Pengfei as the prize they could do no other than to play my game. They arranged for a double-cross story that filtered through to Century House. That caused alarm bells to ring. News that Beijing had traced and were starting to move against one of Six's most valuable deep cover agents could only end in one thing – the call to you, Tommy. Or the recall, I should say. My part was mostly cosmetic, to speed things up a little. And that it did.

'I had Beijing in the palm of my hands. I'm sorry, Tommy, but I used you to keep Beijing interested. You never said anything, but for a number of years I had known about your talent-spotting sideline. I made it my business to learn the names of the students you referred to Century House. When you had your little one-to-one chats with them at the house I had the room bugged so I could hear exactly what was said and if your informal interview went according to plan. For the ones who never even reached the big question "Do You Wish To Serve Your Country?" I forgot about. For the ones who gave The answer "Yes" I made a note of their names.

'Remember those times you took me to your department to show me around, Tommy? Or when I met you there so we could go for lunch together? You didn't seem too surprised that I suddenly became very interested in your academic work place. You should have been. Once given the guided tour, I knew where your room was, where the departmental office was, and where the administration building was, and I made it my business to get access to those places.

'I stole your keys and left the house to get into your files in your room and in the departmental office. I lied about where I was going those evenings, but you were always too wrapped up in your work, whether you were marking papers or writing your latest tome.

'It was easy enough to pick the lock to the admin building, and there I soon managed to retrieve the details of your recruits. I sold them out, Tommy.' Amelia clenched and unclenched her hands and looked into Royle's pained eyes.

Royle, shocked to the core, stood abruptly, projecting his wooden chair across the room, such was the force of his movement.

Then Royle did something he had never done before. Enraged, Royle reached across the table and slapped Amelia – hard, across the face. Speechless, and pale with anger, Royle didn't wait for his sister to recover from the blow. He slapped her again on the other side of her face with the back of his hand, almost sending her crashing to the floor. Only the lightning grip of Li Pengfei saved her from a painful fall.

Li Pengfei gripped Royle's arm with his other hand, preventing any further assault.

Blood trickled from the corner of Amelia's mouth and her face glowed crimson from the double blow. Royle glared at his sister from across the table.

Amelia continued her confession, stifling a sob. 'I suppose I deserved that, Tommy,' said Amelia.

'You deserve more than that Mel,' stuttered Royle.

Amelia took a deep breath, then went on. 'Afterwards, all that remained was for the system to kick into action. That happened very quickly indeed. The fire at home was my idea. I never did like that house. It was a little bit of drama to get the ball rolling.'

'So, now you have found me. Are you here to kill me at last?' said Li Pengfei softly. He had taken hold of her shoulders and gently turned Amelia to face him. He picked up a paper napkin from the breakfast table and gently wiped a trickle of blood from the side of Amelia's mouth, then caressed her reddened face with his other hand.

'Of course not,' said Amelia, her eyes beginning to glisten with tears.

'Why are you here then?' Li Pengfei demanded.

Amelia wiped her eyes with the napkin.

'I came to find you, to be with you, of course. I still love you Li Pengfei.'

*

It was Boxing Day morning and all three boarded a Royal Australian Air Force flight to Hong Kong. From there a flight had been arranged to take them to London. There was some de-briefing to be done, and Royle envisaged it could take some time. Dangerous too, especially for Amelia. The woman, his sister, was a traitor. How could he denounce her? He turned to Li Pengfei, sitting alone across the walkway of the VC10 troop carrier. Amelia was sleeping to his right, in the window seat. Once again they were the only passengers on the flight.

Royle rose to take a seat next to Li Pengfei. Li Pengfei turned, his eyes were brimming with tears. Royle squeezed his arm, feeling the strong, lithe muscle beneath his jacket.

'We can't turn her in,' blurted Royle.

Li Pengfei stared at the blanket of clouds below as the jet soared at 30,000 feet above the South China Sea.

'She played us all for fools,' said Li Pengfei, drawing a sleeve across his eyes. Then he turned to Royle. 'But no, we cannot turn her in.'

'What to do then?' asked Royle.

Li Pengfei stayed silent and continued staring at the cloud bank below.

'Her secret is safe, unless the Chinese decide to reveal her, which is unlikely considering the current state of relations with Beijing. We can just leave her out of the equation. We'll go back, report in; Amelia can return to Hull. End of story,' decided Royle.

'And what a story, eh Thomas?' said Li Pengfei, reclining his seat and closing his eyes to get some much needed sleep.

Royle watched his old comrade for a long moment, then returned to his seat across the aisle. The veteran jungle fighter realized at the moment his sister Amelia had confessed that the story was only now beginning. Dear sister Mel had let her heart rule her head, seemingly for the first time. She had let her love for Li Pengfei distort her own sense of logic. While her deception had resulted in her becoming reunited with Li Pengfei, her lover of oh so many years ago, she had failed to consider one vital aspect of the plan. Beijing would still want Li Pengfei extracted for interrogation and probable execution. And Amelia's part in what was now a double, even a triple deception, could have signed her own death warrant with her Red Chinese masters too.

Royle too reclined his seat and shut his eyes for the long journey to Hong Kong, and whatever that would bring.

HONG KONG, DECEMBER 1974

It was almost as if they were landing in the sea, which in a way they were. The runway at Hong Kong's international airport was built out into the ocean in a narrow strip leading to the heavily built-up and highly populated British-ruled Hong Kong island.

The VC10 taxied to a quiet area away from the international gates. Being the day after Christmas Day the airport was unusually quiet, but still working. As the steps were rolled into place, the VC10's front hatch opened and a British inspector in the Hong Kong Police boarded the aircraft. He was accompanied by a cold blast of air and the stench of aviation fumes. It was winter in Hong Kong. He saluted to Royle, nodded to Amelia and looked at Li Pengfei with narrowed, suspicious eyes.

'Colonel Royle? Welcome to Hong Kong. Inspector Spencer at your service. The message from the embassy in Saigon wasn't too specific. Is this man a prisoner or a guest? I have a sergeant and two constables waiting outside as a precaution.'

'Thank you, Inspector. There are no prisoners here. There are some things you do not need to know, suffice to say we are all together as guests and en route to London.'

'Of course Colonel. Would you, Mrs Harper and Mr Li please accompany me into the airport building? We will bypass the usual procedures. This is after all a diplomatic flight.'

'Very well inspector. Lead on,' ordered Royle, now suddenly feeling very tired indeed.

The inspector led the three emotionally exhausted passengers to the front of the aircraft and down the steps. They were met by a Chinese police sergeant and two Chinese officers, all dressed in their khaki Hong Kong Police uniforms. They boarded a passenger bus which transported them to the terminal building. They were then led through the terminal to the passenger drop-off zone where they climbed into a long wheel-base khaki-coloured Land Rover. The sergeant and a constable seated themselves in the front, the constable driving. The inspector and the second constable sat at the rear of the passenger section of the vehicle, with Royle, Amelia and Li Pengfei up towards the front on padded yet quite hard bench seats. The only windows in the rear section of the police Land Rover were at the rear doors. They were grimy and covered in mesh and difficult to see through.

As they drove through the streets of Hong Kong the hustle and bustle of busy street life filtered through the loud engine noise and rattle of the vehicle. They could feel the vehicle meandering through the noisy narrow streets, then up and up as the vehicle negotiated the colony's hilly terrain. They were headed for the Governor's residence.

It took twenty minutes to reach the mansion house. All the way up they could hear the ongoing Christmas celebrations in the colony. In some areas they could hear exclusively British and Australian voices, but mostly it was the Cantonese chatter of the Chinese population. They too liked a good party, and while many of them weren't Christian they still threw themselves into the Christmas celebrations with gusto.

The police Land Rover ground to a halt on the gravel driveway at the rear of the Governor's residence at Government House. Inspector Spencer led the three bedraggled, and by this time shivering, guests through the kitchens and into a small ante-room where dinner guests would normally play cards, drink brandy and smoke good cigars. A cold drizzly mist had descended on Government Hill on Hong Kong island, where the Governor's residence was located, making them feel even more miserable than they already were.

All three were still dressed in tropical clothes and were left to sit in silence in comfortable armchairs, where they gradually warmed up again, with the aid of a roaring fire in the hearth. None were in the mood for conversation.

Presently high tea was trundled in on a wheeled trolley by a young Chinese woman dressed in a traditional maid's uniform. She placed a china cup and saucer on a small table beside each armchair, poured in the correct amount of milk, then poured the tea from a silver teapot. A three-tiered cake and sandwich plate was brought to a fourth table, then the maid bowed and left without uttering a word.

Amelia rose to offer round the sandwiches, tiny morsels of food between bread with the crusts removed. They appeared to contain cucumber and some sort of fish paste, possibly salmon. The cakes were a selection containing cream and strawberry jam. Tired as they were, the three visitors cleared the three tiers of food and sat back in their chairs feeling relaxed and a little better. They continued to wait.

Then Royle, unable to contain himself any longer, almost shouted in his continuing anger and frustration, 'For God's sake, Mel. Are you saying you did this for love?'

Amelia looked at her brother, then glanced at Li Pengfei. 'Not at first,' she mumbled. She was by now finding it increasingly difficult to think straight in her emotional state.

'I was a committed communist, Tommy,' said Amelia, almost reasonably.

'There are plenty of committed communists around, Mel. Most of them don't end up causing death and destruction in their wake. All those young intelligence trainees I recommended to Six. The ones that made the grade would only be able to expect one result once they infiltrated into country assignments. Death. And you caused that, Mel.'

Amelia nodded slowly. The fancy cupcake she had chosen from the cake stand seemed to turn to ash in her mouth. 'They knew the risks, Tommy. As did you. They knew that any mission abroad could end in disaster for them'

'Yes,' said Royle, 'they would have known the risks of being activated abroad, even in a friendly country. But you changed the equation for them, Mel. You identified them. You may as well have painted a large target on their back, so the Chinese secret service could shoot them right in the bull's eye. Even if their tradecraft had been exceptional it would not have helped them. They would have been watched and intercepted.'

Royle was breathing heavily by this time and felt short of breath as his anger rose again. 'Those who were detained and questioned would have endured hours and days of chemical and physical torture, but after that they would have been disposed of. A quick bullet to the head would have probably done the job. The Chinese aren't barbarians.'

Amelia placed her uneaten plate of food on the small table beside her chair and looked directly at both her brother and her former lover.

'What has been done can't be undone,' she said to both men. 'I believed in what I was doing. It was important to me.

'Tommy, Pengfei, I didn't set out to cause anyone's death. But I got sucked in to the world of international intelligence and there didn't seem any way out. To be honest, I wasn't looking for a way out,' she said. 'I believed my work was important. I still do.'

'You're a traitor, Amelia,' said Royle. His voice shaking with emotion.

Amelia laughed, a single, sharp laugh, more from the nervousness she was feeling than from amusement.

'Then, Tommy, I expect you to do your duty and turn me in. You must disavow me, and then allow matters to run their course, even if it means me being stood against a wall in the bowels of Century House, and shot.' Amelia's head fell forward and she sat there silently without saying another word.

Royle looked at his sister, feeling that she was finally hanging her head in shame, but at the same time realizing that Amelia had confessed everything to him and Li Pengfei, not expecting any special treatment. She expected to be disavowed.

*

It was starting to go dark when the door opened and a man who appeared to be aged in his sixties burst in with a flourish. He was portly, going bald, and had the ruddy complexion of a heavy drinker. He wore a double-breasted grey woollen suit which had seen better days, a crumpled white shirt and a badly creased necktie. His black leather shoes were dull and clearly had not been polished for months, if at all.

The man beamed a smile at the three guests and strode over to Royle.

'Colonel Royle, I am honoured to meet you, sir. Your reputation precedes you of course.' He then turned to Amelia and with a nod of the head simply said 'Madam,' then turned to Li Pengfei, saying 'Mr Li Pengfei, again the honour is mine.

'Allow me to introduce myself, Giles McAdam, freelance journalist of many years standing, darling of Fleet Street, at your service.'

Royle interrupted him and stood up abruptly. 'Fleet Street? Look, I'm very sorry Mr McAdam, but we aren't in a position to talk to the Press at this moment in time. Perhaps later, when we get back home.'

McAdam let out a loud guffaw and helped himself to a large whisky from one of the decanters in the room. 'My dear sir, you didn't allow me to finish. Journalism is just my day job. I am one of C's Hong Kong watchers. Keeping an eye on the commies across the border, not to mention the commies this side of the border.' McAdam smiled broadly and hefted his heavy frame down into one of the chairs facing the three visitors.

'You're with Six?'

'None other, old boy. Here to help as much as possible.'

Royle looked at Amelia, who had become tense when McAdam revealed his credentials. Li Pengfei sat impassively and said nothing.

'I see,' said Royle. 'Well, it's grand to have someone we can rely on Mr McAdam. I have a question. When can we expect to catch a flight to London? I need to present Mr Li Pengfei there for debriefing, I need to be debriefed myself, and need to get my sister, Mrs Harper, back home.'

'Of course, colonel. Of course. My understanding is that your house is still in need of considerable repairs. The police have had no luck with their investigations yet, and they are quite puzzled by the sudden disappearance of Mrs Harper a few days ago. Still, you haven't committed any crime, Mrs Harper,' McAdam looked at Amelia and bowed gallantly. I am sure you will have a good explanation for our boys in blue when you return.'

'Why of course, Mr McAdam. I was just very worried about my brother. I needed to be sure he was all right out in Vietnam. It is still a very dangerous place, you know', said Amelia.

'Indeed it is, my dear lady. Indeed it is. Now, about your flight to London. I will arrange this for as soon as possible. It is Christmas, however, and there aren't many civilian flights available. I will try to arrange passage on a military flight, so we will just have to wait until I can sort something out. In the meantime accommodation has been arranged for all of you here in Government House.

'Please don't take this the wrong way, but the Governor has specifically asked not to meet you, because of your secret status, you know. Can I ask that you confine yourselves to this side of the house?'

'Old Jock the Sock is a grand chap with quite an ambitious agenda. He doesn't want the likes of us secret squirrels spoiling his rise up the slippery pole that is the present day Diplomatic Service ladder.'

'Jock the Sock?' asked Royle, visibly puzzled.

'Why yes, that's what he's affectionately known as … ah, sorry. I'll explain. His name is Murray McLehose. He is a Scot and the twenty-fifth Governor of Hong Kong. Associates and other Brits on the island refer to him as Jock the Sock merely because of his Scottish ancestry and on account of his surname. A little childish, you may think. But the nickname has stuck since he was installed in '71.

'Look, Jock's a good man, but when he's in a spot of bother it's as if one of our famous typhoons has struck – everyone tends to catch it as well.

'He had worked in the Foreign and Commonwealth Office in the Wilson Government of the 60s until a blunder by him led to sensitive papers being lost and only found again by a fellow civil servant. They included a telegram from Wilson to President Johnson about the Vietnam War back in '67. There were calls for him to be immediately dismissed for this stellar breach in security, but instead George Brown, the Foreign Secretary – McLehose was Brown's principal private secretary – sent him abroad. Ironically he became British Ambassador to Vietnam that same year. He's been overseas ever since.

'Then earlier this year McLehose started a crusade against corruption in the Hong Kong civil service and police force. His Independent Commission Against Corruption sparked off civil disobedience protests and a general movement against the Governor. There was violence too. Currently there are moves afoot to get him replaced. So you can see, old Jock isn't in much of a mood for further problems on his doorstep, particularly at Christmas.

'The Governor has agreed to make himself scarce for the next few days and has taken up residence for himself and his family at one of the hotels, just to be on the safe side. He is an ambitious diplomat and does not wish to become involved in anything that smacks of the unsavoury – not that your mission does. But he does not know that, and the less he knows the better.'

'And what do you know, Mr McAdam?' asked Li Pengfei, speaking for the first time since the journalist entered the room.

'Enough, Mr Li Pengfei. Enough.'

*

The next morning, the Christmas holidays over, Giles McAdam called on the trio at Government House. Royle, Li Pengfei and Amelia had all slept well, largely as a result of their exhaustion, and had eaten a good breakfast of kedgeree, toast, orange juice, tea and coffee.

After breakfast, still traumatized by what his sister had told him about her years of treachery and betrayal, Royle left McAdam with Amelia and

Li Pengfei and went to the Governor's study to make a long distance call to Adi's school, first of all speaking to Adi's headmaster and then to Adi himself.

It was 11pm in England and well after lights out time in the school dormitories, but the headmaster gave special permission for Adi to be woken and brought to the telephone.

Emotion began to well up in Royle. He had missed Christmas with his son for the first time, and he wondered how to make it up to him.

'How are you Adi, school treating you well?' said Royle when Adi came on the phone, not sounding sleepy at all.

'Hello, dad. It's been great here at school. Got some friends staying over too, so it's been fun. Their families are away on business too.'

'I see,' said Royle, forcing a laugh at his son's cheerfulness. Royle felt anything but cheerful. 'Sorry we missed Christmas with you, but I'll make it up to you, I promise.'

'Don't worry, dad. I've had a great time,' said Adi. 'Mr and Mrs Peaks have made us all feel at home. We had a fantastic Christmas feast, with presents and games, but I do hope you come home soon.' Mr and Mrs Peaks were Adi's headmaster and his wife.

'That's good, son,' said Royle.

'How's Auntie Mel?' asked Adi.

'Oh, she's fine, bossing me around as always,' said Royle. Adi laughed, then there was a shout in the distance and Adi's muffled voice said something aside. Royle assumed Adi had placed his hand over the telephone speaker while he spoke to someone. He thought it must be one of his friends.

'Dad, we're just in the middle of a midnight feast in the dorm,' said an excited sounding Adi. 'Even though it's not midnight yet.'

'Really?' said Royle. 'Does Mr Peaks know?'

'Oh yes, he laid it on for us. Christmas treat, he said. So I'll have to go now. Hope to see you soon, dad. Tell Auntie Mel I love her,' said Adi

'I will,' said Royle. 'See you soon, and be good for Mr and Mrs Peaks.'

Royle rang off and stared at the Governor's telephone for a long minute or two. Had he compromised his family on this mission? Where was it all leading?

Then Royle made a decision. A new start was needed, and that needed to happen as soon as this mission was over and as soon as he and Amelia returned home. Li Pengfei's future lay in the hands of the British state.

Royle picked up the telephone again to ring his lawyer at home. It was late, he knew, but not too late for Philip Penright, a renowned night owl. Penright was leading partner in Penright Hawthorn, a legal firm in the city of London. They had dealt with the eventual sale of the Royle and Royle-Harper rubber plantations, the purchase of the house in Cottingham, and the family trust that he, Amelia and Adi all benefited from.

Penright picked up the telephone, at first surprised to hear Royle's voice, then with his characteristic bon homie wished Royle a happy Christmas before leading into the purpose of Royle's late night call.

Without hesitation, Royle instructed Penright to put the Cottingham house up for sale first thing in the morning, to dispose of the furniture from the house once the property had been sold, to keep in a place of safety the remaining private documents in the house, and to find and purchase on Royle's behalf another property, perhaps a converted farmhouse or somewhere similar, but a solid, well-constructed house somewhere away from it all. Royle knew their new residence would have to be secured with the latest technology, and it would need to be solidly built in case of trouble. And Royle was unable to shake off the feeling that there was still plenty of trouble ahead.

McAdam walked in just as Royle rejoined his sister and Li Pengfei, a rolled-up newspaper tucked under his left arm. Royle surmised by McAdam's appearance that he must have slept in his dark grey suit, which was more crumpled and unkempt than it had been the day before. McAdam's eyes were bloodshot and his clothes reeked of cigarette smoke and whisky. But the older man seemed alert and appeared to have things to tell the three.

'Well, my dear charges, I think I know why it has been so difficult to get you on a flight home,' announced the cheery MI6 man. McAdam tossed the newspaper, the South China Morning Post, on to the breakfast table in front of Royle, then sauntered over to the coffee pot to pour himself a strong black one.

Royle unrolled the newspaper. Cyclone Tracy had destroyed the Australian city of Darwin on Christmas Day. Dozens had died, and the death toll was still mounting. Emergency flights had been diverted to the region, so no military aircraft were available to ferry the three back to England.

'I see,' Royle said simply, then passed the newspaper to Li Pengfei and Amelia.

'I've got calls in to all the main airlines,' said McAdam, pouring himself a second cup. 'You are on standby. It could take hours or days, who knows? It's necessary for you all to travel together, and I'm told by my airline contacts that this could complicate matters. A lot of people have pre-booked flights for after the Christmas holidays, so they are all full at present,' McAdam said cheerily, pouring himself a third cup.

'So, how about a bit of sight-seeing?' McAdam beamed one of his infectious broad smiles at the trio, and indicated the door with his outstretched hand.

'I thought you wanted us to stay out of sight and out of mind,' said Royle, who couldn't help but smile at this ebullient whirlwind of a man.

'Yes indeed. That was then. Can't keep you good people cooped up here all the time. I'll show you the sights. If any flight to Heathrow has four seats together I'll be paged and we can make our way to the airport. In the meantime I'll show you around Government House, then show you the sights. But first I think we need to get you all kitted out. Don't mean to be rude, old boy, but you all look a frightful sight. Even the dear lady, no offence.'

Royle had to smile again, this coming from the untidiest man he had ever met. But McAdam did have a point. He and Li Pengfei had literally come straight from a war zone at Phuoc Long, and Amelia had travelled in the US Army fatigues she had met them in at Camp Friendship. She did not seem to have any luggage.

'Very well, Mr McAdam. Just one question. You said we are on standby for four seats?'

'Why yes, of course, Colonel. I will be accompanying you.'

*

McAdam first showed them around Government House, inside and out. Inside he led them through the comfortable lounge, then through the ballroom in the building's more recent extension, which was also used for official receptions. They breezed through the dining room, the drawing room and the conference room before heading for the front door.

Outside the south-facing frontage of the mansion house stood the spectacular Victoria Peak, still shrouded in cloud and mist. The air seemed warmer than it was when they arrived. Royle estimated about 65 Fahrenheit, and the sun was trying to break through the thick cloud. To the north, at the rear of Government house, were the central government offices, where Hong Kong's civil service was based. Royle mused, *to be so close to the people you have just launched a thorough investigation against* – the Governor's anti-corruption drive.

They walked across the front lawn and looked at the official residence of the Governor – Hong Kong's legislative chief executive. He was the law. What Jock the Sock said was the law and he held supreme power in the colony.

McAdam explained that Government House had been redesigned by the Japanese after they had occupied the island in 1941, merely hours after the first attacks on Pearl Harbor as the Japanese began their first wave of attacks on western targets to create the Greater East Asian Co-Prosperity Sphere. As a result Government House was now built in a unique Japanese / neo classical style. The new style did not do the official residence any disservice. The Japanese tower and roof gave the building a style all its own.

'The azaleas are beautiful in the spring,' McAdam announced with an all-encompassing wave of his arm around the lawns. 'You should come back to see them then.'

At the rear of the building – set alone amid the greenery of the hill it stood atop – stood the city. Its high-rise banks towered above it, even though Government House was built on a hill. The power of Government House was awesome. It was not the biggest building they had ever seen, but it was set alone and in its own grounds, and in this overcrowded island that itself was a symbol of enormous power.

'Come along now, my children,' bellowed McAdam. Time to go out and about. First we will buy the lady some new clothes, then I will take you gentlemen to Ram's, quite simply the best tailor in Hong Kong.'

'A tailor? We surely won't have time to wait for a suit to be made,' said Li Pengfei.

'You surely will, old boy. Ram can turn a suit round in a day, from measurements to final fitting and any tweaks needed after that. Let's go, a taxi awaits.'

*

Ram's was in the middle of Victoria's buzzing, ramshackle streets. Inside was a hive of activity too, but as they crossed the threshold Ram, the Indian proprietor, rushed to greet them. McAdam explained what was needed and Ram immediately summoned two of his tailors, who arrived gripping tape measures.

Measured up, they left the shop, being told to return at 3pm that afternoon. They walked towards the harbour and took the Star Ferry to Kowloon on the mainland, which with Lantau Island, the smaller Lamma Island, and the vast New Territories stretching to the Chinese border beyond, were all part of Britain's Hong Kong colony until 1997, when the whole of Hong Kong would be returned to communist China by dint of treaty obligations.

'Shame, but it all goes back to China in twenty-three years,' lamented McAdam. 'We only keep it on a 99-year lease, and that will be up in '97. Shame.' McAdam shook his head sadly.

'Have you lived here long?' asked Royle.

'Been here since before the Japanese arrived. I was interned along with many others. That was a horrible time, Colonel Royle. A really horrible time. In my late twenties at that time, working for my father's shipping line and penning a few dispatches to Fleet Street in my spare time. Life was pretty good until the Japanese invasion. Of course, they wanted the deep-water harbour. That's why the British grabbed it in the first place. It's got fantastic strategic advantage. Well, we didn't know what hit us. All of a sudden we were under air attack, then line upon line of troops marched in. For a time I shared a wing of our prison camp with the then Governor. He had also been captured after our feeble defence of the island was doomed to failure. He surrendered and all one-million of us paid the consequences.'

'Probably the only thing to do to save the island,' remarked Royle.

'Oh, indubitably,' replied McAdam as he led them off the ferry and into a cocktail bar back on Hong Kong island.

Royle, Li Pengfei and Amelia refrained from alcohol. They all felt they needed clear heads. But McAdam ordered a whisky and soda. Lunch, apparently.

'So, Colonel Royle,' said McAdam sotto voce so neither Li Pengfei nor Amelia could hear him. 'You are considering a change of residence?'

Royle looked at McAdam for a moment, then nodded. 'Yes, I am, but I haven't told anyone about it yet. Not that I know of, anyway.'

McAdam returned a great broad smile. 'I realise you have been out of the field for some time, Colonel, but I can explain.'

'Don't tell me, you have the Governor's telephones bugged,' Royle said light-heartedly. It was something Royle should have expected, but was too determined to speak to his son and arrange the house sale to care.

'Well,' said McAdam with a smile. 'We do. But that's not how we know about your call to your son's school and to Mr Penright.'

Royle sighed deeply, and indicated that McAdam should continue with his explanation.

'Colonel, you have been out of things for quite some time, but you are still a field officer, so you should know that there is a certain highly secret system in place to monitor telephone calls.'

Royle sat passively, unfazed by the news. 'Of course, it was always so.'

McAdam moved closer to Royle, speaking ever more quietly.

'I don't think you quite understand,' said McAdam. 'We can intercept phone calls. All phone calls.'

'What? How?' said Royle, now with his interest peaked.

'The Government Communications Headquarters at Cheltenham has a new secret system for listening in to phone calls in the UK and abroad.'

'The old code breakers have started listening to gossip now, have they?' said Royle.

'Colonel, GCHQ is working in partnership with the Americans. With the NSA to be precise. They have been working on a new system that allows the interception of telecommunications if a certain target speaks on the telephone, or if certain key words are mentioned in a telephone conversation. That starts the tape recorders working. There's no real need to physically bug phones any more. It can all be done remotely with Echelon.'

'Echelon?' asked Royle.

'Yes, that's the name for the new interception system. It's all very prototype at the moment, but it will have very extensive uses in the near future, I'm sure. We want to know what the IRA are about to do next.

And the Americans are so paranoid these days they want to know what everyone is saying,' said McAdam.

'Even my conversation with my son and with my lawyer,' said Royle, more bemused than angry.

'Well, as I said, it is experimental, but operational,' said McAdam. 'You, sir, being on active service, are a target for Echelon.'

Royle smiled and sipped at his coffee.

The bar began to fill up with office workers – mostly senior management - also out to get a liquid lunch.

Then something strange happened. Royle had been drinking coffee, Li Pengfei and Amelia were drinking green tea. Royle stood up as if in great pain, his head in his hands. An incredible pain suffused his whole cranium and he immediately rose from his seat, starting to leave the table they were sitting at in a state of blind confusion. Then his legs buckled beneath him and he collapsed senseless to the floor.

McAdam was quick to reach Royle, the intelligence officer's sluggish appearance seemingly belying his actual alertness. A crowd began to gather. Then the shots started. Amelia looked alarmed, but Li Pengfei took her by the arm, pulled her to her feet and both disappeared into the crowds outside. Royle would wake up in a few hours none the worse for his ordeal while Li Pengfei whisked Amelia away. The shots fired from inside the bar had wounded two European businessmen who had been sitting at a table next to Royle's drinking cocktails, and injured McAdam in the left hand.

*

Royle woke up in a hospital emergency room. A saline drip was attached to his arm and he was wearing a surgical gown. His head throbbed abominably, his mouth had an indescribable taste, and his arms and legs felt like jelly. Electrodes led from his chest to a monitor on a stand near his bed.

Seeing his movement a white-uniformed nurse, Chinese and efficient, came to him, looked at the monitor, checked his pulse manually, took his temperature, then smiled at Royle before walking away without comment. A few moments later an English doctor appeared, checked the monitor, then said, 'Well, Mr Royle, we'll have you out of here in no time.' Then he walked off.

Royle was struggling to remember what had happened. They had been on the ferry, they had walked into Victoria, then McAdam had taken them into a smart bar where he had drunk coffee. The coffee seemed to taste slightly off, but he dismissed that at the time. Coffee tasted different wherever one went, especially in England where the taste ranged from just ok to awful. The same was true here in Hong Kong, it seemed. But had there been gunfire?

McAdam breezed in at that moment, but his ever present smile was missing. His left hand was heavily bandaged. McAdam loomed up to Royle's bedside slightly breathless.

'How do you feel, colonel?'

'Terrible. What happened?'

'The doctor seems to think someone slipped you a mickey, old boy.'

'A mickey?'

'Mickey finn. You were drugged. Probably chloral hydrate. Nothing lethal, you understand, but you won't be running any marathons for a day or two.'

'Drugged?' Royle was struggling to get his brain to work. *Definitely not chloral hydrate*, thought Royle. *It was something much worse.*

'Yes, in the cocktail bar. Never happened to me before in there. Doubt if I'll be able to show my face there again for a month or so. Anyway that's when the firing started. Two Chinese, Triads maybe?'

Royle just looked at the crumpled, older man.

McAdam returned the gaze with a guilty look. 'We are in a bit of a pickle, colonel.'

Royle continued to gaze at the intelligence officer. McAdam gave out a long, deep sigh. 'Mr Li Pengfei and your sister have vanished.'

Royle was shaken by this news, and with difficulty sat up. The pain in his head spiked horribly as he moved, and he felt he was about to throw up. 'Vanished?' was all Royle could manage.

'Yes, in the confusion. After you passed out. I bent down to see what was wrong. I checked your vitals, they were fine. A small crowd had gathered around. I called an ambulance. Then I looked round for Mr Li Pengfei and Mrs Harper and they were nowhere to be seen. That's when I received this flesh wound.' McAdam held up his bandaged hand. 'Anyway, I checked back at Government House, but they haven't returned. They've gone.'

*

It was going dark when McAdam helped Royle into a taxi and both drove back up the hill to Government House. They sat in silence as the vehicle crunched its way along the gravel path to the front door. McAdam said something in Cantonese to the driver, who then carried on around to the rear door. McAdam paid the driver and gripped Royle by the arm as they walked into the governor's residence. He took Royle to his room and left him to his ablutions. It was patently obvious Royle would be better after a good night's sleep and when the drug had worn off completely.

McAdam walked downstairs in the drawing room, helped himself to a large neat scotch, then slumped down into one of the comfortable armchairs and waited for morning.

After twelve hours of deep, recuperative sleep, Royle awoke feeling famished. It was daylight outside and he felt like he hadn't eaten for a week. Royle slipped a robe over his pyjamas and gingerly went downstairs, holding on to the banister rail. He still felt weak and shaky from the drug he had unknowingly taken.

As he neared the dining room he heard muffled voices through the closed door. He was sure one of the voices belonged to McAdam, but he couldn't identify the others.

Royle walked into the room and was stunned that McAdam's companions, seated before emptied breakfast plates, were his old MI6 debriefer Harrison, and his old colleague from Malaya days Bill Ferney. Royle didn't let his astonishment show. He nodded a silent greeting to the three men then made a bee-line for the kedgeree dish, piling his plate high with the fishy rice breakfast, and filling a glass with fresh orange juice. Royle then seated himself next to McAdam and proceeded to demolish the contents of his plate.

Between mouthfuls, Royle said, 'Good morning. Didn't expect to see you two here. Must be fairly important.' Then he continued finishing the mountain of breakfast before him. He noticed that his hand trembled slightly as he forked in the last of the food, an after-effect of the drug.

'Glad you're up and about again Tommy. No ill-effects, I trust,' smiled Bill Ferney. Royle looked at his old comrade-in-arms. Ferney looked tired and stressed after his long journey from London. His smile was false. Harrison just looked at Royle impassively, his hands clasped together on the table in front of him, as if in prayer.

'Fit as a fiddle,' smiled Royle, equally falsely. Royle's calm exterior bore no resemblance to his true emotions, which were a worry for Li Pengfei and Amelia, and anger at MI6. He was consumed with an almost unbearable desire to know what had happened, but he knew he would need to play the situation out with these three men.

'Are you feeling fit enough to travel, Dr Royle?' asked Harrison, a slight smile on his stubbled face. Slight smile or sly smile? Royle couldn't decide which. Both looked tired and in need of rest. He could only imagine that the two men had just recently flown in.

'To where?' asked Royle, refilling his coffee cup.

'Why home of course, Tommy,' said Ferney. 'It's time to go home. Back to your normal life. Back to your books. Back to academe.'

'And what about Li Pengfei and my sister?' asked Royle, colouring slightly as his anger began to get the better of him.

'Gone, old boy,' said McAdam. 'They disappeared after the debacle in the bar and haven't been seen since.'

'Any idea where you think they could have got to, Dr Royle?' asked Harrison, again that sly, supercilious tone in his voice.

'Of course he hasn't,' spoke up Ferney. 'They made sure he was out of the picture before doing a runner. Question is, who was responsible for the shooting?'

Harrison nodded a diminutive nod and again that sly smile started to curl his lip slightly.

'Are you telling me you still have no idea where they could be?' asked Royle. 'With no transport out, they can't be far.'

'No-one said there was no transport out, Dr Royle,' said McAdam, abashed. He seemed to have had a strip or two torn off him after the fiasco at the cocktail bar. 'There were no aircraft, but plenty of boats. Big harbour,' said McAdam with one of those characteristic hand sweeps.

'And then there's the Chinese border,' interjected Harrison.

Royle fixed Harrison with a cold stare. He had considered arguing against Harrison's suggestion, but after Amelia's confession in Thailand Tom Royle knew this was a distinct possibility. Even the most likely possibility, he realised, especially considering Li Pengfei's background. Li Pengfei had been one of Britain's greatest assets during the Malayan

Emergency. A double agent who was a terrorist leader and knew every move the bandits were to make. The turning of Li Pengfei had been one of the great espionage successes of the war. As he reported back to his MI6 controllers the tide started to turn in favour of the British.

But until now Royle had failed to add Amelia's treachery to the equation. She was Beijing's animal, controlled by the MSS from the Chinese capital. Could she have turned Li Pengfei back and crossed the border with him?

'I'll get dressed,' said Royle. He rose from the table and made his way upstairs to his room. There his newly tailored suit from Ram's was laid out for him, along with a new white shirt and a dark blue tie.

LATE DECEMBER 1974, HULL, ENGLAND

The black cab dropped Royle back home. It had been a long journey from Kai Tak airport in Hong Kong to London Heathrow. Then followed another debriefing session at another hotel with Harrison, who was back in his usual casual interrogator mode, complete with tape recorder, notepad and pencil. Royle had grown to really dislike Harrison.

Amelia's treachery was not mentioned. It proved to be a short debriefing session and soon Royle was given a travel warrant and boarded a train home to Hull, first class.

Royle still felt slightly ill from the after-effects of the drug that had somehow been administered to his coffee in the Hong Kong cocktail bar, but his emotions were overruling his physical complaints. Amelia and Li Pengfei had vanished, his mission had failed at the final hurdle, and his house, he noticed after paying the taxi driver, was still a total mess after the fire that had begun his globetrotting chain of events.

He noted that the windows and doors had all been replaced, and there was still a faint stench of soot and burnt charcoal. But the house was a mess. The carpet had been torn up and not replaced and the furniture stank of acrid smoke. The house was clean, however, and the power supply had been reconnected, as had the water. He looked through the window at the 'Sold' sign in the garden. Looking around Royle was glad to be moving away from this comfortable little bungalow. Penright had sent him a list of properties that may be suitable. One seemed perfect, an old, stone-built house on the bleak West Pennine moors of Lancashire. With the house came two acres of land, and a paddock that had been used for horses, although Penright had warned the stables had been quite ramshackle. He told Penright to purchase it. The house would create a large hole in Royle's bank balance, and the sale of the Cottingham bungalow had been at a loss because of the fire damage, although his house insurance would plug some of that gap.

Royle walked into the kitchen and put the kettle on.

As he waited for his electric kettle to boil he prepared a mug for making tea, then went to pick up a pile of post that had accumulated beneath the letter box of his new front door.

Royle set the mail on a side table, walked into the kitchen to complete the tea ritual, then brought the steaming mug into his lounge, where he sat down to catch up on his correspondence.

Some were utility bills, which Royle placed on one side for dealing with later. One was from the head of his faculty at the university, confirming that his sabbatical had been granted and that he would be expected back at his desk in six months, preferably with a manuscript in his hand. Royle couldn't help but smile. At least Ferney had arranged this for him at short notice to cover his tracks as he trailed Li Pengfei.

The rest was composed of junk mail, a short letter from a student explaining why he had probably failed his second year exams and – one with familiar handwriting, from Amelia.

Royle tore the envelope open.

Dearest Tommy

By the time you get this we should be far away living a life we should have begun twenty years ago. I don't think it would be a good idea to pursue Pengfei again, or myself for that matter. We want to be on our own and catch up on the years we lost together. None of us are getting any younger and we feel we haven't a moment to waste. Keep well, dearest Tommy. Thank you for all your love and care over the years, but now is the time for Pengfei and I. I'm sorry.

Love, Amelia.

So, that was that. Royle picked up the envelope. Airmail, posted from Kuala Lumpur. Back there after all this time? Well, why not, there were worse places to live.

Royle's morning paper hadn't arrived, presumably cancelled by the efficient Detective Constable Redpath. Royle put on his overcoat and shoes then strode off into the village to buy a newspaper.

The air was cold and damp, with an overcast sky. It could rain later, thought Royle. He reached the Cottingham Stores and bought that morning's edition of *The Times*, *The Guardian* and the *Daily Telegraph*, for the variation, then began to stroll back to his house. Later he would start his treatise on the Malayan Emergency again, although he suspected he would need to find another publisher.

Back home, he sat down again with another mug of tea and unfolded *The Times*. He looked at the dateline and was surprised when he saw it was New Year's Eve - 1975 was just around the corner. In the paper there was news about more unemployment and gloomy news about high interest rates and a looming economic recession. Oil prices continued to rise, as did inflation. It wasn't a good picture to come home to.

Royle flicked through the three newspapers, but was unable to concentrate. He kept thinking about Amelia's letter. He had been cut off from his only relative and one-time greatest friend. And it meant he would need to hire someone to look after Adi when he wasn't in school. He made a mental note to visit his son in school on New Year's Day. Royle threw the newspapers on the floor in anger, mainly at himself. How could he not have noticed someone putting a drug – certainly not chloral hydrate as McAdam had suggested - in his coffee?

He never was much good a tradecraft, he decided. *Give me the jungle any day. You knew where you were with a jungle. Jungles could be uncompromising and could be your greatest enemy. They could also be your greatest friend. You just needed to know what you were doing. Once under the canopy it was like being in another world. A wild world of danger and safety*, mused Royle.

Royle sat down at his writing table to read a letter from his son. He realised it was too long since having seen Adi. And his mission overseas meant Adi had to spend Christmas at boarding school. He vowed to make it up to his son, and think up some story to explain his Aunt Mel's disappearance. Royle began to write a cheque to pay for Adi's board and lodging over the Christmas holidays.

The squeak of his garden gate opening and then crashing shut brought him back to the real world. After a short pause the doorbell rang.

Royle let out a deep, exasperated breath. The last thing he wanted at the moment was a joining of conversation with a visitor, whoever it was. Whether it be a brush salesman, a Jehovah's Witness, or a neighbour inviting him to a New Year's Eve party, Tom Royle was determined to send them away and enjoy his melancholy alone.

Royle rose reluctantly from his chair. The remaining newspapers that had been resting on his knee slid to the floor with a collapsing crumple.

Peering through the spy-hole in the door, Royle recognised a student – no, an ex-student. Malcolm ... Michael ... Somebody?

He was still trying to recall the name as he opened the door, saying 'Ah, hello. Not seen you for a while. How's the graduate life treating you ... er?'

'Matthew, Dr Royle. Matthew Skelton. And post-university life is treating me very well, thanks to you.'

'Why of course, Mr Skelton. How could I forget? A First in combined South East Asian History and Oriental Languages, if I remember rightly.'

'You do, sir.'

Royle looked at the young man with a new spark of recognition. Matthew Skelton was dressed in a leather jacket and flared blue Levi jeans. Despite the chill he wore a red Che Guevara tee-shirt and a university scarf. His feet were shod in light brown suede boots. Still a student by appearance, but Royle noted his once collar-length black hair was now neatly shorn. Royle remembered another thing about young Mr Skelton. Royle had recommended him as a possible MI6 recruit in his unofficial role as SIS talent spotter on campus.

'Please come in, Mr Skelton. Tell me all about yourself.'

Royle opened the door wide and showed Skelton into the house. 'I must apologise for the mess, but we had a bit of a fire a few weeks ago and I have only just returned home.'

'Yes, I heard about it, Dr Royle. I'm glad you're all right. And your sister?'

Royle looked sharply at his former star student, but remained silent. In the lounge, Royle indicated a chair for Skelton to sit in.

'So, Mr Skelton, what brings you back?'

Skelton smiled, and looked a little embarrassed. 'I know you put my name forward. I was recruited and I have been given the post of junior case officer.'

'Ah,' said Royle, nodding sagely, his eyes boring into those of the younger man.

'Dr Royle, you're my case.'

'How very inappropriate,' said Royle.

'Perhaps,' said Skelton. 'But your mission isn't finished yet, Dr Royle.' Royle continued to gaze at his former student, but remained silent.

'Dr Royle, I have been assigned to you so that you can now complete your mission.'

'I see,' said Royle.

'Sir, I've seen your file and your service record. I know your mission to retrieve Li Pengfei was beset with problems. I also know that Li Pengfei has surfaced again in Kuala Lumpur.

'Yes he has,' said Royle, and handed Skelton the letter from Amelia.

After a quick read Skelton handed the letter back. 'This could complicate things,' the young MI6 officer ruminated. 'How long have they ...'

'Known each other?' interrupted Royle. 'In both the platonic and the biblical sense, since the Emergency. It ended when Li Pengfei's communist forces faced final defeat and he was forced to disappear. It began again in Hong Kong a few days ago.'

'We must bring Li Pengfei to London,' said Skelton, seemingly unable to think of anything else to say. 'His life is in danger. We believe Chinese intelligence agents want him dead and we need to get vital information out of him.'

'And then what, Mr Skelton? Set him loose to fend for himself?'

'I don't know. That's not my decision. What I do know is that Li Pengfei is a maverick and should be reined in.'

'Perhaps my sister has succeeded in reining him in, as you say. They have gone back to the place where they first met and fell in love.'

'Dr Royle, I don't know the background to your sister and Li Pengfei, but I do know that the Chinese MSS have him in their sights. He's a marked man, and if your sister gets in the way she will be killed.'

Royle leaned back in his chair and exhaled deeply. 'I'm tired, Matthew.'

'I understand that, sir. But we need you, we really do.'

Royle nodded slowly, then regained his composure and sat up straight. 'What's my status currently?'

'Still active ... Colonel Royle.'

'Dammit,' muttered Royle. 'Well, in that case, when do we leave?'

'In a week, sir. If you can put all your affairs in order in a week, I will arrange everything else.'

Royle reached for the telephone. He needed to ring Adi's school to extend the boy's stay.

*

Royle and Skelton's Boeing 747 landed at Kuala Lumpur International Airport under an early January cloud-leaden sky. It was a comfortable 26 degrees Celsius at mid-day and both men felt cool in the light business suits they had selected for the journey.

They rented a small Japanese-made Datsun car and drove into the city centre. They had rooms booked at the plush Sheraton Imperial, a 38-storey building in the heart of Kuala Lumpur's business and commercial district. It suited their cover as visiting businessmen.

As Skelton drove through the maze of roads and streets into the centre, Royle stared through the front passenger window, always startled by the changing face of Kuala Lumpur. In his Malaya days, his visits to Kuala Lumpur were infrequent. The now glittering and bustling city of concrete and glass was then little more than a small, untidy, backwater town. Now it had grown, and was still growing, as the commercial capital of modern Malaysia. Royle had visited the city a number of times in an academic capacity, and the ongoing metamorphosis of Kuala Lumpur never failed to make him catch his breath. The independent Malaysia had done well, and a small part of Royle felt immensely proud that his actions had played a part in that success.

On arrival and after check-in they had arranged to meet in the hotel bar after taking their luggage – one small suitcase each – into their separate rooms. Twenty minutes later both were sitting in a secluded bar alcove, sipping a cold beer compliments of the management.

'It's 2.30pm now. We'll meet the SIS resident in an hour here.' Skelton slid a small street map across the tiny square table so Royle could see it. Skelton pointed at the Cathedral of St John's. 'It's a 30-minute ride across town by taxi,' said Skelton. 'Especially at this time. The roads are manic and it's the first week of the new year. Everything will be frantic.'

They finished their drinks, changed into casual clothes, then picked up a cab from the front of the hotel – Skelton was back in his jeans and suede boots, only this time wearing a striped shirt with the top two buttons undone and a light windjammer jacket; Royle wore Chinos, loafers, a plain light blue shirt open by a single neck button, and a lightweight canvas jacket. Twenty-five minutes later they were dropped off on Jalan Bukit Nanas, the road where the cathedral complex was located.

After ten minutes a portly figure emerged from the cathedral book shop. Royle couldn't believe his eyes. The last time he had seen Reginald Campbell was during the closing days of the Emergency. Royle had been a successful MI6 intelligence gatherer against the communist Malayan National Liberation Army, and was gearing up for retirement.

Campbell had been a member of Military Intelligence and was a Major. He had worked as liaison with SIS during the war and remained with MI6 during the Emergency. It seemed that whenever Royle had planned anything, or required covert aircraft or submarines to infiltrate Royle behind Japanese lines, Campbell always seemed to be there to mess up the arrangements. They did not get on well together.

Royle put on his broadest smile and stretched his hand out in greeting. Campbell was the first to speak.

'Well I never, Tommy Royle. I thought we'd seen the last of you 14 or so years ago.'

'Ditto, Reggie. Ditto,' replied Royle.

'I see you are both acquainted,' said Skelton.

'Acquainted?' laughed Campbell. 'We were very nearly joined at the hip in the old days.'

'Not quite joined, Reggie. More like attached. A bit like a mosquito, or a leech,' said Royle.

'Don't be like that, old boy. We're on the same side now,' Campbell went on, still laughing, but now with an edge to his voice.

'We should have been on the same side then Reggie. But you were always a secret squirrel first and foremost.'

'As were you, Tommy. We just had different priorities.' Campbell then turned to Skelton in a loud aside. 'The SOE were always too gung-ho for their own good, even when they change their spots.'

Skelton looked at the veteran agents and realised that there was an enormous amount of ill-feeling between the two. It was going to make his job all the harder if they didn't put aside their differences. And this being Skelton's first big mission, he was determined to make it work.

Skelton lightly gripped both men by the arm and light-heartedly said: 'I suppose you can talk about old times later. Right now we have got a fish to land, and we need to get to him as soon as possible. Where can we talk?'

'We can go to the Paradise Bar, just across the road. It's loud,' said Campbell, then walked off, dodging the traffic and entering a dingy-looking bar with a day-glo pink awning over the door. Royle and Skelton followed. A wall of music struck them as they walked in and found Campbell in a corner booth, a gin and tonic already in his hand. The two men sat at Campbell's table, Royle raising a hand to attract the barman's attention. Blaring out of a visibly vibrating wall speaker was Alice Cooper's "School's Out", a three-year-old chart hit.

'Now then, down to business, gentlemen,' said Campbell, barely making himself audible over the racket. 'We have managed to trace Li Pengfei and his little woman ...' Royle gave Campbell a murderous look. '... Sorry, old boy. I mean to say your errant sister Amelia. Anyway, we have traced them both to a small place on the coast, Kuala Selangor, about 60 miles from KL. They are ...'

The barman came over and took their order. Beer for Royle and Skelton, another gin and tonic for Campbell.

The music changed to T Rex and "Children of the Revolution". The barman left and Campbell continued: 'As I was saying, they are living in a rented house at the end of Jalan Karamat Tanjong, in Kuala Selangor. You can't miss it. Just drive to the end of the road until you come to a modern white walled bungalow with a red tiled roof. It doesn't seem to have a street number – none that I could find anyway. But there is a yellow post box outside with the name Sederhana written on it. I believe that means "lucky" in English.'

The barman returned with a tray of drinks and threw the slip of paper containing the bill vaguely in Campbell's direction. Campbell slid this, together with the slip containing the price of his first drink, towards the centre of the table.

'You take the E1 out of KL then bear left onto the E35 until you hit Route 54. The road's also known as Sungai Buloh.' Campbell took a long swig of his drink, finishing half of it, then placed it noisily down on the table, missing the paper coaster the barman had provided. 'After that, follow Route 54 all the way to Kuala Selangor.'

'Nice seeing you Tommy. It has certainly been a long time. Perhaps if you get the chance we can catch up a little when all this is over.' Campbell finished his drink, wiped his mouth with the back of his hand, stood up and left.

Royle and Skelton looked at each other, decided not to finish their beer, and went out of the bar, leaving some ringgits on the table to cover the price of the drinks.

As they left the music was still stuck in a 1972 time warp as Roxy Music's "Virginia Plain" roared, filling the empty yet mysteriously still smoke-filled bar.

As they emerged the sun was beginning to break through a solid ceiling of cloud and they hailed a taxi back to the Sheraton Imperial.

They arrived in time for afternoon tea and sat in one of the hotel's ornate lounges drinking tea in comfortable armchairs.

'We leave tomorrow morning,' said Royle.

*

Royle and Skelton went down to breakfast at 8am. Royle tucked in to a traditional Nasi Kandar, a fragrant fish curry served up with meat in chilli and boiled eggs. Skelton picked almost nervously at his Nasi Dagang, a glutinous rice served with a fish curry, coconut and cucumber pickle. It was a culture shock for Skelton, but a taste of home for Royle.

After the traditional Malay breakfast, Royle felt a new man, especially after the long flight and the strained meeting with Campbell.

They set off in their hired Datsun along the route described by the SIS resident in Kuala Lumpur, fought their way through heavy morning traffic, then settled back into a leisurely drive through the outskirts of the still growing city, rapidly making its name as the newest of the economic Asian Tigers. High-rise buildings were flying up in KL as the city became a hub of international trade. Mining, agriculture and rubber production were no longer the staple markets of Malaysia. It was quickly establishing itself as an important industrial nation. The proof could be seen in the smog of the city centre, which depleted as one radiated out and into the countryside. The tropical forest was a constant feature as they left the city – that and the flat fields where rice was cultivated. Villages flew by as they made their way to Kuala Selangor, arriving in the small town nearly two hours after leaving the hotel. Malaysia's roads, even the main auto routes, still left a lot to be desired.

They found the house as Campbell had described it, at the end of the long and winding Jalan Karamat Tanjong road. A white detached bungalow with a red-tiled roof amid a small patch of land consisting of grass but mostly clay-coloured soil and dust. Outside stood a yellow post box bearing the inscription Sederhana.

They parked the car at the front and walked up the uneven, crazy-paved driveway.

Royle took a deep breath and knocked. There was no answer. After knocking a second, then a third time, Royle and Skelton wandered back to the car. They got in and drove a quarter of a mile to a left turn. They took the turn and parked the car near the mouth of the Selangor River, which flows into the Straits of Malacca. Kuala Selangor turned out to be a pretty seaside town, popular with KL city-dwellers seeking weekend relief from their hard labours. On a hill overlooking the town was a quaint old lighthouse which warned shipping of dangerous currents, rocks and landfall at the mouth of the river. All around the two men silverleaf monkeys silently gathered, waiting for any food tidbit the men may have had for them. The simians were to be disappointed as the men walked to a nearby tea house for some shade and refreshment. The noon-day sun was beating down at a warm 28 degrees in a blue sky littered with cotton wool clouds. They decided to hang around and try again mid-afternoon.

Mid-afternoon came and went. Two further visits to the house ended in failure. A look through the windows front and back confirmed the building was being lived in but was so far unoccupied. Royle and Skelton decided to move the car a little down the road, in view of the house so they could see when Li Pengfei and Amelia arrived. Instead of a straightforward meet, greet and retreat operation, this was becoming a complicated stake-out.

After a dramatic tropical sunset over the Selangor River, night came as if someone had turned off a light.

It was coming up to ten at night when a car drew up at the house. It was a black 1970 Plymouth GTX with a white vinyl top. It looked scratched and dented, but its engine sounded tuned and fast.

Li Pengfei emerged from the driver's side of the car and walked up the crazy-paving towards the house. As he walked he looked left and right at the ground. As Li Pengfei reached the door he stopped and crouched to examine the ground, then quickly walked to the back of the house.

Another car appeared, a silver-coloured Ford Capri. It stopped behind Li Pengfei's Plymouth and Amelia stepped out. She was wearing a beige linen trouser suit and her hair was swept back into a pony tail. She looked younger, thought Royle.

Amelia began to walk up the driveway when Li Pengfei came running down from the back of the house. He looked distressed, thought Royle, then he realised that Li Pengfei had detected their earlier visits. In the split second it took Royle to smile and give credit to Li Pengfei's superior tradecraft, Royle had left the Datsun and began striding towards the house, waving his arms wildly to attract Li Pengfei's attention. Looking first confused, then determined, Skelton followed.

Li Pengfei saw Royle walking towards him seconds before Amelia. She turned and looked dumbfounded as Royle approached them, followed by a younger man who looked like a student, she thought.

As Royle got within five metres of Li Pengfei, the double agent and erstwhile colleague of Tom Royle pulled a gun – an old Webley service revolver – from his inside jacket pocket, and pointed it directly at Tom Royle's chest, the widest part of the body, hence easier to hit. He held the handgun in a classic double grip that showed an intention to use it. Royle stopped abruptly and instinctively raised his hands, palms facing Li Pengfei.

'Are you mad?' blurted Royle.

'Maybe, Thomas. What are you doing here?'

'Unfinished business, Li Pengfei. Have you forgotten, I've travelled half way around the world – twice – to bring you back to London.'

'I haven't forgotten,' Li Pengfei said, then swivelled his aim towards the approaching Skelton. 'Stay where you are.' Li Pengfei directed his gaze back on Royle. 'Who is this boy?'

Royle was unable to stop himself from grinning. 'Let me introduce you to Mr Matthew Skelton. A former first-class student of mine ... and currently my designated case officer.' Li Pengfei looked at the younger man and did not seem impressed.

'Is there anyone else with you?' asked Li Pengfei.

'Just us,' said Royle, hands still raised. 'Are you going to shoot us, or can we come inside and talk?' Royle said.

'Inside,' Li Pengfei ordered, still holding the gun on the two men as he led them up the driveway and into the house.

'Your tradecraft is still far better than mine,' said Royle to Li Pengfei as they entered the house.

'It was always so, Thomas. It was like a herd of elephants had trampled all around the house.' For the first time Li Pengfei smiled and clicked the weapon's safety catch back on. He placed it in the waistband of his trousers and beckoned the two men to sit. Amelia followed them in after making sure her brother was telling the truth about there being just the two of them.

'This is a fine welcome, I must say,' said Royle jovially.

Then Skelton spoke up. 'If I may, perhaps I could explain our position, Mr Li.'

Li Pengfei looked suspiciously at the young man, then nodded.

Skelton cleared his throat nervously, then spoke. 'Mr Li, Colonel Royle and I have been sent by SIS to request that you accompany us back to London for your final debrief before retirement. We understand the difficulties you faced last time in Hong Kong and we appreciate the situation you find yourself in. Your travel expenses will be taken care of, as will those of Mrs Harper. I must stress that it is imperative that you return with us. After that you will be free to go your own way. We can offer you a very good pension and a house anywhere in the United Kingdom, or possibly elsewhere in the Commonwealth if necessary.'

Li Pengfei looked at the young operative for long moments, then said, 'How did you find us?'

Skelton looked exasperated. It was not the response he had expected.

Royle was less surprised. His old comrade was security conscious to his very soul. He and Amelia had disappeared off the map and Li Pengfei had been careful to cover their tracks. Did he know of the letter Amelia had sent, and which may have helped give away their position?'

'I'm sorry, Mr Li, I cannot reveal our methods ...' Skelton was saying, when Royle interrupted.

'Campbell,' said Royle. Skelton looked shocked, as if Royle had been revealed the Fourth Man, the missing high profile MI6 spy who had been working for the Russians along with the traitors Kim Philby, Guy Burgess and Donald McLean.

Royle turned to Skelton and said acidly, 'Don't be so surprised, son. Li Pengfei and I go back a long way. We've dealt with enemies and treachery more times than you've sucked at your mother's tit.'

'Campbell!' exploded the normally unruffled Li Pengfei.

'He found you,' said Royle.

'He's even worse at tradecraft that you are, Thomas,' Li Pengfei laughed. Then he grew serious again. 'If Campbell found us we are in trouble.'

'Why, because he's so useless?' laughed Royle.

'No Thomas, because he is so compromised,' Li Pengfei revealed. 'I never had proof, but I am certain Campbell has been selling information to the highest bidder.'

'Nonsense, old friend. What secrets does he possess? None.'

'Precisely, Thomas. He's been stuck here in Malaysia for quite a number of years now. Malaysia isn't exactly Espionage Central, Thomas. Not anymore. He knows he's been stuck in this backwater to keep him out of the way. It's a sunset posting, and he has no means of bettering himself after all these years. He hasn't had a promotion since 1965.'

'We can't accuse a fellow officer of corruption just because he's not very good at his job and because we don't like him very much,' said Royle.

Li Pengfei's shoulders stooped and his face seemed to turn grey. His unhealthy pallor reminded Royle of the sick Li Pengfei who trekked out of the jungle to talk peace and was almost murdered by the army after the peace talks broke down back in 1957.

'It isn't just that, Thomas. Look how he was. When we were SOE, Campbell was always the most vocal of his SIS colleagues to berate our operations. His operations always came to nothing. In fact he seemed to work hard trying to sabotage our work. And he succeeded more times than I like to mention.

'Remember our early attempts to land on Perak? Back in 1942 when we were trying to increase our SOE operations on the mainland? The only way was by submarine, but Campbell – and Six – made sure we couldn't get hold of any British boats. Any British submarine that became available was snapped up by MI6. There weren't many to start with because at that time the priority was fighting the war in Europe. But we had our own struggle to get back to Malaya. We both went through guerrilla training – SIS tried to disrupt that. They took our submarines, so we had to find our own – thanks be to the Dutch. The Royal Dutch Navy was still active in the area, out of the Dutch East Indies – Indonesia as it is now. They helped us more than our own, until the Japanese took them out of the equation.

'It was an old school thing, Thomas. They are under the umbrella of the Foreign and Commonwealth Office, we were under the Ministry of Economic Warfare, at least until Mountbatten became Supreme Allied Commander South East Asia and SOE formed its special group for Malaya – Force 136. You must remember the struggles we had, Thomas? Not just against the Japanese.'

'I remember, old friend. They made a very difficult time almost impossible. But we ploughed on and succeeded better than they, or even we, could have imagined,' Royle explained. 'But our mutual dislike is no reason to believe Campbell has sold us out. Despite all his faults …'

Skelton then spoke. 'Gentlemen, now we have cleared the air, perhaps we can agree to travel fairly soon?'

Then Amelia stood in front of the three men and said, 'Why can't we stay here. Malaya – Malaysia – is our home. It always has been and always will be.'

'It isn't part of the British Empire any more, Amelia. There is no British Empire any more,' said Royle.

'I know that, Tommy. I'm not stupid. We want to stay.'

Royle looked at Skelton. After all, the junior man was in charge of this operation despite Royle's higher rank.

Li Pengfei interjected before anyone could say anything else.

'My old friend, Thomas. Amelia. I am afraid that whatever we are allowed to do in the long term, in the short term we must go away from here. Immediately.'

'You're convinced Campbell is compromised?' Skelton said.

'I am, Mr Skelton,' said Li Pengfei.

'All this on a mere feeling?' wondered Skelton.

'Mr Skelton … Matthew,' said Royle. 'Mr Li Pengfei here is famous for his finely tuned sixth sense. He seems to know when danger is around. He knew there had been snoopers – us – at his house today. He knew this before he even began looking for signs. In our Force 136 days he knew when a camp was going to be raided by the Japanese. Not through any outside intelligence. He just knew. When he came to the peace talks at Baling in 1957 Li Pengfei knew there was an extreme danger he may not survive, and to his credit and supreme courage, he came anyway. He has a knack for sniffing out danger. That's why he's been off our radar for so long. Even though there is a lack of concrete evidence, if Li Pengfei has a feeling that our dealings with Campbell has compromised his safety, then I for one am willing to listen. Why do you think London was content to keep Campbell in relative obscurity for so long? A virtual lifetime, in fact. They had their suspicions but couldn't prove anything. Rather than face an embarrassing situation of having a rogue officer they just abandoned him here. Now he must be ready to retire, and a nice little bit of treachery against Li Pengfei here would be a handy supplement to his pension. I must agree with Li Pengfei. We should leave this house now.'

'Yes, I agree,' Amelia said.

'Very well,' said Skelton, resignedly. 'I will bow to the superior experience of both of you. I shouldn't really say, but I have been a little in awe of you both since reading your files for the first time.'

'All right then. Li Pengfei, Mel, do you want to pack a few things before we leave?' asked Royle.

'Just a few things, our passports and our money,' said Amelia.

'Forget the passports,' said Skelton, now back in control of the situation. 'We'll head for the British High Commission in Kuala Lumpur and we'll arrange fresh documentation for you when we get there.'

Minutes later the four were ready to leave.

Again Skelton took the initiative. 'May I suggest something? As Mrs Harper is an innocent party in all of this, perhaps she should take our hire car, just in the very unlikely event of Mr Li Pengfei being right about Reggie Campbell. If Campbell is bent, then it stands to reason he has both your cars tagged. I should take Mrs Harper's Capri, and Colonel Royle and Mr Li Pengfei should travel in the Plymouth.'

'Excellent thinking, Skelton. That's a good plan,' said Royle, smiling to himself that Skelton still believed Amelia to be innocent, when in fact she was a principle player. 'Anyone know where the High Commission is?'

'It's at Jalan Ampang in the city centre,' replied Skelton. 'Mrs Harper?'

'Yes, I know it. We've visited,' she said.

'I can guide you, Thomas,' said Li Pengfei.

'All right,' said Skelton. 'Let's go. Keep to traffic laws and we'll rendezvous there. Good luck everyone.'

All left the house for their respective vehicles. Despite Skelton's scepticism about Li Pengfei's suspicions, both he and Royle could not help but feel a heightened sense of awareness of their surroundings, and an unaccountable mounting fear that something terrible was going to happen.

In the Datsun hire car, Amelia carried out a u-turn in the road and headed back towards Kuala Lumpur. Next, with Li Pengfei in the driving seat of his powerful Plymouth GTX, he and Royle set off following Amelia, with Skelton taking up the rear in Amelia's Ford Capri.

The three vehicles had been driving in convoy for about an hour when Skelton flashed the Capri's headlights three times in quick succession followed by one long flash. It was the time honoured signal that they were being followed. On a quiet stretch of Route 54, Skelton's Capri moved up alongside Li Pengfei's Plymouth. Skelton shouted through the open window, 'I'll move up to the front and look for somewhere to pull in. Somewhere busy with people, hopefully.' Royle gave the thumbs up sign and Skelton moved up alongside the Datsun driven by Amelia Harper. 'Mrs Harper,' he shouted. 'I'm going to lead and stop somewhere.' Amelia nodded, her hands tight on the steering wheel. Skelton accelerated to move his Capri to the front of the line.

Ten minutes later Skelton spotted a large, busy looking late night outdoor market. He indicated left and turned to park in a street nearby. Amelia and Li Pengfei followed in their cars.

'Are you sure we were followed?' asked Royle.

'Fairly sure,' said Skelton.

'I think we were tailed,' agreed Li Pengfei. 'There were car lights behind us all the way from when Skelton overtook us. They slowed when we slowed and sped up when we did. I know we weren't really being very evasive, but it looked suspicious to me.'

'Who could it be?' asked Amelia, sounding worried.

'Perhaps it's Campbell making sure the pick-up goes according to plan. After all, he's the only other person who knew your whereabouts,' said Royle in his most reasonable and reassuring tone of voice, although he didn't believe a word of it.

'That's what I feel worried about,' said Li Pengfei gloomily.

'Well, let's head into the market. We should get something to eat as it's getting quite late and I for one am quite famished,' said Skelton.

The four headed into the throng of the market and soon found a street-food stand with tables and chairs all around. They ordered a meze of dishes, which included Malay delicacies satay, nasi goreng, rojack, and char kway teow, all washed down by tea from the Cameron Highlands.

After they had eaten they wandered the market aimlessly, all the while keeping an eye open for possible assailants.

At a stall selling children's toys Royle spotted something that would help them on their journey. It was a two-way radio set for the US-made GI Joe action figure. Each pack contained two two-way radios for children to play soldiers with. The radios were very short range, merely a matter of metres, but they would prove useful to three cars in close convoy with no other means of communication, especially if trouble appeared for them again. Royle bought two sets so that each car would have a radio transceiver, plus batteries to power them.

After an hour of shadow watching, and finding none, the four decided to head back to their cars and continue on their journey.

As they walked into the street where their cars were they knew immediately that something was wrong. The street was deadly quiet, whereas before it had been bustling with people when they arrived. The four stood in the shadows watching for signs of movement. They stood watching for a good twenty minutes, and finally seeing nothing decided to continue to their cars.

They emerged into an area lit by street lamps, illuminating where their cars were parked. But as they neared their vehicles a figure moved out of the shadows. He was Chinese and carried a long-bladed knife. Another Chinese moved into the light. He too carried a long-bladed knife.

Skelton, Royle and Li Pengfei moved to the front of Amelia, ready for the inevitable fight.

But Amelia pushed her way forward so that she was standing at the front, facing the two armed men.

'Oh my God,' she muttered. Then simply said 'hello' to the two armed Chinese in a loud voice – 'Ni hao.'

They responded with a sneer. 'Ni hao, Amelia Harper.' Then they bowed respectfully and went on, 'Jiuwen daming,' a greeting signifying extreme respect.

Skelton looked at Amelia and for the first time was truly confused. Why should these men show such great respect for this woman?

Li Pengfei said, 'Their accents are not Malay. These men are from the People's Republic. They are MSS.'

Royle nodded. It must have beden the MSS who had attacked them at the Hong Kong cocktail bar. He had been drugged and the Hong Kong SIS resident slightly injured. Their target was Li Pengfei. The MSS never forgot about double agents, and they regarded Li Pengfei as a traitor because of his activities in Malaya during the Emergency and most recently with the Viet Cong. On the other hand MSS never forgot a friend either, and they regarded Amelia Harper as one such friend, even though she was irrevocably linked to Li Pengfei through love.

'I say we split up and run,' said the inexperienced Skelton.

'No,' said Royle. 'We stand and fight. They want Li Pengfei and it's our job to get him back to London, remember?'

'Yes sir, of course,' responded Skelton. 'I hope you're still in shape, Colonel Royle. These boys look pretty handy with those knives.'

'I don't suppose you're carrying a gun by any chance?' asked Royle, knowing the answer would be 'no'.

'It's not company policy, sir,' said Skelton, who was now starting to look nervous as the two Chinese agents started to close in. Skelton shifted his stance into a better fighting position.

The three men again took up a position shielding Amelia, with Royle in the centre and Li Pengfei to his left.

Royle looked at Li Pengfei and shrugged. 'After all we've been through we appear to be seriously outmanoeuvred.'

'I don't think you know me at all, Thomas,' said Li Pengfei. With that he smiled at his old companion, unbuttoned his jacket and reached into his inside pocket to produce the old Webley revolver he had earlier pointed at Royle outside his home. Li Pengfei had switched it from his trousers waistband to the jacket pocket as they left the house for the last time. Li Pengfei went into a crouch, held the weapon with both hands and fired off two shots in quick succession. The two Chinese agents dropped. Their long knives clattered to the ground as they crumpled to the pavement.

'Get in the cars,' ordered Li Pengfei. Then turning to Royle said, 'I'll be along momentarily.'

Li Pengfei walked towards the two fallen men, his revolver still smoking in his hand. Both men were mortally wounded and groaning in pain. Royle watched as Li Pengfei said something to the men in their native language, then casually – expertly – broke their necks.

Li Pengfei returned to the cars and told Skelton to lead off. They would continue on their journey to the High Commission in convoy, all the while watching for enemies.

The three-car convoy slid away, back on to Route 54 and bound for KL. After a five-minute drive on the empty road blue and red flashing police lights began to approach from ahead. Two police cars, sirens screaming, sped passed them heading towards the market. The bodies had been found.

Royle looked at Li Pengfei driving the Plymouth. 'It won't be safe on this road for much longer. We need to find somewhere to lie low for a while.'

'I know a place,' said Li Pengfei.

'All right. I'll tell them we're taking the lead.' Royle picked up his toy radio, pulled up the telescopic aerial at the top and pressed the transmit button. 'Skelton, this is Royle, are you receiving, over?'

The radio's speaker crackled, but with no response. Royle repeated the call, with the same outcome.

'These bloody toy radios have too short a range. They won't even reach Skelton in the lead car,' said Royle.

Just then his radio crackled into life and Amelia's thin, tinny voice came through. 'Tommy, if you can hear this then I can relay a message to Skelton if you wish.'

Elated, Royle spoke through his radio to his sister. 'Thanks, that should work. We need to disappear for a while and we know a place to take cover, but we will need to take the lead, and Skelton will need to take the rear to watch for any other cars following us, over.'

'Will do,' crackled Amelia's voice, then came silence.

After a few minutes Amelia's voice came through again. 'He'll do it.'

Li Pengfei's Plymouth indicated to overtake and accelerated to take over as lead car. Amelia then overtook Skelton in the Datsun hire car to again be in the middle of the group.

Soon Li Pengfei's lead car began to slow and indicated a turn down a narrow track surrounded by pitch black jungle. The other cars followed.

They drove slowly along the bumpy track for about a mile before turning off into a clearing in the trees. They secreted their cars behind jungle bushes, then turned off their car engines and lights.

Royle and Li Pengfei got out of the Plymouth and moved over to the other cars. 'We'll stay here for the night,' said Royle. 'We should remain in our cars, but roll the windows up to keep out mosquitoes, and anything else that may want to bed down beside you for the night. Pengfei, if you want to join Amelia in the Datsun, I don't mind. We'll come up with a plan in the morning. I will take first watch, followed by Skelton then Pengfei. It's almost two o'clock in the morning now. We'll take an hour each, by which time it should be dawn. Sleep well everyone.'

*

The sunrise was almost as dramatic as the previous evening's sunset. None of the four fugitives had slept much, although all had managed to doze a little. Thanks to their late supper they did not feel hungry, which was fortunate because there was no food to be had. The four gathered beneath the tropical canopy to work out a plan of action.

'We should continue to KL,' said Skelton. 'Our priority is to get a flight back to London.'

'Our priority is to stay alive, young man,' rebuked Royle. But Skelton was undeterred.

'My mission is to bring Li Pengfei back to London for his final debrief. What you or Mrs Harper does is entirely up to yourselves. But Mr Li Pengfei is my responsibility and my priority,' said Skelton. He was clearly tired and angry.

Li Pengfei and Amelia watched the exchange as it became heated.

'Look Skelton, you said earlier that you would defer to my wider experience in these matters. Now my experience tells me that the British High Commission is the last place we should be seen near. They will be watching for us.'

'I am aware of that, Colonel Royle, but once inside we will be safe ...'

'Don't be so damn naive, Skelton. It's a High Commission, not a secure embassy building. Security is minimal and it's staffed by pen-pushers. If we were to be attacked by letter then it would be the ideal place, but I doubt if they would be able to repel knives and bullets. We need a fall-back plan.'

Skelton fell silent. Royle, Li Pengfei and Amelia were all watching him hopefully.

'Well, of course I have a fall-back plan. That's standard procedure. Unfortunately it involves Reggie Campbell again,' said Skelton, now feeling considerably foolish. Li Pengfei shook his head slowly, visibly disappointed.

But Royle kindly placed his hand on Skelton's shoulder. 'That's quite understandable, Matthew.' Then he turned to the rest of the group. 'He couldn't have known that Campbell was less than trustworthy. Even if he isn't on the take, and we still don't know for sure, Campbell has always been pretty useless. But as the local SIS resident he was the obvious provider of any Plan B we may have been in need of. What we need now is a Plan C.'

As they struggled to form a new plan, the jungle seemed to come alive around them. Royle and Li Pengfei suddenly felt at home. But in some ways the situation they now found themselves in was more dire than in the days when they fought the Japanese from secret jungle bases, or when they tackled the MNLA from beneath the canopy, with Li Pengfei the inside man.

The sounds of newly awakened jungle wildlife drowned their deliberations.

'I believe,' said Royle, 'That the best course of action would be to dump the Plymouth and Capri here and all set off in the Datsun. It's far less conspicuous, and of course it isn't known, whereas your vehicles are.'

Royle turned to Li Pengfei. 'How many rounds do you have for your handgun?' he asked.

'Just the four remaining bullets in the chamber,' Li Pengfei said thoughtfully.

'Is there anything else in any of the cars we can use as weapons if the need arises?' queried Royle.

They rummaged through the cars' interiors, producing tyre levers, a couple of screwdrivers and a claw hammer.

Royle looked at the 'weapons'. 'We will have to make the best of a bad job. Next, I suggest we drive north, into Thailand, and head for the British Embassy in Bangkok. It's a long drive, but once there we will be able to get back in touch with SIS, get new documents and fly back home.'

It was a 900-mile journey north to the Thai capital, an arduous drive in the unsuitable Datsun. But by now all were convinced it would be suicide to use the Plymouth and the Capri on open roads anywhere in Malaysia. Police could be on the look-out for them after the killings of the two Chinese MSS agents, and Beijing's Ministry of State Security agents must surely know the cars for them to have been tailed in the first place.

They waited until nightfall again before abandoning their vehicles and setting off in the small Datsun. A driving rotation was agreed and Skelton agreed to be the first of the four to take the wheel. By this time they were all feeling very hungry. They stopped at a small roadside fruit stall and Skelton bought food to keep them going.

Six hours and 300 miles later they approached the Thai border having experienced no further mishaps en route. It was midnight.

The border post Royle had selected was manned by two Thai guards and no-one on the Malaysia side. The border took the form of a gate and barbed wire fence, all dimly lit by an inadequate floodlight. The Thai flag flew at the other side of the gate. As their car approached the two border guards appeared from a blockhouse, both carrying machine guns. Unsmilingly the guards appeared bored. Royle put on his best tourist face and handed one of the guards his British passport. Tucked inside was £50 in sterling. Skelton did the same for the second guard. Having been paid, the two guards opened the gate and waved the car through without even asking for further passports and checking the passengers. The Datsun drove into Thailand and headed towards Songkla before turning north up the isthmus towards Bangkok, another 600 miles away.

At five in the morning dawn was coming up fast as they approached Thung Song, a major town on the isthmus. A poor road had slowed their travel time, but in the town they found somewhere to breakfast and rest a while before filling up the car's tank with petrol and continuing on the journey.

It was late in the day when the outskirts of the Thai capital approached. The road system got better the nearer they got to Bangkok. And as the roads got better the air quality gradually grew worse. They drove into the city mayhem of traffic, traders and pedestrians crossing roads seemingly with a death wish.

They were given directions to the embassy by a cop on traffic duty and they abandoned the faithful Datsun in a side street close to the embassy compound on Wireless Road, in Pathumwan, Bangkok's main business area. Then watching for danger all the way to the embassy gates they walked in.

Skelton asked for the military attaché, giving his name and identity number to confirm his credentials, and the party of four – described as the Skelton party by embassy staff – were shown to an ante-room.

After a wait the attaché's secretary entered and invited them to a meeting. They were taken in a lift to the second floor and into a nondescript office with a large map of the world on one wall. A window overlooked the busy street outside and a desk was topped by tidy paperwork, two telephones and a green-shaded desk lamp. Behind the desk sat a man in his mid-forties, besuited and wearing horn-rimmed spectacles. His hair was cut in military style.

He stood to greet the Skelton party, smiling as he said, 'Good day to you, my name is Captain Drummond, military attaché. Welcome to Bangkok. What can we do for you?' Drummond indicated two chairs with an apologetic shrug.

'Thank you Capt Drummond, I'm Matt Skelton. I appreciate you seeing us unannounced.'

Drummond nodded, and still smiling concentrated his attention on the three older people with the young SIS officer.

Royle then took the initiative and spoke. 'Capt Drummond, we are grateful for your kindness at seeing us. I am Colonel Thomas Royle, and this is my sister Mrs Amelia Harper.' Then indicating Li Pengfei, Royle went on, 'I would like to introduce Mr Li Pengfei, an extremely important asset to the United Kingdom government for the past 30 years.'

Drummond look startled, but remained silent.

Skelton said, 'We need to take Mr Li Pengfei back to London for a final debrief, but unfortunately we ran into a little difficulty in Kuala Lumpur. We're hoping for better luck getting home from Thailand.'

'I see. Couldn't the High Commission in Malaysia help?' asked Drummond.

'Not secure enough, sir,' replied Skelton. 'There was an assassination attempt on Mr Li Pengfei's life by the Chinese counter-intelligence service. I'm afraid there was some shooting and we thought it best to leave the country.'

'Capt Drummond,' said Royle. 'Do you know the SIS resident in Kuala Lumpur?'

'Can't say I do, Colonel,' said Drummond. 'But I'm sure our own resident will know him.'

'I see,' said Royle. He looked at his companions, then focused his attention back on Drummond. 'I'll confide in you. We aren't sure that the SIS resident in KL can be completely trusted. Only he knew where to find Mr Li Pengfei, yet we were followed by the Chinese MSS and we were attacked.'

'Good grief,' expounded the military attaché, for the first time looking truly surprised.

Skelton added, 'I will need to contact the office to make them aware of our concerns.'

'Of course,' said Drummond. He then looked straight at Royle and said, 'All I know about you, sir, is that your name is Royle, you're a colonel and you have brought your sister with you.'

Royle smiled. 'That's really all you need to know, Captain Drummond. However, if you contact Fred Conti at the Saigon embassy I know he'll vouch for me. And for Mr Li Pengfei here.'

'You know Conti, colonel?'

'Just ask him, captain,' replied Royle.

After a brief moment of thought, Drummond pressed a button on his desk intercom and called his secretary in. She walked in immediately and Drummond said, 'Will you take these good people to the ante-room please, and give them some refreshments. They've had a long journey.' Then turning to the group said, 'I will join you shortly.'

An hour passed and the Skelton party enjoyed plates of sandwiches and cups of tea, courtesy of the embassy.

Then Drummond walked in, visibly more relaxed. He addressed Royle. 'Well, colonel, your story checks out with Conti. Good opportunity to catch up with him, we served together in Northern Ireland. Things are looking fairly grim for Saigon. Conti is busy making emergency evacuation plans.'

'Yes, things were looking bad when Mr Li Pengfei and I were there before Christmas,' said Royle.

'Now then,' said Drummond, addressing the whole group. 'We can't get your travel documents together for at least two days, so you are welcome to stay as guests of the embassy until such time that you are able to leave the country. The major difficulty is with travel documents. Only Colonel Royle and Mr Skelton have passports, and it would be best not to use them. So you need four emergency passports, which we are arranging now.'

Drummond opened the door and summoned a Royal Marine. 'This is Sergeant Dempsey. He will show you to your rooms. Let me reiterate, you should not leave the embassy grounds.' Drummond left the room and Sgt Dempsey showed the four to three guest rooms. Royle was to share a room with Skelton, while Li Pengfei and Amelia were given separate rooms.

In the event the documentation did not arrive for three days, and the Skelton party were becoming stir crazy as they waited. They took regular walks three or four times a day around the almost 13 acre embassy site, avoiding the section adjacent to the busy, smelly, six-lane Ploemchit ring-road; spent a lot of time in the grounds, taking in the park-like areas, the embassy's own lake, the statue of Queen Victoria and the imposing embassy war memorial. All the while they were accompanied by Sgt Dempsey.

On the third day Drummond reappeared. The Skelton party had not seen him since that day in his office. Now he had called them all to his office, where a large folder bulged with documentation.

'Thank you for your patience,' said Drummond. 'Your papers are now ready.' Drummond thrust his hand into the folder and retrieved four UK passports. 'Mr Skelton, yours is in the name of Smith – sorry. Lack of imagination in the registration office. Colonel Royle, yours is in the name of Rogers. Mrs Harper goes under the name of Hill, and Mr Li Pengfei has a British passport in the name of Lu Chen.' Drummond handed out the passports then produced air tickets.

'Your flights are business class to Heathrow leaving tomorrow morning. In addition Sgt Dempsey will accompany you to the airport with two other Royal Marines, all in civvies of course, as your security detail. Once in the air I'm very happy to say you will no longer be my responsibility.'

'We are eternally grateful, Capt Drummond. Please accept our thanks,' said Skelton.

*

Departure day arrived. Even though the sights and smells of the vibrant Thai capital beckoned, all in the Skelton party knew it would have been foolhardy to venture outside the embassy compound. Who knew what dangers awaited them in the vulnerable outside? The security detail, headed by Sgt Dempsey, was waiting at a side door. He and the two Royal Marines with him wore light suits, shirts and ties. All were checking the Browning 9mm semi-automatic sidearms they would carry in shoulder holsters beneath their suit jackets.

Mixed feelings at the departure played on the faces of the Skelton party. Skelton himself, the young SIS officer on his first important assignment, was merely relieved the operation was coming to a conclusion. He still felt unsure how he would write up his report, especially Campbell's part in things. His phone call to his MI6 headquarters at Century House on arrival at the Bangkok embassy, would surely have set the cat among the pigeons by now.

Royle too was glad to be heading home. He had endured a traumatic and distressing three months travelling many thousands of miles to end up in the thick of intrigue and danger, a life he thought he had waved goodbye to over a decade ago. His excitement at being homeward bound and a long awaited reunion with his son was tempered by the still damaged state of his house, and the pending move to the countryside.

Amelia Harper was worried. She had confessed her treachery to her brother and Li Pengfei. Would the two dearest people in her life reveal her sordid secret? Does anyone at MI6 know about her? She knew that now she had no choice but to go where her distinguished brother and her double agent lover took her. The trip back to England was a fait accompli as far as she was concerned.

Li Pengfei too was anxious about the trip to London. Although he had served London for more than 30 years in one way or another, remarkably this would be his first journey to the English capital, indeed to Europe. Yet his anxiety revolved around this final debrief. He felt he had not finished his work. Why else would he risk his life as a cadre leader for the Viet Cong, only to be pulled out of Vietnam just as the North Vietnam Army was starting its final offensive? Why should MI6 cut him loose now after all this time? And was it a coincidence that the Chinese version of the Soviet KGB, the MSS, was on his trail for the sole purpose of assassination?

Captain Drummond came down to see the party off and wish them good luck, shaking hands with each of them warmly.

He then turned to Skelton and said, 'Young man, you have done a splendid job so far. You should know that I have arranged a pick-up for you all at Heathrow. It will take you straight to Century House, and then individually on from there.'

'Thank you, sir. You have been most helpful, and I will include that in my report.'

It was time to leave.

The three Royal Marines and the Skelton party climbed aboard a 1972 VW Camper Bus, one of the Marines was driving, and it crunched along a gravel drive, through the embassy gates, and off in the direction of Bangkok International.

At the airport they emerged from the minibus to the pungent odour of aviation fuel in the atmosphere. The soldier driving the bus parked at the airport entrance and remained there while the remaining two Marines, led by Sgt Dempsey, shepherded the Skelton party towards check-in. This was a very quick affair as the party had no luggage. The soldiers then escorted them to the international departure lounge, leaving the airport premises only once the four had passed safely through passport control into the secure area where bored travellers awaited their various flights.

They bought books, newspapers and magazines and found seats as they settled down to wait for their flight. It was scheduled to leave in another two hours.

Amelia stood up and beckoned her brother to follow her. They converged on a queue at a coffee stall. Through a large window at the stall they were able to watch line upon line of airliners parked and awaiting passengers. Further in the distance one of the take-off runways was getting steadily busier as the morning wore on, with aircraft climbing into a cloudless morning sky.

'You know, Tommy. I was never a bad person,' said Amelia. 'I just did what I thought was right.'

'It was a bad thing you did, Amelia. I'm not sure I can forgive it.'

'Was it any worse a thing that Li Pengfei has done? He betrayed his people and you benefited.'

'Li Pengfei was an undercover operative working for the British Government all the time …'

'Even when he was out in Malaya killing British soldiers, planters and mine owners, creating terror wherever he went?'

Royle remained silent. He was well versed in this contradiction and he had wrestled with it for decades, never really coming to an adequate conclusion.

'Tommy,' continued Amelia. 'We were both double agents, only he is the hero because he worked for you. Forgive me.'

'I can't,' said Royle, a tremor in his voice betraying his emotions.

He walked away from the coffee stall and watched the aircraft through the concourse window. Amelia followed him.

'I know I can't change the past,' Amelia said quietly, 'But we can rebuild the future. Li Pengfei and I have come to terms with my actions and we are still in love. We want to be together more than anything else in the world. If he can forgive, then why can't you?'

Royle remained silent, but walked away shaking his head. Amelia returned to the other two.

'The coffee?' asked Skelton. Amelia looked non-plussed for a second, then said, 'Oh, yes, the coffee vendor wouldn't take sterling, and I have no Thai baht.' It was a feeble excuse, but it would have to do, and Skelton looked satisfied. Li Pengfei, however, gave Amelia a puzzled look.

Presently Royle returned to his seat, but remained broodingly silent, ignoring all attempts of conversation by members of the group.

*

The flight to Heathrow was uneventful and after 14 hours the Skelton party touched down. London's premier airport was getting quieter as the evening drew on. The night sky was clear and cloud-free, and where light pollution didn't dazzle the stars blazed. It was just touching minus-two Celsius and a hoary frost was settling.

The reception committee was waiting for them airside. Two young, well-built men from Century House had been assigned to escort the four to SIS headquarters.

They took the party through, bypassing passport control at the British end, and led them towards two powerful black Jaguar XJ6 saloons, each with its own driver, parked on an unused taxi-way by the airport fire station.

Skelton and Li Pengfei entered the back of the lead car, Tom Royle and Amelia Harper got into the rear vehicle. The two SIS escorts got into one car each in the front passenger seat.

The two cars' 2.8 litre engines roared to life almost simultaneously and the lead vehicle set off, followed by the rear car, along a wide turning circumference to head for the perimeter gate. They were waved through by airport security officers and headed for London the long way round.

Both vehicles drove at a steady pace on a country road which led to the south and away from the motorway into the city. For one of the quieter roads around Britain's biggest international airport, it seemed remarkably busy, considering the hour. It was approaching 11pm, yet there was a constant stream of traffic, mostly going in the opposite direction.

All the way from the airport Royle puzzled about Amelia's confession. *Could that be it?* he wondered. *Had the British, the Americans and the Chinese got their knickers in such a twist, brought me and Ferney out of retirement, and chased each other half way round the world for my sister's indiscretions all those years ago?*

Royle watched the street lights blur as they sped past. Houses were thinning out now as they began to head into a stretch of open countryside where the road bisected farmers' fields. *There has to be something more. And it has to be Li Pengfei.*

Royle decided action was necessary, and he needed an urgent word with his old comrade-in-arms Li Pengfei in the other car.

'Driver, I need you to pull over. I'm going to be sick,' shouted Royle. It was the oldest trick in the book, and for a good reason. The ruse usually worked on the unsuspecting.

The car pulled over and the SIS man in the front passenger seat radioed the lead car to tell them to do likewise. Royle jumped out of the car and feigned vomiting into the grass verge. The lead car containing Skelton and Li Pengfei signalled, slowed to a stop, then reversed nearer Royle's car.

Skelton got out of the car, followed by Li Pengfei. 'Probably after effects of stress and a long flight,' Skelton said to their SIS minders.

To their surprise, Royle immediately stood upright and, grabbing Li Pengfei by the arm, pulled him to one side.

'Pengfei, I have a question.'

'Yes, Thomas. I wondered if you would have.'

'Rather late in the day, old friend, I know. But what is this really all about.'

Li Pengfei looked away, into the inky blackness of the darkened fields they had parked alongside. Then he looked earnestly at Royle and nodded, more to himself than anyone else.

'After the death of Ho Chi Minh on 2nd September 1969, the Hanoi government was in a state of flux. They had followed Ho since 1945. Even before that.'

'All right, and …'

'Weren't you ever curious that Ho died on the exact anniversary he made his declaration of independence in Hanoi in 1945? Same day, same month. That enabled them to grab power, at least north of the 17th Parallel as soon as the big war ended.'

'Are you saying Ho didn't die of natural causes?' Royle queried, starting to feel out of control as a huge conspiracy seemed to be unrolling before him.

'That is exactly what I'm saying,' said Li Pengfei.

'So, what happened?'

'Ho's declaration of independence pretty much emulated the American declaration of independence, which upset some hawks in the US establishment. Not government, Thomas. Establishment. As you know, he did this in an effort to win support for his cause by the Big Three: Britain, the United States and the Soviets. Mainly the United States, who held all the aces in post-war negotiations.

'Remember, in 1969 the Cold War was at its height. But at the same time the American establishment became irked at the memory of Ho's words, and approaching 40,000 US servicemen killed in the Vietnam War by then, and the Russians became tired of financing what they – and the Americans – began to see as a never ending conflict.

'So the two big Cold War powers got together to assassinate Ho Chi Minh.'

Royle gaped at Li Pengfei for a long moment. He said, 'How?'

'I don't know the details of the conspiracy itself, but a very senior government official of the People's Republic of China – I'm talking an extremely powerful man in Beijing – was recruited to carry out the task. It was bankrolled by the Americans and negotiated by the Russians, who promised this Chinese statesman political asylum for doing their dirty work as one of only a few non-Vietnamese Ho was willing to completely trust. This Chinese statesman was extremely highly placed, but certain corrupt practices had come to the notice of other party leaders, most importantly Mao himself. So an escape plan was required, and this seemed to be the perfect opportunity, as long as he carried out this specific task.'

'You're telling me that America and Russia formed a secret alliance – in the middle of the Cold War and just seven years after both sides had been at the brink of annihilating each other with nuclear weapons – to kill the man who was keeping the Vietnam War going, simply because one was offended by him and the other found his war to be a drain on their resources?'

'That's exactly what I'm telling you, Thomas.'

Skelton approached the pair. 'Everything all right over there?'

'Better now,' said Royle. 'But I need to speak to Li Pengfei. We'll need to travel in the same car. You all right on your own in the lead car?'

'It's a little irregular, sir,' said Skelton. *In other words*, thought Royle, *he's been ordered to keep a close eye on Li Pengfei.*

'I need to fill in some blanks. I was out of it for a while if you remember, and these two disappeared together. It's for my own peace of mind.' Royle looked Skelton in the eye.

Or you all want to get your story straight before your separate debrief, thought Skelton. But Skelton relented, nodded, and made his way back to the lead car as Li Pengfei and Royle walked to the other vehicle, where Amelia sat waiting.

Once in the car Royle sat in the middle on the rear seat, with Amelia and Li Pengfei on either side. Both cars began to move off into the traffic, which had thinned out considerably during their short stop.

'Continue,' Royle said to Li Pengfei. Amelia looked at them both wondering just what had taken place between the two men at the side of the road.

'In 1969 the Soviet economy was starting to slide. The previous year they had invaded Czechoslovakia to crush the reformist government there, and suffered the ire of the free world as a result. In addition their planned economy had started to fail because it didn't match up with world markets. The Soviets were spending billions arming revolutionary groups around the world, propping up the Castro regime in Cuba – a highly prized Soviet asset in the back yard of the United States of America - but most of all keeping North Vietnam armed and in the war.

'At the same time the Soviet Union was starting to discuss detente with the United States and arms limitation talks had begun. The nuclear arms race was becoming unsustainable for the Brezhnev government, which decided something needed to be done urgently to prevent the Soviet economy from crashing.

'They had already begun to engage the nuclear problem with America, but North Vietnam remained a thorn in their side, while cooling relations between Moscow and Beijing meant that arms supply to Hanoi would continue to flow from Russia, with China only contributing a small amount. It was a huge drain on the Soviet economy.'

'Very well,' said Royle. 'I get it. The big picture was that the Soviet economy was struggling and the only way out of it was talks with Washington and … what? The Russians are still sending arms to Hanoi.'

'That's true, but now there are no Americans to fight, just the Republic of South Vietnam,' said Li Pengfei.

'So what has all this to do with Ho Chi Minh's death?' asked Royle.

'There were talks within talks,' said Li Pengfei. 'Washington and Moscow cooked up a plan to assassinate Ho, using a very high ranking member of the Politburo in Beijing.'

'How high ranking?' asked Royle.

'The third most powerful man in China.'

'You mean Bin Lao?' asked Royle, shocked at Li Pengfei's revelation.

'Yes, Bin Lao. A hero of the Long March and the civil war. He was one of the generals who led the People's Liberation Army into Beijing at their victory. He became First-ranked Vice-Premier, a marshal of the People's Liberation Army, and the Minster of National Defence. Mao named him as his successor to be Chairman of the Chinese Communist Party and therefore supreme leader. Bin Lao was beyond reproach and to all intents and purposes untouchable, and only Mao and Premier Chou En-lai were his superiors.

'He was also in the pay of Moscow,' said Li Pengfei in a whisper, his head close to Royle's.

'He was a KGB mole?'

'Yes,' said Li Pengfei, 'and had been for years. He was the man Moscow Centre went to, to rid them of their Vietnam problem. Bin Lao was corrupt, he loved the thought of acquiring all the women he wanted on a whim, of stealing funds from state assets; of feathering his own nest, all with the help of Dzerzhinsky Square and the KGB.

'Bin Lao's corruption had been discovered early in 1972. It was felt better to let sleeping dogs lie to avoid a scandal within the Politburo. His role in the assassination was discovered later on, in September '72. That was the last straw. His treachery left Mao and Chou no option but to take action against their old friend and comrade. When Bin Lao realised he was about to be arrested he fled in his private plane with his wife and children, along with a pile of cash and gold – a small fraction of his true wealth. Bin was en route to Russia when his plane was shot down over Mongolia and he was killed. He had become too much of a liability even for the Soviets.'

'Yes, I remember the incident,' said Royle.

'So do I,' said Li Pengfei. 'I was the one Bin recruited to carry out the act.'

'You killed Ho Chi Minh?' asked Royle, astounded.

'Yes, Thomas. Marshal Bin Lao personally supplied me with an experimental drug that would make Ho's death seem like a heart attack. I was trusted in Hanoi – that's where I disappeared to after Malaya. I was highly regarded as a travelling guerrilla leader. I made many trips to Hanoi between forays in the South. I was always asked to share coffee with Ho whenever I reappeared in Hanoi. We always met in private to discuss how the war was going in the South. It had been going well for the North, so Ho was very happy to talk in private. It was during one of these conversations in Hanoi – and it was stipulated by my handlers that it must be on that date, mainly to please the Americans - when I slipped the drug into his drink.'

'Just like you did with me in Hong Kong,' said Royle. Li Pengfei remained silent as Royle brooded.

Then Royle said, 'So, not only were you working for the British Government and the Chinese, you were doing the dirty work of the Russians and the United states? A quadruple agent.' Still Li Pengfei remained silent as he watched the dark countryside fly past his window.

'That's why the Americans and Chinese want you dead,' said Royle. 'But why are they interested in Mel?'

'She has been connected with me for many years, Thomas. We were lovers, as you now know, and she really was a spy for the Chinese. She had nothing to do with Ho's assassination, but I suppose they see her as a loose end that needs to be eliminated.'

The cars slowed down as they approached a major road – the A315 London Road – and headed to the capital from there.

They had just joined the A315 in order to drive east to London, and were approaching a quiet section near Hounslow Heath, when the driver of the rear car, containing Royle, Li Pengfei and Amelia Harper, spoke in a low voice to their SIS minder. He pulled down a sun shade which contained a second rear view mirror. A pair of headlights shone in them. He picked up a microphone from the car's dash and spoke into it. Neither Royle nor his sister and Li Pengfei could hear what was being said, but their hackles went up when they observed the body language of the two men in the front go to full alert.

A response came from the lead car over the vehicle's intercom. Again Royle, Li Pengfei and Amelia were unable to make out what was being said. But almost immediately both cars began to accelerate. The mystery car behind them did the same.

It was at this moment when the rear car minder turned in his seat and said to Royle, Li Pengfei and Amelia, 'It appears you were expected. We have an unidentified pursuer. We will need to take evasive action.'

'If it's the people who hit us in Hong Kong and again in Malaysia, the betting is that it's Chinese MSS,' said Royle. The SIS minder nodded without speaking, then relayed the same message over to the lead car.

Both cars sped off and re-entered a built-up area, then heading into Houslow turned up and joined the A4 Great West Road. They accelerated fast, approaching Kew Gardens but still within the safety of a heavily built-up district. The rear car's SIS minder turned in his seat again and said, 'If they were following us, then we appear to have lost them, so we can continue …,'

That was the last thing he said. As Royle was looking at him an unnatural movement through the windscreen caused him to take his eyes off the man. The lead car took off skywards as an orange ball of flame erupted beneath it. It flipped on to its roof and slid backwards along the busy road, throwing out a shower of sparks as the road surface gouged into the Jaguar's metal roof. Oncoming vehicles braked, screeched and skidded as the drama unfolded.

Next, Royle and Amelia's driver swerved to avoid the wreckage of the lead car. They must have hit a treacherous patch of black ice in the road, for the next thing Royle remembered was being inside a slow motion carousel as the second Jaguar traversed uncontrollably into the road's central barrier.

Time became real again as the car crumpled into the barrier with a loud report, then stopped, facing the wrong way.

They had gone past the first car, which was smouldering badly, and were now facing it. The lead car's front wheels had flown off in the blast, and the passage of the car on its roof created a deep trough in the road tarmac.

All five in Royle's car climbed out of the driver's side, and legs shaking with adrenaline walked slowly and alertly towards the crippled lead Jaguar. There was movement from the rear and Skelton staggered out of the wreckage, blood streaming from a head wound. Royle's minders ran to the front of the car, crouched to look inside, then turned back.

'They're both dead,' said the minder who met them at the airport. Both minder and driver then pulled out handguns, Brownings, similar to those carried by the Thai embassy Royal Marines. The SIS minder and driver held their weapons in readiness as they led their charges to the roadside. A crowd was gathering as the pile-up caused more minor accidents on both sides of the carriageway. There was almost immediate congestion in both directions.

Skelton ran back to the stricken first Jaguar, reached into the front passenger seat and retrieved that man's side arm. Now there were three weapons defending the three charges.

Another vehicle, headlights on full beam to dazzle them, howled up the pavement on their side of the carriageway, ploughing into parked vehicles, rubbish bins, bushes and fences to the houses which lined the road.

The car stopped. It was clearly the car that had been spotted following them on the A315. Four men emerged as the mystery car stopped. From the opposite direction, two more men approached on foot, one carrying a grenade launcher.

One of the SIS men, the surviving driver, swore under his breath. 'They used a wombat gun.'

Skelton asked, 'A what …?'

'That's what the Australians called them in Vietnam. It's an M79 grenade launcher. Unusual if they are Chinese agents. They usually use their own versions of Russian weapons. The M79 is US-made.'

'So, we're in trouble, I take it,' commented Royle, no stranger to firepower, but now looking around he considered their position to be considerably disadvantaged. An old soldier who had often found himself in sticky situations, Royle never admitted a situation could be lost, but he recognised the position now to be such.

As the assailants closed in the sound of a police siren began to come closer from the same carriageway, from the direction of Hounslow. The blues-and-twos of the police patrol car stopped a quarter of a mile away. It was the closest the two officers could get to the accident epicentre.

'Colonel Royle, Mrs Harper, Mr Li Pengfei,' said Skelton breathlessly. Take cover behind the first Jaguar.' He pointed at the smoking wreck as he spoke, and the three ran towards the smouldering ruin, which still contained the bodies of two SIS officers.

It was a stand-off. Three good guys carrying 9mm semi-automatics against six bad guys wielding God knows what.

One of the six bad guys from the car with the glaring headlights peeled off and headed towards the police officers. That left five bad guys against three, with one of the bad guys carrying a grenade thrower. These were not good odds.

The three stood back to back, two facing what was now the three from the mystery car, and one against the grenade launcher pair. They were joined by Tom Royle, who had gone to the wrecked SIS car and reached in to the driver's side to commandeer the dead driver's weapon.

'Now it's four against six,' said Royle through gritted teeth. 'Odds are getting better all the time.'

Royle and Skelton faced the approaching grenade launcher pair. The flow of blood had abated from the gash on Skelton's head. As the pair came closer the man carrying the grenade launcher seemed to be wearing blue denim jeans and an ex-military combat jacket, the type people bought in army surplus stores. The other assailant appeared to be wearing a dark-coloured suit, white shirt and dark tie. He appeared unarmed.

Behind them they heard a man's voice. It sounded cultured, well educated. He was speaking very good English, with a slight but obvious Chinese accent. 'Please, put down your weapons. We have no wish to harm you. However, we will have no compunction to do so if you do not comply with our demands.'

'Same here,' came an American voice – the partner of the grenade thrower.

Royle and Skelton looked at each other. Chinese *and* Americans. 'It seems they're all out to get us, Matthew,' said Royle, with a grim, low laugh.

The assailants, the three Chinese agents approaching from the Hounslow side, and the two Americans facing them, had stopped.

Skelton again took charge of the situation, hopeless though it now seemed. 'Gentlemen, you are all on British soil engaging in illegal operations. In the name of the British Government I require you to withdraw immediately.'

No reply came. Neither party moved.

'Ask them what they want,' said Royle.

Skelton seemed to grow as he stood out of his armed crouch and peered at both groups in the face-off. His weapon hung loosely in his hand, by his side but ready for action in a split second.

'Why are you here?' Skelton said to both groups.

Almost simultaneously the two sides spoke the names of two people. From the Chinese side the cultured voice said, 'Mrs Harper.' On the other side, the American in the suit said, 'Li Pengfei.'

The suited American made the first move. He stepped forward, arms slightly raised with palms facing outwards, so the British could see he was not carrying a weapon.

'Hand over Li Pengfei and we'll be on our way,' the American said. Then he nodded towards the Chinese and said, 'Sorry about these guys, but I don't think we can help you there.'

Royle then stepped forward to face the American. He too held his arms out. He had pocketed his weapon and held out the palms of his hands to reassure the American.

'Why on earth would you want Li Pengfei?' said Royle.

'Colonel Royle, is it?' the American asked. Royle nodded, tension knotting his jaw. 'Well, Colonel, you of all people should know that Li Pengfei is one of the most wanted terrorists in the world. He raised hell during your Malaysian campaign and he's been raising Cain with our enemy the Viet Cong over in 'Nam. Colonel Royle, he's responsible for the deaths of countless Americans. One of these was a colleague of ours, killed in the line of duty last month. We're supposed to be on the same side. How can you not hand him over to us?'

'This colleague wouldn't be Charles Kravitz by any chance, would it?' asked Royle.

The suit replied, 'Chuck Kravitz, yeah.'

Royle shook his head and a slight smile stretched his stressed face. 'Charles Kravitz and I go back a long way. Back to his OSS days in Vietnam, incidentally.'

'So you shouldn't have a problem handing Li Pengfei to us, then,' said the American, his face still hidden in the gloom of the night. Somehow his voice floating over to them amid the noise of the queuing traffic behind and ahead of them was beginning to sound familiar.

'Oh yes, I do have a problem,' said Royle forcefully. 'You fools, don't you realise it was Kravitz who helped me to find Li Pengfei in the first place? He interrogated – tortured - a Viet Cong cadre member to death to find out for me. He was working in co-operation with me and by inference MI6. His CIA brief took him into a battle zone and the heavy invasion by North Vietnamese forces led to his death. Not Li Pengfei. We need to get Li Pengfei to Century House.'

'Not convinced, Colonel,' said the American.

'Look, get your embassy to contact our military attaché at the British Embassy in Saigon. A man called Fred Conti. He will confirm my story.'

The American did not reply, but lifted his left arm to his face and seemed to speak into it. He was wired and this operation was being monitored by the CIA at Grosvenor Square, thought Royle.

Then Royle turned to the Chinese group. Their leader, the cultured one, was standing slightly ahead of his colleagues. The fourth man had returned and had joined the party. All were spread out, weapons still aimed at the British, but in a relaxed stance.

Royle bowed slightly, in the Chinese traditional manner, then spoke to their spokesman. 'Mrs Harper is my sister, and as her only surviving family member I demand to know why you wish to take her.'

The man took a step closer. His face became illuminated by a street light. He seemed to be quite young to be in charge of a mission like this, perhaps in his late twenties. He was smartly dressed in a suit and tie. He too had pocketed his side arm and returned Royle's courteous bow.

'Colonel Royle, it is an honour to meet you. Your methods are taught at our academy. However, I must humbly ask once again for your sister to come with us. I think you know why, colonel.'

Skelton whispered, 'What's he talking about, Colonel Royle?'

Royle ignored the younger man and continued to face the man who seemed to be the MSS extraction squad leader. Royle knew that if the American now in contact with the US Embassy in London managed to discover the truth about Li Pengfei through Fred Conti then the Americans could become a possible ally. Failing that he would have to explain that Li Pengfei had possibly shortened the war when he assassinated Ho Chi Minh. The only hope for this to happen would be to play for time with the Chinese.

'Yes, I know why. But first, to whom do I have the honour of addressing?' asked Royle, in his most amenable tone.

'My name is not important, Colonel Royle, but time is of the essence. We must leave immediately, and we must take Mrs Harper with us. Now, hand her over and we will leave you in peace. This is a matter for our government, not yours.'

'What about the police officers your man has dealt with?' asked Royle.

'They are unharmed, colonel. They are bound and gagged at a lamp post a little way down the road.'

'You didn't kill them out of hand then?' asked Royle.

'Your suggestion dishonours us, colonel. We have no quarrel with your police force, nor with your country. We simply wish to claim ownership of Mrs Harper. She faces conspiracy and espionage charges.'

'It sounds as if there is already a bullet waiting for her. Has she already been tried and found guilty?' asked Royle.

The MSS leader did not respond.

Just then, Amelia emerged from behind the cover of the wrecked Jaguar. She walked into the open towards the Chinese group and stopped equidistant between the MSS leader and the British group.

'Get back, Amelia,' shouted Royle.

'No, Tommy. I have to hand myself over. They've been chasing me since Hong Kong. Longer than that, probably. And it will solve your problem of what to do with me, and Century House's.'

'No, Mel,' said Royle.

'I must,' she said, and walked towards the MSS squad, her arms raised.

Before Royle could put his hand in his pocket for his gun, Li Pengfei dashed from behind the upturned Jaguar towards Amelia Harper. His only weapon was a length of jagged metal rod, part of a component from the damaged car's front steering array. He had managed to prise it loose as they crouched in witness to the complicated impasse scene before them.

One of the MSS agents raised his weapon toward Li Pengfei as he surged forward, but the experienced guerrilla fighter hurled the rod at the agent's gun hand, sending the weapon flying away and into the gutter with a metallic clash.

Li Pengfei grasped Amelia Harper by the shoulders and propelled her towards the SIS group, which automatically opened up to receive her as a four-man body guard. As Li Pengfei hurled Amelia into the MI6 group one of the Chinese agents took two long steps sideways and with his weapon raised fired two shots into Li Pengfei's chest.

The veteran guerrilla fighter was spun round by the velocity of the bullets and fell to the ground.

'Pengfei!' shouted Royle, as he ran to his old friend's side. Li Pengfei was lying in a twisted position in the roadway. Royle turned him over and saw the spreading blood stains on his shirt. 'Pengfei,'

Li Pengfei looked up at his old friend and collaborator, and smiled faintly. 'Did you ever know what my name means, Thomas?' Pengfei said, huskily, each effort causing him spasms of pain.

'No,' replied Royle, his eyes smarting with tears.

'Pengfei, my given name, it means *flight of the Roc*, a legendary bird.' A shadow of a smile transformed Pengfei's face almost beatifically. 'Now, I fly,' croaked Li Pengfei as he closed his eyes.

Royle said softly. 'Oh my God.' There was no pulse. Li Pengfei had stopped breathing. Royle stood slowly and walked back to the bodyguard, who were now physically restraining a distraught Amelia Harper, preventing her from breaking away from their protection and falling on to the body of her lover.

Royle walked over to the Chinese lead agent, his arms outstretched. He walked up close and said softly in his ear, 'Do you realise you have been chasing the wrong one? Li Pengfei had been working with the man your people have revered since he was killed two years ago. He was Bin Lao's weapon of choice. You will need to seek much higher clearance to discover what Li Pengfei did at Bin Lao's bidding. Much higher.'

The Chinese agent looked nonplussed at Royle's comments. Royle had twisted the truth in order to confuse. He knew these MSS foot soldiers would never find out the secret that had led to the marshal's death, or Li Pengfei's involvement. He looked back at his men. None appeared to have overheard Royle's whispered half-explanation. Royle walked back to his group.

Royle had observed that the Americans had now joined the MI6 group. The man with the grenade launcher was poised to fire at the Chinese squad, who were again on high alert to complete their mission to extract Amelia Harper.

'Well colonel,' said the suited American, 'I knew you'd be trouble when I first clapped eyes on you.'

Royle looked at him, his face now fully illuminated in the street lights. 'Joe Guardino? What the …'

'In the flesh. Got taken out of Saigon. The firm sent in lots of reinforcements. Can't say I'm sorry.'

'Are you here to help us now?'

'That's the way of it, colonel.'

All six armed men faced the Chinese group, weapons raised. Amelia was protected behind the human shield of MI6 and CIA operatives.

'Well, colonel. It's your call,' said Guardino. In Saigon, Royle was wary of the then deputy CIA station chief in South Vietnam. He appeared suspicious and tense at the US Embassy in Saigon, and unaccountably belligerent towards Royle. Now he was putting his life on the line for the British.

More police sirens began to sound, this time from both directions.

'Mr Skelton, I believe the ball is back in our court. Would you mind?' said Royle.

'If it's all the same to you, sir, I think I can take it from here,' said Skelton. Royle nodded, then let his eyes fall on the lifeless body of Li Pengfei. Amelia's sobs could be heard from behind.

'Gentlemen,' said Skelton. 'I say again, leave now. And I mean leave the country. Put down your weapons and go. You have twenty-four hours to get out, then you will be hunted down with maximum force.'

The Chinese squad leader was visibly livid, but he knew he had lost. He said something to his men, and all four simultaneously placed their hand guns on the road, turned and walked away into the night.

Amelia dashed to Li Pengfei's body, deathly still in the frigid night air. She knelt beside him, and tenderly held Li Pengfei's hand as she softly wept, her body swaying with grief.

Skelton then looked at Royle and Guardino.

'Your sister was a double agent for the Chinese?' he said to Royle, then to Guardino said, 'You killed two of my men for no reason.'

Royle interceded, 'Joe Guardino, this is Matt Skelton. He's in charge of this mission.'

'Mr Skelton,' Guardino said, pocketing his own weapon. 'My apologies, but we needed to stop you before the MSS got to you.' Then turning to Royle said, 'However, I am as nonplussed as Mr Skelton here. We thought the Chinese were after Li Pengfei, to take him home. We just wanted to get to him first. Turns out they wanted your sister, colonel. Care to elaborate?'

Royle started to feel the weariness of years of intrigue and fighting weigh down on him. He slowly walked over to his sister and placed a hand gently on her shoulder.

'Mel, it's time to go. I think Mr Skelton would like to speak to you.'

CENTURY HOUSE, LONDON, 30th JANUARY 1975

Colonel Tom Royle was seated in a nondescript, windowless office deep within the bowels of the headquarters of the British Secret Intelligence Service, MI6. Seated with him opposite a television monitor and video tape recorder was Matt Skelton, the deputy director of Six, Sir Hugh Pearson, and CIA guest Joe Guardino.

They had just come to the end of watching the last of Amelia Harper's interrogations at the secure safe house she was being kept in, somewhere in north London. As a Chinese agent Royle knew Amelia would have to be intensively interrogated.

Amelia looked tired and drawn, but she had kept her composure throughout the lengthy sessions. Most of the time she had conversed with SIS interrogators. On the odd occasion the CIA were given access to her, mainly to appease the chiefs at Langley that Mrs Harper had not stepped on any American toes during her years of spying for the Chinese. They seemed satisfied that Amelia Harper was purely a British problem, and Joe Guardino had been tasked to make sure the rest of the interrogations did not implicate the CIA in any way. They did not.

The Harper File, as it would be known after being processed by Registry and filed in the basement beneath Century House, was complete. Amelia Harper had admitted her treachery, her pre-war recruitment to communism, her complicity in the deaths of British soldiers and planters, including her own husband, during the Malayan Emergency, and then she had stopped her activities after moving to England with her brother.

She had decided to take action when she discovered Tom Royle's new manuscript contained a great deal about Li Pengfei during the Emergency years. She knew there was nothing incriminating that could reveal Li Pengfei's – or Royle's – secret status, but she realised that once the name of Li Pengfei was again made public, the hunt would be on by the Chinese to capture him. She had no reason to believe it would be the Americans who were most adamant in their attempts to find and redact him. She was mortified when she realised that her own interference by attempting to find Royle and Li Pengfei first – as they had been ordered to make contact by the SIS – would reactivate the hunt for America's public enemy number one, and China's realisation that Amelia Harper was again on the scene and needed to be taken out.

Amelia had insisted that Tom Royle and Li Pengfei had known nothing of her allegiance to the Chinese communists, which was true up to the point when she confessed to them in the functional back room of a US air base bar in Thailand on Christmas morning.

All were satisfied they now had the full story from Amelia Harper.

Sir Hugh Pearson stood and switched off the television monitor. 'Thank you for attending Mr Guardino. I trust you are satisfied there is nothing for CIA to get involved with?'

'Yes sir, that's the case as far as we're concerned. Thank you for your time.' Guardino turned to shake hands with Royle. 'See you for a drink afterwards? I'm in town for the next few days.'

'Of course, Joe. I'd like that,' said Royle. Guardino gave Royle a friendly slap on the back before leaving the room.

Pearson turned to Royle. 'Colonel, I have to admit I found it hard to believe that you could know nothing about your sister's dalliance with the Chinese MSS.'

'I would have found it difficult too, Sir Hugh.'

'Yet there it is. You have a devoted sister,' said Pearson, never letting his gaze leave that of Royle. Royle knew Pearson did not believe Amelia when she said that neither her brother Tom Royle, nor her lover Li Pengfei, had known of her betrayal.

Earlier, Royle had divulged Li Pengfei's big secret during a private conversation with Pearson, a piece of information that Joe Guardino and the CIA would never hear of, although there would be a file buried deep in the CIA's own registry at Langley, Virginia, spelling out the ultra-secret Cold War deal between hawkish members of the USA establishment and the Soviet Union to be rid of Ho Chi Minh – a charismatic figure in the United States and throughout the western world who needed to be liquidated quietly and efficiently. Who would have believed that the man they believed to be the number one terrorist in Vietnam would be the same person responsible for Ho's death? Only a few among the Russians, the Chinese, the Americans and the British now knew of Li Pengfei's attempt to shorten the Vietnam War by killing Ho Chi Minh, and that was a secret that would be very closely kept hidden.

'So what now, Sir Hugh?' asked Royle anxiously.

'Now we place her into your care, Colonel Royle.'

'So there will be no charges brought against her?' asked Royle, tension mounting in his voice.

'No criminal charges. It's such a long time ago, colonel. Yet we must suspect that she had been directly responsible for deaths because of her treachery. No proof of this, of course. She worked actively, and I must say enthusiastically, against the State. We can't forgive her that, colonel. It is fortunate that you and she enjoy independent means because the revenge we intend to exact will be somewhat tempered by that fact.'

'What revenge is that?' asked Royle.

'Oh, the usual. She will become persona non grata,' Pearson explained. 'Her National Insurance number has been deleted, so she will not be able to get a job anywhere, and she can expect no state aid – ever. She will be required to make monthly visits to a police station of her choice, to register with them and make sure she is not up to any more mischief. She has had her passport revoked, so she can never leave the United Kingdom, legally at least, and she will have her mail intercepted for the rest of her life.'

Royle realised Amelia had got off lightly. The authorities could easily have secreted her away and thrown away the key, or simply have put a bullet into her brain. He felt the new knowledge of Li Pengfei's activities had also tempered the severity of Amelia's punishment. While Li Pengfei had been helping the Russians, albeit unwittingly, he had also been helping the Americans and the British by taking out North Vietnam's most resistant of leaders and ensuring the exposure and death of one of the most powerful, influential and dangerous men in the People's Republic of China.

'Thank you, Sir Hugh.' So that was that, thought Royle. No thank you from the deputy chief for coming out of retirement and risking life and limb for him. The mission had not gone according to plan, this was quite obvious. The man he had been sent to Vietnam to retrieve, Li Pengfei, his friend and colleague over many years and one of Britain's top intelligence assets, had been killed, literally at the final hurdle.

'You can collect her in a couple of days, colonel,' announced Pearson abruptly. 'Goodbye, colonel.'

Pearson walked out of the room, leaving Royle to reflect on Amelia's – and his – fate.

FEBRUARY 1975

A winter sleet pelted the window panes at the new Royle residence, situated in the wilds of the West Pennine Moors.

The wind howled outside. The house was atop a hill above the bleak moorland that stretched for miles and miles. It was perfect, thought Royle. Away from civilization and just the postman for company whenever his red-liveried Royal Mail van drew up outside.

But it was dark now. Night time here. So dark that nothing could be discerned outside.

Installed outside was some of the most advanced security equipment currently available. Floodlight systems activated by infra-red sensors in the grounds would alert the occupants visibly if any intruders happened to trespass on the Royle property. An audible alarm would also sound within the house once the outside lights were activated by anything larger than a badger.

MI6 had had a hand in procuring some of this equipment, at Royle's request. He had made the case that there were still some bad people out there who wanted to get hold of Amelia, and himself for that matter. The request had gone up to Pearson himself, who signed off the request for security equipment personally. The last thing he wanted was for Amelia Harper's secrets being uncovered. Certainly not on his watch.

In addition to outdoor security, there was a hi-tech system that could detect intruders to the house itself, and a split-screen TV monitor to capture images from the closed circuit television cameras dotted around the outside of the house, and around the perimeter of the land now owned by Royle.

'Auntie Mel, can I have another piece of cake?' asked a smiling Adi.

All three were playing a board game on a rug in front of the warming fire.

'How many pieces of Christmas cake have you had already, young man?' asked Amelia in a mock stern voice.

'Just one,' lied Adi, giggling while drinking from his glass of squash to hide his laughter.

'Very well, just one more,' said Amelia. She looked up and smiled at Royle, who was standing by the window. Royle smiled back at his sister.

Just then the floodlights flashed on, and the internal alarms sounded. Royle dashed to the monitor screen and flicked through the cameras, but could see nothing.

'I'd better go out and have a look,' said Royle, smiling reassuringly. Royle reached for his all-weather oilskin coat and hood on a hook at the back of the door, then placed his feet inside hefty wellington boots and went outside.

Amelia watched him nervously on the monitor screen as Royle trudged from security point to security point, then along the perimeter, pointing his flashlight in a wide arc as he walked.

Soon Royle returned, dripping wet, but still smiling.

'Nothing there. This security system must need another tweak. Can't have the weather setting it off at all hours, day or night. Especially here at the top of this hill. Everything gets thrown at us here.'

Royle took off his waterproofs and took his seat by the fire to warm up again. He had poured himself a scotch and water and sat watching the flames flicker in the grate.

Soon Adi went to bed, leaving Amelia and Tom alone downstairs.

'Will we ever be safe, Tommy?' asked Amelia.

'I could lie to you and say "yes". But the fact is you have a lot of enemies, who want to take you away. They may want you dead, Mel. I can't let that happen,' said Royle. He put his glass down on the hearth and took Amelia's hand. 'We three are all that's left of the Royle family. I have been shocked by your crimes, and what they have caused, not least the death of Li Pengfei.

'But we are a family, and we must remain a family. You are my sister and I still love you, Amelia. We both love Adi. We have to be out of public sight, but we must also remain safe. And we must be in this thing together now, because we are all that's left.'

They heard the light slide of the front door letter box and the unmistakable sound of an envelope falling to the stone floor.

Royle jumped at the slight sound, physically alert. He had seen no-one during his search of the property, yet somehow someone had made their way to his front door undetected except by the infra-red system. *At least that worked, but whoever had pushed an envelope through his front door must be invisible*, thought Royle.

He shot from his chair and checked the closed circuit TV monitors again, switching from every point, but again could see nothing. A phantom had delivered an envelope to his door, it seemed. Royle went to the door and picked up the envelope. It was a standard-sized plain white envelope, slightly damp round the edges from the sleety squall outside. Nothing special.

Royle tore it open and extracted an ornate piece of paper. At the top was the crest of the People's Republic of China, and the address was the Chinese Embassy in London.

'What is it, Tommy?' asked Amelia worriedly.

'It's an invitation.'

'What kind of invitation, Tommy? Who would trudge through miles of moorland in the pitch black, in weather like this, through our detect-all security, and yet not be seen in order to deliver a letter of invitation?' said Amelia.

'It's an invitation to me, Mel. From the PRC. They want me to meet with someone about you,' said Royle, returning to his chair by the fire. He picked up his whisky glass again and drained it, then went to the table where his scotch bottle stood and poured himself a straight shot.

'So who wants to talk about me, Tommy?' she asked.

Royle handed his sister the letter.

She picked it up and read the contents. A formal invitation, to her brother alone. It was requesting his attendance to meet a very important person, via a circuitous, unofficial route. It was requesting Royle to make contact in Hong Kong and then cross the border into communist China. The letter said it was on a matter of utmost secrecy and concerned her personal future. But she wasn't invited along to discuss her own life.

Angry, Amelia thrust the letter on to the floor. Royle looked at her grimly.

'Who will you be seeing, Tommy?' asked Amelia.

'It doesn't say,' said Royle.

'But you must have some idea,' accused Amelia.

'Some, but I can't be sure,' said Royle. 'I can only surmise it's someone from the People's Republic's secret service. Maybe the fellow on the road from Heathrow.'

'Are you going?' asked Amelia, now concerned for her brother's safety.

'I don't think I have a choice, Mel,' said Royle. He picked up a code book, turned to the page for that day, transcribed a message, then rang the number for Century House, where he delivered his coded message to a silent duty officer.

*

It took a day for Century House to get back to Royle. Royle had no way of knowing that his coded message had caused a flurry of furious activity among the upper echelons of the Secret Intelligence Service. And to Royle's dismay that reply simply said "stand by".

A further week passed before Matthew Skelton arrived at Royle's front door. Skelton was to be Pearson's personal messenger, he told Royle, on what he described as a matter of utmost importance to the state.

'Nice place, sir,' said Skelton, shaking Royle's hand as he was invited inside.

The weather had turned bright and sunny, and was set fair for the next few days. Cotton wool clouds floated slowly across the big sky above the Royle residence on its moorland hilltop.

'Sir Hugh didn't want to trust the telephone, even scrambled and coded,' said Skelton. 'So he sent me.'

'Pearson seems to be getting more paranoid by the minute,' said Royle, frowning. It was good to see his former student, latterly his case officer during the Li Pengfei debacle, but he knew Skelton's unexpected appearance could only mean trouble for him and his sister.

Skelton shrugged. 'You are aware of our own telecommunications interception system of course, colonel?'

Royle nodded, pouring both of them a mug of coffee from the bubbling percolator on the Aga. Royle looked at his watch. Amelia had left the house to take Adi back to school and would not return for hours.

'Echelon, our interception system, is of course shared with our cousins across the Pond. We don't want our coded messages reaching the ears of Langley,' explained Skelton. 'Hence my presence.'

'Very well, I understand,' said Royle, taking his seat by the fire and indicating to Skelton that he should do likewise opposite him. 'And your message is ...?'

'Colonel, we think the source is someone in the PRC politburo.'

Royle's eyebrows raised at that. 'Not our friends from the A315 encounter?' asked Royle.

'We don't believe so, sir,' said Skelton.

'Who then?' demanded Royle.

'That we don't know, colonel,' said Skelton. 'Perhaps this would be a good opportunity to find out.'

Royle sighed deeply. The long-awaited book, the one that had caused all this trouble in the first place, would have to be delayed a little while longer.

Printed in Great Britain
by Amazon